The Christmas Window

The Christmas Window

Melissa McClone

TULE

PUBLISHING

The Christmas Window

Tule Publishing First Printing, September 2018

The Tule Publishing Group, LLC

First Publication by Tule Publishing Group 2018

ISBN: 978-1-949707-14-4

A matchmaking aunt wants her nephew to find love under the mistletoe...

All doggy daycare owner Callie Andrews wants for Christmas is to win first prize this year. The annual window display competition is a huge event in Silver Falls, and she's determined to showcase her success when her family visits her small town. It's time for her parents and three older brothers to realize the "baby" of the family is thriving on her own.

The last thing Brandt Winslow wants to do is rehash the past, but returning home to Silver Falls means confronting the reason he left. His vacation, however, takes an unexpected turn when his well-meaning aunt meddles in his love life, and he finds himself caught up in her misguided efforts at matchmaking.

Despite their reluctance at being paired up, Callie and Brandt discover the holidays are full of surprises...and romance. But is the magic of Christmas strong enough to keep the couple together through the new year?

Dedication

For Jane Porter,
an amazing author, publisher, and friend.
This book wouldn't have been written if not for you!

And to my family…
A summer deadline wasn't in our plans,
but thanks for being so understanding!

Chapter One

DECEMBER MIGHT BE six days away, but Silver Falls was ready for Christmas with fresh garland strung across First Avenue, streetlights decorated like candy canes, and twinkling lights, well, everywhere. The scents of pine and cedar hung on the air. The dusting of snow resembled pixie dust, another reminder of the magic of the season.

As Callie Andrews walked toward Wags and Tails, her doggy daycare, warmth flowed through her despite the freezing temperature on this overcast Monday morning. She loved how her small town celebrated the holidays. Loved the Christmas traditions of the First Avenue Business Association. Loved the nonstop cheer that overflowed from Thanksgiving to December twenty-fifth.

Who was she kidding?

She loved everything about this place.

Silver Falls was home.

Moving here and buying a business were the best decisions she'd made. This year would mark her third December in Silver Falls. She wanted to make the most of the holidays, especially with her family coming to visit. This Christmas would be perfect. Especially if her plans—updated last night on the flight home after spending Thanksgiving with her family in Los Angeles—worked out.

Why wouldn't they?

Up ahead, a blue compact SUV parked in front of Tea Leaves & Coffee Beans, the only coffee shop in town. Raine Hanover—owner and barista extraordinaire—slid from the driver's seat, opened the hatchback, and removed a large wreath.

"Good morning." Callie stopped in front of the coffee shop's window display of potted poinsettias, large bags of coffee beans painted with Norman Rockwell-type Christmas images, and twinkling white lights. "I hope you had a good Thanksgiving."

"It was great, though I need to lose ten pounds after eating too many slices of pumpkin pie smothered in whipped cream." Raine shut the hatch. "Thank goodness for leggings. No way could I zip my jeans this morning."

"I know the feeling."

A man wearing black sweats, a gray hoodie, and tennis shoes crossed the street toward them. He couldn't be out for a morning run. Not without a hat and gloves. Must not be from around here.

He stepped onto the curb, giving Callie a full view of his face. Her jaw nearly dropped. He was gorgeous.

Her stomach fluttered.

Raine inhaled sharply. She must have noticed, too.

"Good morning." His light brown hair was carelessly styled, almost as if he'd crawled out of bed and used his fingers as a comb.

Callie double-checked to make sure she wasn't drooling. His stubble was sexy. Glasses gave him a nerdy vibe, but did nothing to dull his vibrant eyes. Drowning in those pools of blue would be so easy to do, but what a way to go.

He glanced at the door and then back at her. "Is the coffee shop open?"

As Raine stared—okay, *leered*—she hadn't seemed to hear his question. Understandable. The barista's boyfriend, Emmett, might not think so, but this wasn't the typical eye candy found in Silver Falls.

Callie nudged her friend, trying to be inconspicuous. Luckily, the large wreath hid what she was doing.

"Uh, yes. Sorry." Raine appeared dazed, but Callie didn't blame her. This guy could be the next Bachelor of the Year, if the town awarded that title. "We're open. Someone's behind the counter. I'll be right in."

Raine's words tumbled out one on top of the other as if she were nervous or flustered. Funny how an attractive guy could take intelligent, successful women right back to their tween days.

As he adjusted the right corner of his glasses, Callie couldn't stop herself from gawking at him. He glanced at her, not seeming to notice her staring…or at least pretending he hadn't. His grin—full of straight white teeth—sent her pulse sprinting.

"Have a wonderful day."

His deep voice left her breathless. Or maybe that was his smile. Could have been his eyes.

Before she could think of anything to say, he went into

the shop.

"Whoa." Raine stared at the closed door. "Do you know him?"

"I've never seen him around. Trust me, I'd remember meeting someone with a face like that."

"Me, too." Raine whistled. "He's hot."

"Smokin'."

Her mouth quirked. "He was eyeing you heavy. Want to call dibs?"

"Dibs?" Callie laughed. "No, thanks. You can."

"Emmett would have an issue if I did that, but you—"

"I don't have time for dating." The words cascaded from her mouth like water over the falls this town was named after. "As we have talked about several times before."

Raine feigned innocence like she hadn't been trying to set up Callie with Emmett's friends. "You made time for Rex."

Callie shrugged. "A dog is different. I can take him to work with me."

"All work and no play…"

Not ready to have this conversation again, she motioned to the coffee shop's door. "There's nothing wrong with looking, so get in there and enjoy the view while you can."

"You don't have to tell me twice." Raine grinned as if she were holding a winning lottery ticket. "I'll bring by your usual order later. We can talk about our weekends, and if I find out more about the hottie stranger, I'll let you know."

"Please do." A vanilla latte would give Callie a much-needed jolt of caffeine to get through the day after arriving home late last night. And even if she wasn't interested in dating, the guy piqued her curiosity. She wouldn't mind knowing who he was or what he was doing in town. "Thanks."

"See you soon." With that, Raine hurried into the coffee shop.

Strolling along First Avenue, Callie hummed "Winter Wonderland." The impressive window displays overflowed with red, green, silver, gold, and white. Some themes were subtle, almost monochromatic. Others burst with a kaleidoscope of color. Lights—from miniature fairy ones to icicle and snowflake shaped—glowed brightly.

The elves, aka her fellow business owners, must have binged on iced sugar cookies to manage all this decorating over the Thanksgiving weekend. Only Raine hadn't finished, but she was close. Wags and Tails must be the only shop not decked out for the holidays.

An empty feeling settled in the pit of Callie's stomach. One that had nothing to do with skipping breakfast.

Stop.

Callie had chosen to spend Thanksgiving with her family. She'd known taking off from Wednesday afternoon through Sunday night would put her behind. Being the last to finish didn't matter. Not much, anyway. The First Avenue Business Association required stores to be decorated by the end of November. That gave her five days.

Plenty of time.

Judging for the holiday window display competition didn't happen until December twenty-third. Some store owners worked on their entries until the last minute. Last year's winner had added a Christmas-inspired wedding cake to her bakery window the day before judging. Pure genius and talent that deserved the grand prize—a gift certificate to the town's best restaurant, a shiny plaque, and bragging rights for the entire year. Taryn Lawson had made no secret of wanting to repeat as winner.

Not if Callie had anything to say about it.

This year, she planned to step up her decorating efforts. She had the time now that she employed two full-time and two part-time employees. To be honest, she'd never cared or thought much about the award itself, but after listening to her parents' and her three older brothers' recent accomplishments over the weekend, she was determined to grab first place. *Winning* was her new goal.

Metal scraped against cement.

Callie glanced across the street to see Mr. Jones setting out a display of snow shovels in front of his hardware store. The older man—some said Harry was in his late sixties while others claimed he was pushing eighty—wore a red-and-black padded parka and a hat with fleece flaps over the ears.

She waved a gloved hand. "I hope you had your fill of turkey, Mr. Jones."

"More than enough." He patted his stomach. "Did you enjoy visiting your family?"

"Yes, I did."

Thinking about being with her parents and brothers brought a mix of emotions. She loved her family, and they loved her, but she wasn't like them. Unfortunately, none of them recognized that or could see she had different goals. They misread her love of dogs as a sign of immaturity, treating her as if she were a little girl who needed help to get through the day instead of a twenty-eight-year-old business owner.

That would change when they arrived in Silver Falls on the twenty-fourth of December. Once they saw Wags and Tails thriving, they'd realize the *baby* of the family *could* take care of herself and run a business. And had been doing that for nearly three years despite their concerns.

Maybe then her brothers, who took overprotectiveness to the max, would relax. Flynn and Garrett had texted last night to make sure she'd arrived home safely, and Keaton had called earlier this morning in case she'd overslept. She appreciated they cared and watched out for her, but she didn't like when they told her what to do or how to do it. The big bro stuff she could live with. The other made her feel bad and needed to stop.

"But I'm happy to be home," she admitted. "I may have been born and raised in LA, but the big city no longer appeals to me. I'm a small-town girl at heart."

Mr. Jones beamed, more like a pleased grandfather than a happy lumberjack. "We're happy to have you here."

In Silver Falls, *we* could mean anything from Mr. and Mrs. Jones to the First Avenue Business Association, but Callie stood taller. She'd never felt as if she truly belonged anywhere until discovering this town. "Thanks."

He held onto one of the shovels. "We thought your employees would decorate while you were away since you're open seven days a week, but Wags and Tails was closed for four days."

Four and a half if she wanted to get technical. Callie didn't. "I gave my staff the time off."

"That was generous." He arranged the last shovel before moving the sale sign closer to the display. "Hope you don't regret that decision. The Association will issue a fine if your store isn't decorated by the deadline."

He didn't sound upset. Add him to the list of people concerned about her. Unlike her family who made her feel as if she wasn't good enough and needed validation, Mr. Jones was one of the many people who looked out for one another around town. Association fines added up fast. No one wanted to see another person penalized if they could avoid it.

Callie appreciated the sense of community, both as a business owner and resident. She adjusted the strap of her tote.

"I'll be finished well before that." If the setup didn't hit any snags—it shouldn't—the window would be ready tomorrow night. She crossed her fingers.

"Good to hear." Relief softened his stance. "Holler if you need a hand."

"Thanks, but everything will be okay," she reassured him, knowing she had this, like most things, under control. "I have a plan."

Her plans had never failed her. This one wouldn't, either.

Chapter Two

A FEW MINUTES later, Callie opened the door to Wags and Tails. The bell jingled, welcoming her into the lobby area where customers dropped off and picked up their dogs. Warm air enveloped her as did the familiar scents of dog and grooming supplies.

Home.

She'd been away for only a few days, but that was long enough.

A bark cut through the air.

Her heart swelled with affection. Callie placed her tote bag on the floor, dropped to her knees, removed her gloves, and held out her arms. "Rex."

Her dog, a part lab mixed breed she'd adopted from the local animal rescue, lumbered toward her with the happiest expression on his face.

"It's so good to see you, handsome boy." She wrapped her arms around him. His brown fur smelled clean and fresh. "You got a bath."

"Everyone at my house gets a bath on Sundays." Anna Kent, the shop's groomer and Callie's best friend, stood behind the counter. With her blonde hair pulled into a ponytail, Anna resembled a college student more than a woman who'd turned thirty last month. She wore the shop's hunter-green apron with *Wags and Tails* embroidered on the front over a white long-sleeved T-shirt and jeans. "Before you ask, Rex was a perfect guest. No trouble at all. He even let the cats sleep on top of him. I'm hoping his good behavior rubbed off on my bad dog."

"Milo isn't bad." Callie ruffled Rex's back. His fur was soft against her fingers. "He's…spirited."

Anna rolled her eyes. "Well, the spirited dog is in a crate in the back."

Oh, no. Milo, a West Highland white terrier mix also adopted from the rescue group, was known for getting into mischief, but he was a total cutie. "Doggy time-out?"

"Unfortunately. Five minutes after we arrived and…" Anna threw up her hands.

Callie rubbed Rex's side. "You're my sweetheart. Help Milo stay out of trouble, okay?"

Rex's tail wagged at twice his normal speed. As he rubbed his muzzle against her, her insides melted. The house had felt lonely without him there last night.

"How did I get so lucky to find you?" She kissed Rex's head again before smiling at Anna. "Thanks for watching him."

"Anytime." Anna came around the front of the counter. "I was surprised you only texted while you were gone. Sam was sure you'd miss Rex so much you'd call to talk to him."

"I missed him, but I was trying to be strong for both our sakes."

"Thanks for that." Anna grinned. "Sam owes me five bucks."

Standing, Callie grimaced. Sam worked for her full time. He also took a couple of classes at the university in Summit Ridge, the nearest town to them. Still…

She placed her hands on her hips. "You two bet on me?"

"It was Sam's idea. He was positive you'd call every day since this is the longest you've been away. I knew you wouldn't because you'd be too busy with your family."

"That doesn't make betting right." Callie glanced at Rex. "What are we going to do with Aunt Anna?"

Rex tilted his head, making Callie think he understood what she was saying.

"You're not doing anything with me. At least not until you tell me about your trip." The curiosity in Anna's gaze matched the tone of her voice. "How was Thanksgiving at your parents' house? Was it fun? Lots of yummy food? Did your brothers fix you up with any of their attractive friends?"

Trying not to laugh at the barrage of questions, Callie led Rex behind the counter to his dog bed. He circled twice before curling up on the large pillow. This was his spot when he needed a break from daycare activities or when only a few dogs were here.

"Imagine me going out with a lawyer, doctor, or professor." A giggle escaped. "They wouldn't know what to do with my dog and small-town talk. They'd be bored or lost, maybe both, and so would I listening to them babble on about their high-powered jobs."

Having no common ground was only one reason dating

her brothers' friends would never work. Flynn, Garrett, and Keaton were hardworking, successful men, but their friends likely had the same overachieving type-A personalities—men who would tell her what to do and how to do it.

All. The. Time.

Whether she was in Silver Falls or Los Angeles.

No, thanks.

She'd had enough of that.

Callie strived to be successful in her own right. She worked as many hours, maybe more, than the two doctors, two lawyers, and the professor in her family, but she did so because her job made her happy. When they were passing out the family DNA, someone bypassed giving her the claw-to-the-top-in-a-cutthroat-field gene.

"The trip went well. No travel issues. Perfect SoCal fall weather. No drama other than a heated debate about homemade cranberry sauce versus canned."

"Homemade."

"Agreed."

The tablet on the counter buzzed. Anna picked it up before raising an eyebrow at Callie. "Any dates with an old acquaintance or maybe a new one?"

Callie pretended not to notice her friend's hopeful tone. "Nope."

"Bummer."

She shrugged. "Not really since I'm head over heels in love."

Anna's eyes widened. "Say what?"

Somehow, Callie managed to keep a straight face. "You

know him."

"Who? How did I miss this?" Anna leaned forward so much Callie was afraid she might fall over. "Spill. Now."

Better not drag this out any longer. "Chewie, the labradoodle. He and Rex got along like best buds when he was here last Monday. I haven't stopped thinking about the cutie pie. Might have to meet at the park for a playdate."

"Grrrr." Anna clutched the tablet to her chest. "This is for me betting on you, right?"

"Maybe, though I have a type I regularly fall for."

Anna scoffed. "Four-legged, furry, and barks isn't a type."

"Shh. Rex might be hurt if he hears you." Callie covered his ears, half in jest. Her dog was the love of her life. "Not all of us can have a handsome contractor named Davis wooing us."

Anna's cheeks turned bright pink. "We've only gone out a few times."

"That's more than I've dated."

"You could if you wanted."

Callie shrugged. She hadn't tried to meet men since moving here. "Owning a business and taking care of Rex doesn't leave much free time. I'm okay with that."

Everything she wanted, she'd found in Silver Falls—her own business, cottage, and friends. She didn't need anything more right now, including romance.

An image of the hottie outside the coffee shop popped into her mind. So handsome…

Nope. Not even him.

"But I'm happy you met Davis."

"Thanks, but things are so new. Who knows what will happen?" Anna studied whatever message was on the tablet as if the survival of mankind was at stake. That suggested she didn't want to talk about the new guy in her life.

No problem. Callie pointed to the Christmas figurine sitting on the counter. The lighted Christmas tree with dogs in Santa hats on the branches had been a present from the doggy daycare's former owner before he moved to Florida.

"What's this doing out?" she asked.

Anna glanced up. "I grabbed it from one of the Christmas boxes in the storage room in case anyone mentioned our lack of decorations. You know how serious Silver Falls is about Christmas."

"Crazy serious." Callie wound the knob on the bottom. Strains of "We Wish You a Merry Christmas" played. "But by the time I'm finished with the window display, people will forget we didn't decorate at the same time as the other shops."

"Uh-oh." With a do-I-want-to-know expression, Anna set the tablet on the counter. "The last time I heard that tone was when you took over the travel agency's space next door and doubled the size of Wags and Tails. Should I be worried?"

"Not at all. It's just…" Callie stared at the window display currently housing an area for smaller dogs. Milo loved playing in there, and folks passing by enjoyed watching the pups' antics. "We're going to win this year."

"Win what?"

Determined, Callie raised her chin. "The annual holiday window display competition."

Anna's mouth gaped. She closed it. "But you've never taken the competition seriously. Last year, you said your time and resources were better spent elsewhere. You claimed the contest didn't matter."

"I did." Callie had no problem owning up to what she'd said in the past. "Those things were true my first two years here, but now I've had a change of heart."

"Because..."

"The Christmas windows are important to the town."

Anna's nose crinkled. "And..."

"Business is booming after our expansion. I have more resources and time since hiring part-time help."

"And..."

Anna knew her too well. "My family is visiting over the holidays. This will be their first time in Silver Falls."

"I can't believe they haven't come to see you yet."

"I didn't want them here while I was trying to build the business and redo the cottage. If they'd come before I was ready, they would have tried to convince me to give up and go back with them." Callie hadn't wanted her family to see her struggling to pull her business and home together or telling her what to do. She wanted to show off her new life from a point of strength and success. "Now that everything's going well, I invited them to visit."

Anna scratched her cheek. "That doesn't explain you wanting to win."

Callie sighed. "This weekend was a lovefest over the

awards and acknowledgments my parents and brothers recently received. I'm proud of them…"

"But you want them to be equally proud of you."

She nodded. "Listening to them go on, seeing the social media posts, the certificates, and the awards, I became that baby sister again, the one who didn't like sports—who never received even a participation medal to add to the family collection. Unlike my three older brothers who brought home medals and trophies for whatever they played."

Compassion shone in Anna's eyes. "You never told me that."

Callie shrugged. "It's silly, but the competition this year is important to me. I want to show my family what I've accomplished and make them proud. Winning the award will do that."

"Oh, sweetie. Emphasis on accomplished." Anna circled her arm in a sweeping gesture around the lobby as if to make her point. "You own a business. Volunteer. You're a fixture in town. Everyone loves you…and not only the four-footed barking residents."

"Thank you." The compliment touched Callie. She was doing well. "But I want my parents and brothers to see the person I've worked hard to become. To acknowledge me and stop thinking I'm the baby who plays with dogs all day and is barely supporting herself."

Flynn and Garrett had offered to pay her plane ticket home this past weekend. She'd said no and then booked the trip herself much to their chagrin.

"Don't get me wrong. I'm happy for my family's successes. I really am. But hearing them go on about everything made me feel…less than." She imagined the first-prize plaque hanging on the wall behind the counter. That would impress her parents and brothers. "Trophies and awards matter to them, so I decided to go for it."

"If that's what you want to do, great." Anna always had her back. The same way Callie had hers. "But your family doesn't need a shiny award to be proud of you. You shouldn't need anything to be proud of yourself, either."

True, but… "I realized last night on the flight home, I want to win. Not only for my family, but also for all of us at Wags and Tails, too. Bragging rights for a year, remember?"

"I forgot about that part of the grand prize." Anna rubbed her chin. "Okay. I'm in. Just tell me what to do."

"Thanks." Callie's muscles tightened as if preparing for the work ahead.

Nothing would stand in the way of her winning. She would show her family how well she was doing in Silver Falls and that she could take care of herself. Her parents and brothers would see she was as successful as they were, only in a different way. Working with dogs wasn't playing or a temporary job. Owning a doggy daycare was not only a viable profession in a growing marketplace, but it was also her passion.

She bounced on her toes.

Soon. Very soon.

Chapter Three

AFTER THE DETOUR to the coffee shop, Brandt Winslow parked his all-wheel-drive car on Aunt Margot's driveway. He hadn't been back to his hometown in six years—six years trying to forget what had happened here. Even though he hadn't needed the money, he'd taken contract computer programming assignments and found professional success. He could work wherever he wanted and had. Too bad he'd yet to find a new place to call home.

Not that he still considered Silver Falls as his home, but an extended vacation at his aunt's house was what he needed. Aunt Margot was the perfect combination of second mom and best friend with her unconditional love, acceptance, and unlimited supply of homemade desserts she'd made for him when he'd been growing up and then returned here to live after college.

He grabbed the drink tray holding the two coffees and a pound of coffee beans, slid from the driver's seat, and then closed the car door. The cold bit into his lungs and stung his skin.

"Brr." His breath hung in the crisp, fresh air, the temperature a reminder he was no longer at sea level. San Jose and the Bay Area were thirty-plus degrees warmer. He'd forgotten how cold Silver Falls could be, but crossing the street to the coffee shop had reminded him fast. Gloves, a hat, boots, and a heavier jacket were must-have winter gear that belonged on him—not in his suitcase.

But as he'd prepared for the trip, summer had come to mind. He'd left Silver Falls the week after Fourth of July. As he packed his car, sweat had rolled down his back. The blistering heat was a perfect match for his boiling anger.

Forget about that.

Holding the drink carrier in his left hand, Brandt swung his laptop bag over his right shoulder and grabbed his suitcase. As he headed to the porch, his shoes left footprints in the light layer of snow.

Halfway to the door, barking sounded.

He froze.

Dogs.

His muscles bunched. And then he remembered…

His aunt owned two dogs.

He didn't relax, but tension seeped away.

Aunt Margot had said they were friendly mutts. He hoped so.

Brett wasn't afraid of dogs per se. He was, however, uncomfortable around them because he'd never had a pet due to his mother's severe allergies to anything furry. His aunt hadn't gotten dogs until his parents moved away from Silver Falls after he'd left town.

He continued to the front door and knocked.

The barking intensified, a cacophony of noise with one

higher-pitched yelp and a deeper growly one.

The door opened. Two furry creatures—a small tan one and a medium gray-and-black one—bolted to sniff his shoes and legs. Tails wagged, and paws pounced.

"Leave your cousin alone," Aunt Margot chastised her two pets, but her indulgent tone didn't stop their behavior. She grinned at Brandt. "Angus is the feisty little one who loves belly rubs. Sadie is older and a love bug. They might sniff and lick you to death, but they're harmless."

"I suppose there are worse ways to go," he said in a lighthearted tone, even if he wasn't sure what to make of the two dogs yet.

"Let's not find out," she teased back, her blue eyes twinkling. She took the drink carrier from him. "Thanks for answering my panicked call about being out of coffee."

"I was happy to stop." Seeing the pretty woman with chestnut-colored hair standing outside the coffee shop had made his return to Silver Falls a little brighter. "I can't survive a morning without caffeine myself."

"Your dad's the same way. A family trait."

The Winslow clan shared a few of those. "I'm sorry I didn't arrive yesterday as I planned, but the traffic was so bad. I was tired and needed to stop for the night."

"I'm glad you did. Better safe than sorry." She motioned toward the open door behind her. "Now get in here before you catch a chill and end up sick."

Same old Aunt Margot. She was ten years older than his dad and doted on everyone she met, but especially Brandt, her only nephew. She'd never married. As far as he knew, she didn't date. Her passion was quilting. She owned the quilt shop on First Avenue but only worked part time since hiring a store manager.

He'd last seen Aunt Margot at his parents' beach house over Labor Day weekend last year. She dressed as bohemian as ever in a patchwork quilted jacket, a floral-print skirt that swished around her ankles, and a hip-length sweater. The lines around the corners of her eyes and mouth had deepened with age. Her hair had turned fully gray, too, but the sparkle in her eyes still lit up a room.

The dogs ran around the front yard. "My two cousins want to stay outside."

She handed him his coffee. "Drink this."

He did. The hot liquid warmed his insides.

"Nice and toasty now." He took another sip and then winked. "But in case you haven't noticed, I'm not a kid you need to keep an eye on. I wasn't one when I moved away."

"You may have lapped the sun a few more times since you were here last, Brandt Winslow, but you can't fool me." She poked a finger against his chest. "You're the same kiddo who ran away to my house whenever he didn't like something his parents did."

"I remember those days." This house had been his sanctuary. He'd left clothes in his aunt's guestroom, so he hadn't even needed to pack before running out the front door. He laughed at the memories. "I guess some things haven't changed. Mom and Dad are going on a three-week Christmas cruise, friends of theirs are staying at their condo on the Oregon coast, and here I am."

Aunt Margot's expression softened. "You've always been welcome, and you always will be."

"I know, and I appreciate that." He didn't want to make her feel like his second choice this Christmas. She wasn't. "There's no place I'd rather be than here with you."

She pushed back her shoulders. "I plan to make the most of your stay."

His aunt appeared determined. Good, so was he.

He would make up for the years he'd stayed away. Whatever his aunt needed him to do or wanted to do with him, he was game. He raised his cup to hers. "That makes two of us."

Something caught his attention. Rather, something that should have been on the front porch but wasn't there. "Where is the old plastic snowman and the other Christmas decorations?"

"You said you wanted to help me with my holiday to-do list."

His aunt had always decorated on Black Friday. He gripped his coffee cup so hard the lid nearly popped up, so he loosened his fingers. "You waited for me."

"I've missed having my number-one helper." She glanced at the bigger dog trotting around the front yard. "It'll be like old times."

A sense of nostalgia flowed through him. Regret, too, for not being a better nephew and visiting her. He had been working crazy hours, but that wasn't the reason he'd stayed away. He'd needed time to get over the betrayal of his former best friend and business partner. That healing had taken time...*years.*

Was he ready to face the past?

He wasn't sure, but he'd wanted to spend this Christmas with his aunt so here he was.

"Thank you." Words weren't enough, but that was all he had to give her. "I haven't decorated in…far too long."

"When was the last time?" She drank her coffee.

Brandt tried to remember the last Christmas tree he'd put up. "When I lived in Silver Falls…"

His aunt shook her head. "You helped your mom and me decorate. You were barely at your apartment."

"You're right." Work had been insane then. He dragged his hand through his hair. "It's been a while."

As Aunt Margot gave him a one-armed hug, her vanilla-and-floral perfume brought back memories of living in Silver Falls. Happy times he'd pushed aside along with the bad ones.

"This old place wants its halls decked. Today!" She bounced from foot to foot with excitement. "Are you ready to spread some holiday cheer?"

"I'm ready." More than he realized.

She whistled. "Inside, you two fur monsters."

The dogs scrambled into the house, their wet paws slipping on the hardwood floor.

Brandt followed his aunt. He set his luggage and bag on the wide-plank hardwood floor, hoping the two pieces would be safe from the dogs, who ran to the kitchen.

Warmth surrounded him. Whether from forced-air heating or the crackling logs in the fireplace, the cold disappeared from his skin. A knot in his gut—one he hadn't realized was there until now—loosened.

Her house looked identical to the last time he'd been here. Even the delicious aroma of fresh bread baking in the air was the same. Only the fresh-cut flowers from her garden that had been on her dining room table were missing.

He needed a minute, so he sipped his coffee. When he finished, the emotions hadn't faded but grown. "I've missed this place."

Staying away from Silver Falls had seemed like the smartest way to leave the past behind and move on. Now Brandt wondered if he'd made the right decision. Aunt Margot had visited him, but he'd never thought about coming to see her. Not until now.

"And you." He swallowed around the lump lodged in his throat. "I'm sorry it's taken me so long—"

"No apologies needed." Aunt Margot squeezed his arm, her voice full of understanding he didn't deserve. "After Nick sold the company behind your back, I don't blame you for staying away and not wanting to see him again."

Nick Baxter, his best friend since preschool.

Make that former best friend and business partner.

A chill ran the length of Brandt's spine. From the time they were kids, Nick had wanted to be the one to shine, and Brandt had let his cofounder be the face of NiBrTech—a company they'd founded in college. But he'd never expected Nick to buy into the hype of being the brains behind their start-up and let his control-freak ways get the best of him.

"I'd prefer to avoid him while I'm here." Brandt's anger sparked. He took a calming breath. One of the many techniques high-priced therapists had suggested to him over the years. "What happened is in the past."

"Where it should stay," Aunt Margot agreed.

If he ran into Nick, so what? The guy was nothing to Brandt. Nick had been a selfish jerk, thinking only of himself and his pregnant wife. He'd been offered options—solid ones that would have solved his marital problems and lowered his stress level when the pressure got to be too much for him—but the guy hadn't wanted to take a step back. Selling the company to a competitor who wanted to take their technology—algorithms Brandt had created—and put them out of business had been a better solution.

"I'm thrilled you're back where you belong and staying until the new year." She stared over the lip of her cup. "I plan on spoiling you, so you won't want to leave."

Holding back a grin, he raised a brow. "Are you supposed to be telling me your nefarious plot?"

"I'm not one for keeping secrets." Aunt Margot relished her role as town gossip. Her quilt shop had the reputation of being rumor central. "Besides, you're so smart you would have figured out my plans after a day or two of being home."

Home.

Standing in Aunt Margot's living room was the closest he'd gotten to being home since he'd left Silver Falls. No other place had felt this way, and he'd tried to find one that had.

Brandt shifted his weight between his feet. "I'm better debugging code than figuring out people."

She pursed her lips. "Give yourself more credit."

"What can I say? Computer programming is easy." Relating with others, not so much. That'd been one reason Nick had taken on the role of CEO while Brandt ran the technical side of the company.

Stop thinking about the past.

Grab and hold on to the present.

Which was what he would do now.

The spot near the front window had been cleared out and vacuumed, ready for the Christmas tree.

"Let's not waste any time." Brandt downed the rest of his coffee. He couldn't forget there were more wonderful memories in Silver Falls than bad ones. This time with his aunt would create new ones. "It's time to turn your house into a winter wonderland."

Chapter Four

THE NEXT MORNING, Brandt stood in his aunt's living room. A good night's sleep on the comfortable mattress in the guest bedroom and a hot shower had taken away the soreness after carrying boxes from the attic and climbing a ladder to decorate the house inside and out. The results, however, had been worth the aches and pains.

"Not bad." He was pleased with how Christmassy the house looked. "Mom would be proud."

Multicolored lights twinkled on the artificial Christmas tree. After a spider infestation due to a freshly cut tree two years ago, his aunt wouldn't allow another live one in her house. Scented sticks hanging near the tree trunk filled the room with a pine fragrance.

A Christmas quilt was folded on the back of the sofa. Different fabrics made up the blocks, but the green, red, and gold colors remained consistent on each. A patchwork teddy bear his aunt had made years ago sat in a small rocking chair Brandt had used as a kid.

A strand of garland with white lights was strung across the front of the fireplace mantel. On top was a display of snowmen. Two quilted stockings, made by Aunt Margot, with each of their names embroidered on the cuffs, hung below them. He made a mental note to buy stocking stuffers so his aunt's overflowed with gifts and candy on Christmas morning.

A nativity snow globe sat on the coffee table. Lighted porcelain village pieces were displayed on bookcase shelves. Not one flat surface in the room, or house, was without some type of holiday décor—candles, candy bowls, figurines. The two bathrooms were themed, too, with Santa in one and angels in the other.

Every decoration brought back memories of Christmases past.

Satisfaction flowed through Brandt—a way he hadn't felt in years.

"Admiring our decorating?" Aunt Margot exited the kitchen with a coffee cup in each hand. The dogs followed her, but both stayed out of the living room as she continued toward Brett. She handed him one.

Steam rose from the cup. He took a sip. Perfect. "You remembered how I like it."

"Two splashes of milk and a teaspoon of sugar." She pointed to the side of her head with her free hand. "I may be old, but my brain still works."

Aunt Margot had decorated past ten o'clock last night. Her energy level hadn't faded once, even though his had sapped. "You're young."

"Young at heart." She struck a pose, a cross between Voguing and random silliness, and then burst out laughing.

Greatest. Aunt. Ever.

A delicious smell drifted from the kitchen. The scent wasn't too strong, especially with the coffee cup near his mouth, but the hint of enticing goodness made his mouth water.

Cinnamon rolls? Swedish tea ring? Baked French toast? She'd made those dishes for him over the years. "What are you cooking?"

"A sundried tomato and spinach strata."

Visiting Aunt Margo had been the right decision. The home cooking was an added bonus.

"It'll be ready shortly." Moving closer to the tree, she glanced out the window and clucked her tongue. "The snow is coming down hard."

He didn't like her concerned tone. "I'll drive you to the quilt shop."

"I appreciate the offer, but I've been driving in snow since I was sixteen. I'll be fine." As she faced him, the lines on her face were deeper than they'd been minutes ago. "It's the dogs I'm worried about."

Brandt didn't understand. "Don't they like snow?"

"They love it, but they also enjoy being walked to their doggy daycare on First Avenue." She glanced at the two dogs. "But I can't chance hitting an icy spot along the way. Angus and Sadie will be so disappointed."

He didn't associate that emotion with animals, but walking the dogs seemed important to his aunt. That made the task important to him. "I'll take them for you."

"Oh, that would be wonderful." Her shoulders relaxed a bit, but her smile didn't widen as he expected it would. "Are you sure?"

Neither dog acted rambunctious. Both had kept their distance last night. Today, they sat patiently outside the living room. That suggested they were well-trained.

"Positive." How much trouble could walking two dogs a couple of blocks be? "I don't remember a doggy daycare on First Avenue."

"Wags and Tails opened the year after you left. It's next to the flower shop. The travel agency used to be on the other side, but the doggy daycare expanded into that space earlier this year."

He pictured the street lined with shops and cafés. It had seemed different yesterday morning, but he'd been in a rush so hadn't paid close attention. He remembered those businesses his aunt mentioned and the gift shop that used to be between them. "There have been some changes since I've been gone."

"Several shops closed. New ones opened." A note of mystery crossed her face. "But the changes have been good for the town. Not all the business owners are from here."

Trying to decipher Aunt Margot's hidden meanings was a waste of time. He'd learned at age eleven to just ask her. "What do you mean?"

"Silver Falls needed fresh faces. New blood. People moving to town for business opportunities made that happen." Mischief gleamed in his aunt's blue-eyed gaze—the same color eyes as him and his father. "In fact, a couple of those faces happen to be female. Your age or a few years younger. I'll introduce you."

Oh, no. Brandt held up his hands, palms facing his aunt as if that would stop her. If need be, he'd grab garlic cloves from the kitchen or whatever else would ward off her matchmaking.

Memories of her wanting to find him a date to his senior prom still lingered. The nightmares, too. Spending the month being fixed up on blind dates didn't appeal to him in the slightest. If anything, his skin prickled as if ready to break out in hives. He needed to stop her before she began.

Dating wasn't part of his plans for his visit. If it were, he'd still tell his aunt no and find out the name of the pretty brunette who'd been standing outside the coffee shop himself.

"I'm in town to see you, not to meet fresh female faces." Lowering his arms, he kept his voice calm. No reason to panic yet. "Or date. That's not happening while I'm here."

As she adjusted an ornament on the tree, a playful grin tugged at her lips. "You're in Silver Falls until New Year's."

"To spend time with you." He sipped his coffee.

"I have to work at the shop."

"Only part time." His aunt set her own hours. She didn't have to go in each day, but she enjoyed visiting with customers and keeping her hand in the business she'd founded over three decades ago.

"You'll be alone." She sounded like he needed a babysitter.

"I'll be fine. I finished an app before I came. I'm working on a mobile game now." That was what he did for fun between contracts. The fact he earned money from his creations was icing on the cake. "I have plenty to do while you're at work."

"Did you know geeks are as sexy as superheroes? At least according to the cover of a magazine I saw at the grocery store."

"Learn something every day." Brandt sipped his coffee. "Maybe I should take off my contacts and put on my glasses instead."

"No need. You're attractive with or without glasses." Her stark appraisal made him feel like a slab of beef on display at the butcher shop. "Which is why I'm shocked you're not dating someone."

Bummer. He thought they'd moved on from this, but his aunt tended to get tunnel vision about certain things. "Nothing wrong with being unattached."

"No, but you're a catch. Thanks to your mother's interior design influence and my color instinct, you have an eye for decorating, which many men don't have." As Aunt Margo sipped her coffee, she continued to stare at him. "Sweatpants aside, you also dress well. There's no reason you shouldn't be dating one or more women while you're here."

She wasn't going to give up, but he was willing to argue his case so she would back off.

"I've gone longer than a month without a date and survived." He could calculate how long, but he didn't want to give Aunt Margot any ammunition. Playing matchmaker was her second favorite hobby after quilting. He wanted no part of it. Now or ever. "December will be no different."

"It's still November."

He gave her the stink eye.

Aunt Margot sighed.

Brandt would try again. "You introduced my parents and they're still together, but I don't need to meet anyone right now. I'm happy being single."

She harrumphed. "You're thirty-two."

"My biological clock is not about to go off," he joked.

"At your age, you should be dating or married," she countered. "Not programming or gaming or whatever it is you do."

"I date," he countered.

People always wanted to fix him up with their sisters or friends when he started a new job. He usually said yes, but he worked and moved so much that getting involved in a serious relationship didn't make sense. Besides, he preferred pulling an all-nighter at his desk, sleeping when he could, and fueling on caffeine to having a romantic dinner for two.

Coding was more than a job to him. He derived immense pleasure and satisfaction from the projects he worked on. Nothing else compared to the rush of taking a product live. Forget that he wasn't an actual employee of the companies who hired him. He liked having the freedom to choose the jobs and the places he worked. Why would he want to do anything differently and tie himself down?

No way.

Aunt Margot and the women he'd dated didn't understand how much fun he had working. "I promise I'll date when the new year rolls around and I'm settled in a new job."

The set of his aunt's jaw told him she wasn't convinced.

"I'll text you pics when I go out so you'll have proof."

A compromise, but one he hoped would appease his aunt.

Although…if she became interested in playing matchmaker to someone else, he'd be off the hook. One of her employees or customers? There had to be someone in Silver Falls who wanted help finding love this Christmas. He didn't care who as long as it wasn't him.

"Deal?" Brandt asked.

A beat passed. And another. She tapped her chin with her index finger. "I'll consider it."

That was better than a no.

"Fair enough." He hoped she decided to say yes.

The oven timer beeped.

Aunt Margot glanced toward the kitchen, but she didn't appear to be done talking.

He was. "I'll pull out the pan, then set the table."

That would give his aunt time to realize he wouldn't humor her matchmaking efforts or, worst-case scenario, have her double-down to find him a girlfriend, not a date.

Brandt had to prepare himself for either happening. He'd once been caught off guard and lost his company, his hometown, and his faith in friendships and partnerships.

That would never happen again.

Chapter Five

AFTER BREAKFAST AND helping his aunt prepare the dogs for their walk, Brandt closed the front door behind him. In his pocket was a roll of purple potty bags. He hoped he didn't have to use one. He transferred one of the leashes to his other hand.

A blanket of snow fell. No problem. He'd unpacked his winter gear. With a fleece-lined beanie, heavy parka, top-of-the-line gloves, and snow boots, he was prepared for whatever Mother Nature threw at Silver Falls today.

"This will be fun." Angus and Sadie wore matching sweaters, red ones with thin green stripes. They pulled against their leashes. "Hang on."

The dogs didn't acknowledge him. They kept moving, their paws sinking into the inches of snow on the front walkway.

Brandt followed, not that they left him any choice unless he wanted to fall onto his face. "Impatient to get going?"

Ignoring him, the dogs quickened their pace. Guess they enjoyed being out as much as his aunt had said.

Medium-sized snowflakes pricked Brandt's cheeks. Nothing like the tiny ice pellets he remembered, but he would wear a scarf the next time he went outside. "Hold up a minute."

The dogs stopped, snow clinging to their sweaters, but their tails kept wagging. Brandt raised his collar to keep snow from falling inside.

"Good dogs." The edges of his mouth curled upward. "Let's go."

The dogs scrambled forward as if they were on a mission. Brandt didn't care. Other than the dogs pulling to go faster, walking them was easy. He could do this each morning, so Aunt Margot wouldn't have to go out in the snow. Everyone, dogs included, would be happy.

When they reached the sidewalk, Angus turned left. Sadie went right. The leashes crossed in front of Brandt's legs, nearly tripping him.

"Whoa."

He held out his arms—well, tried—to steady himself. The tread on the bottom of his boots kept him from sliding or falling, but if he didn't do something quick…

He untangled the leashes. "We're going the same direction. Come on."

Sadie pulled toward the right again—the wrong way, but she didn't tug Brandt off-balance because he was prepared. Angus darted between his legs, lassoing Brandt with his leash.

"What are you doing?" The dogs stared at him with their heads tilted. He wasn't amused. "According to memes, cats are the ones who plot to kill people—not dogs."

Angus panted as if taking a breather, probably so he

could cause more havoc.

"Stop pretending to be innocent," he said to Angus, trying to step out of the mess of leash around his legs. "Don't forget, you're smaller than me. I can carry you."

Sadie, however, was too big.

Tail wagging, Angus barked. Sadie's head bounced between the smaller dog and Brandt.

"Your name should be Trouble with a capital T, not Angus." Brandt unwrapped the leash. "This way."

Sadie barked.

"Not you, too." The dogs would not get to him. He continued toward First Avenue. "I bet you don't give Aunt Margot any problems."

Given the devilish gleam in Angus's brown eyes, maybe they did.

Sadie stopped and squatted.

Brandt groaned. "Are you kidding me? You have to go to the bathroom now?"

Ignoring him, Sadie did her business. At least Angus stayed out of the way.

"You could have done this in your own backyard. When I wasn't around." Cringing, he used a potty bag to clean up the mess. He didn't get anything on himself, but still… "Now I'm going to have to disinfect my gloves."

As if on cue, Angus raised his leg and sprayed a bush.

"I hope that's all you have to go."

It wasn't.

The dogs ambled as if they were in no rush, pausing to smell trees, plants, or rocks despite the snow. "If you two don't speed up, the doggy daycare will be closed by the time we arrive."

Okay, not really, but the dogs had turned into immoveable sniffing machines who weren't making any measurable forward progress.

"Come on," he urged. "I didn't plan for this to take all morning."

Or day.

Ignoring him was their best skill. Poor Aunt Margot. She must have her hands full with these two.

"You didn't want to go on a walk." Brandt's words rushed out. If it weren't so cold, he'd be sweating in frustration. "You wanted to take a scratch-and-sniff adventure."

Neither barked. Of course not. That would mean lifting their noses from whatever inconsequential piece of matter had grabbed their attention.

"Your silence must mean you agree with me."

After more cajoling, they reached First Avenue.

"I'm ready for a nap." He stifled a yawn. "Maybe there's a comfy dog bed I can borrow at Wags and Tails. After I wake up, I'll have the energy to research obedience classes."

What he said didn't bother Angus or Sadie. Of course not. "Why am I talking to dogs who don't understand me?"

Brandt didn't expect an answer. Thankfully for his sanity's sake, he didn't receive one.

Seeing the sign for Wags and Tails propelled him forward. "Almost there."

A couple bundled up in heavy coats with fur-lined hoods headed toward him. The man nodded. "Good morning."

"Hello." Brandt didn't recognize the two, but he couldn't slow down even if he had. The dogs might sniff the people or take another bathroom break.

At the doggy daycare's front door, he brushed the snow from the dogs' sweaters and himself. A young woman stood behind the counter inside.

Movement in the front window to his left snagged his attention.

He turned that way and...

His breath caught in his throat.

An angel.

A living, breathing Christmas angel.

Glowing white surrounded a beautiful woman with chestnut hair. Bright light shone around her. Was that a halo and wings?

His heart stuttered.

Who is she?

Wanting to find out, he stepped closer. Only knowing she could see him if she raised her head kept him from pressing his face against the glass.

Wait a minute.

Were those white cords and small bulbs?

He blinked. Once. Twice.

Not an angel.

The woman kneeled in the middle of thousands of miniature white lights. His aunt called them fairy lights. The jolt of reality placed his feet firmly on the ground. Probably better she was human and not heaven sent. Still, the sight of her mesmerized him.

Wait. He'd seen her before.

Outside the coffee shop yesterday.

Her hair had been loose under her hat. Today, she wore it in a single braid. Loose strands framed her face, making him want to tuck the stray pieces behind her ear.

High cheekbones and wide-set eyes would be the envy of model-wannabes, yet she didn't wear a lot of makeup. He liked the natural look, which was one reason he'd noticed her before. Unfortunately, he couldn't make out the color of her eyes.

Hazel? Green or blue?

Something nudged his legs.

Sadie's muzzle pressed against his knee.

The dogs, right. He was supposed to drop them off. For his aunt. Inside.

Like the woman in the window.

His tiredness vanished. Energy surged. As Brandt opened the door, a bell jingled.

With a surprising bounce to his step, he entered the doggy daycare. Angus and Sadie went to the counter, pulling him along. He peeked over his shoulder to see the woman's profile. She appeared oblivious to him. Good. He didn't want her to see him gawking like a teenager with a crush.

As she fiddled with a strand of lights, the tip of her tongue stuck out between her lips.

Would she taste sweet or spicy?

Not that he should be thinking of kissing a stranger when he wasn't interested in dating, but something about her...

"Welcome to Wags and Tails."

Hearing a female voice made him face the counter.

A twenty-something woman wore a green apron over her clothes and her blonde hair in a ponytail. "Good morning, Sadie and Angus."

The woman stared at him expectantly as if not knowing who he was. He didn't recognize her, so she must not have grown up in Silver Falls.

Was this one of the fresh faces around his age his aunt had mentioned? The woman in the window, too?

Maybe he should reconsider having Aunt Margot play matchmaker.

Wait. What was he thinking?

No way. His aunt's matchmaking was never a good idea. She'd had a few successes like his parents, but several attempts had led to broken hearts.

Brandt cleared his voice. "I'm dropping off the dogs for Margot Winslow."

The woman picked up a tablet from the counter and then tapped it twice. "Angus and Sadie are checked in. I'll do a quick search before they go back to the play area."

"A search for what?" he asked.

"Fleas."

Ick. A shiver shot down his spine, and he hoped she didn't find any. If she did, he'd have to take them back to his aunt's house and he wasn't ready for another battle.

Not wanting to think about fleas, he glanced at her tablet to study the app displayed on the screen. He'd been curious what they used after his aunt mentioned reserving spots for her dogs online. She could also watch Angus and Sadie at the facility. Whatever app they used offered multiple features based on the interface.

"Such a good boy," the woman cooed to Angus. "It's Sadie's turn."

Angus must have mad acting skills because he was the definition of a bad boy. Rather, a bad dog. He needed his picture taken with a sign around his neck that said: *Nearly killed my human cousin today*. The day was just beginning, so who knew what would happen later.

Multicolored lights were strung around the counter. Colorful dog bones tied with green and red ribbons hung from the ceiling, but a Christmas tree figurine with different dog breeds on the branches captured his attention the most. Each canine wore a Santa hat. The decoration was cute, something his aunt would like, since two of the dogs resembled hers.

He pointed to the tree on the counter. "Did you buy this in Silver Falls?"

"It was a gift from Wags and Tails' former owner. I've never seen another around here." The woman gestured from where she was checking Sadie. "There's a knob on the bottom if you want to hear the music."

He did, and a familiar song played. Spending Christmas with his aunt would be merry. He was hopeful about the upcoming new year, too. All he needed to do was figure out where he wanted to work next. Several jobs were available. Silicon Valley offered plenty of programming positions if he wanted to stay there, but a change of scenery might be good for him. He had a month to decide.

Brandt set the figurine on the counter.

A young man whose blond hair fell into his eyes appeared from the back. He wore a forest-green apron over his clothes, too. "Are they ready?"

She handed over the leashes. The dogs trotted next to the guy like the most well-behaved animals in the world.

Traitors.

"Those two always have fun here," the woman said in a pleasant at-your-service tone.

"I'm sure they do." Better here than with him. "Do you need anything from me?"

"Sadie and Angus are set." Her voice was bubbly. "Enjoy the rest of your day."

"Thanks." Brandt turned toward the front door, but he found himself heading toward the window instead. He wasn't searching for a date—he'd meant what he told his aunt—but saying hello wouldn't be a big deal. Maybe he could figure out the color of her eyes.

Halfway across the store, he noticed the stacks of decorations and extension cords. A large box showed a picture of a waterfall. Something like that should be self-contained, but…

A funny feeling settled in the pit of his stomach.

None of his business.

But the memory of a water feature gone wrong at one of his old apartment complexes made him want to say something. Cautioning her based on his experience wouldn't come across as mansplaining. He was being…helpful.

Brandt continued to where she kneeled. The window platform was the same height as the bottom of the glass pane.

"Hey." Not the most eloquent opening, but women usually came onto him, so he'd never had to up his game. "Looks like you're using a water feature in your Christmas window."

The woman's gaze traveled from the lights she was placing around the edge to him. She blinked.

"Oh, it's you." She seemed to catch herself. "I mean, I saw you outside the coffee shop yesterday morning."

"You did." She was prettier than he remembered. Her bright green eyes reminded him of the grassy meadow where he and his parents picnicked.

Home.

That was what staring into her gaze felt like.

Coming home.

Except he wasn't here for that.

Focus. "The water feature."

"I'm using one." She motioned to the box he'd seen. "A waterfall."

"Cool." He wanted to cringe for saying that but managed not to. "Those fountains are self-contained, right?"

"This one is." As she gathered more lights, her features tensed as if she didn't know what to make of him.

That was how he felt being around her. Unsettled, not sure where his next breath would come from.

"Good." He forced the word from his dry throat. "Do you have a backup plan to contain the water in case something goes wrong? A tub underneath the window's platform might work or something else like that?"

Rolling her eyes, she released an exasperated sigh, but a smile returned a second later. A forced one. "This is a brand-new, highly rated fountain. I researched the manufacturer, and I read the reviews. It's not going to break."

Her tone was pleasant, but the underlying tightness suggested she wasn't happy with his questioning her. "I didn't mean to offend you."

"You didn't." She spoke too quickly for him to believe her.

"It's just..." He might as well say what prompted him to speak up. "I lived in an apartment building where an indoor fountain failed. That led to water damage and a fire."

She raised a brow. "Water and fire sounds like an oxymoron."

"The damage was real." If she didn't want to listen and take precautions, that was her problem. "Three units were affected, and residents had to move out."

"That's too bad, but the same thing won't happen here."

Her confident attitude was so much like...

A boulder settled in the pit of Brandt's stomach.

Talking to this woman was a bad idea. Their conversation reminded him of ones with Nick where Brandt had ended up feeling the same frustration. Even now, his nerve endings stood at attention, unsure whether fight or flight was the correct response.

Flight.

He'd learned that was the best course of action. "Good luck."

"Thanks." Another forced smile appeared. "I'll…consider your suggestions."

No, she wouldn't.

Her words said one thing, but her tense face and stiff posture told another story.

"Anything else?" she asked, but she was only humoring him.

"Nope." He hurried to the door, pushed it open, and stepped out of the shop.

The temperature had dropped while he'd been inside, but that wasn't what chilled him to the bone.

Brandt fought the urge to glance back at her one more time.

He'd thought the woman was beautiful, the closest thing he'd seen to an angel on Earth. But after seeing what she was like…

His opinion had changed.

Ignoring the falling snow, Brandt wandered down First Avenue. The snow stuck to the pavement, accumulating where someone had recently shoveled.

A good thing he wasn't interested in dating her or he might be disappointed. He only hoped her fountain worked perfectly.

He stepped out of the way of a delivery man dressed in brown carrying boxes.

The Tea Leaves & Coffee Beans sign caught his eye.

Wait a minute.

His stomach dropped. He'd headed in the wrong direction. Maybe he hadn't slept as well as he thought. No, that wasn't the reason. The woman in the window was.

Not a problem.

All he had to do was stop thinking about her.

How hard could that be?

Chapter Six

UNBELIEVABLE.

As the shop's door closed, Callie took a deep breath before unclenching her fists. Her muscles remained knotted as if the stranger's words had twisted each one before turning them inside out. He hadn't been *rude*—though his "Good luck" bordered on a slam—but he shouldn't have said anything to her in the first place.

Since seeing him yesterday, she'd been curious. Now she was annoyed.

She took a breath and then another. "That guy had some nerve."

"I saw him talking to you." Anna hurried around the counter. "What happened?"

Callie flexed her fingers, hoping to lessen the tension in her shoulders and her spiraling blood pressure. A glance out the window told her the guy was no longer around. Good. He might be attractive—okay, gorgeous—but she didn't want to see him again. "He acted like I was totally clueless about installing the waterfall."

Anna's jaw dropped. "He said that?"

"Not exactly." But he might as well have given his

pompous posture and I-know-better-than-you tone. So different from their brief interaction on the street. Too much like Callie's family.

If you keep holding the knife that way, you'll cut your finger.

I'll drive because you still hug the shoulder.

Attending veterinary school will lead to a better career for you than playing with dogs all day.

As if that was something she wanted to do at twenty-eight, when it hadn't been her dream at eighteen or twenty-two or ever.

Callie shouldn't let others make her feel inadequate. She wasn't. Not when she was living the life she wanted.

She shrugged. "He asked me about having a backup plan if the water feature breaks, but worded his question so he was giving me a suggestion as if I hadn't thought of one."

That had been subtler than what her family would say, but still…

"Do you have a backup plan?" Anna asked.

"Of course." Callie had researched, watched videos, and asked questions at the hardware store to understand how the waterfall worked. She'd planned this theme months ago, but she hadn't decided she wanted to win until this weekend. "I lined the platform and floor underneath with two layers of plastic yesterday. Any splashes or drips from the waterfall won't soak through. But I wasn't about to tell *him* that."

As Anna folded her arms over her chest, her lower lip stuck out. "Why not?"

"It's none of his business."

A resigned expression crossed Anna's features. "I know

what that means…"

Callie narrowed her gaze. "What?"

"You got all huffy after being told what to do, then let a smokin' hot guy with killer baby blues leave instead of asking him for help."

"I didn't get all *huffy*." Callie repositioned the tree that had fallen over. The guy had great eyes and an amazing smile. But once he opened his mouth, he'd ruined the gorgeous fantasy guy she'd been daydreaming about since yesterday. "I was polite."

But he must have sensed her frustration given his quick apology.

"It's just…" She rolled her shoulders to lessen the tightness in the muscles. "I know what I'm doing. I don't need help."

Blowing out a breath, Anna rubbed the back of her neck. "I have either failed as your best friend or you are hopelessly doomed to remain single forever."

"Not funny." Maybe Callie was overreacting, but Anna's lack of understanding hurt. "I thought you had my back."

"I do. Always, but this was a missed opportunity. A huge one." Exasperation laced each of Anna's words. She sat on the window platform. "I know you're not interested in dating, but handsome guys like him do not walk into this place every day. Or month. Year, even. And to have one approach you…"

"Okay, I get your point."

The guy was handsome enough to make Callie's heart bump when she saw him. Both times. She'd blinked to make sure she hadn't wished him into existence. Full lips softened his chiseled cheekbones and straight nose. Dazzling blue eyes had been plucked from a cloudless sky. A beanie hid his hair today. No stubble this morning. His smooth skin was freshly shaved. Many women might be attracted to a gorgeous man like him.

If Callie were in the market for a date, she might have been. But she wasn't. And besides...

"Except whatever hotness factor disappeared when he told me what I should do with the waterfall." Callie stared at the decorations, trying to remember where she'd been before being interrupted. "Guys like him are full of themselves. I don't date jerks."

Not that she had time to date, but it was the principle of the matter. If she were going out with someone, she wanted a nice guy. A gentleman with manners who cared about her and understood she could take care of herself. An equal partnership was her ideal, not something lopsided where one person took care of the other.

Anna ran her finger along the branches of the silver Christmas tree. "That's a huge generalization."

"Yes, but my brothers have provided more than enough data." If she added in her parents' comments, Callie could write a paper worthy of a PhD. She picked up the strand of lights and then placed the cord around the edge of the window.

"The guy might have been nervous." Anna, who'd grown up in a town smaller than Silver Falls, saw the good in people, choosing to ignore any signs that might suggest the opposite. She'd suffered more than her share of heartbreaks because of that trait, but she was also a loyal, if not an opinionated and nosy, friend. "Not all men have A-type personalities and are outgoing."

"He didn't sound nervous." The guy had exuded confidence. Callie remembered what else he'd said. "He mentioned water damage and an electrical fire being caused by an indoor water fountain at his apartment building, implying I might burn down or flood the shop."

Anna's forehead crinkled. "You've been interpreting what he said."

Her friend sounded more like a lawyer than a dog groomer. "His meaning was clear."

"You *can* be hypersensitive when people offer help."

"He wasn't offering help." Even though what Anna said was true. "I'll be the first to admit I don't take constructive criticism well, but I can't help it. My family doesn't accept me as I am, and they talk to me as if I can't do anything by myself. Before I left this weekend, my parents brought up vet school again. It doesn't matter how many times I tell them that's not who I am or what I want to do…"

Anna grimaced. "They won't give up."

"Nope." Callie straightened a cord that had twisted. "If I hadn't stopped listening to them when I did, I might believe I was incapable of doing stuff on my own and who knows where I'd be?"

Most likely not in Silver Falls.

Callie shuddered at the thought.

"I'm sorry." Anna's gaze softened. "I shouldn't be getting

on you about him, but he was so…"

"Hot."

Anna nodded dreamily. "You deserve to be happy."

"I am happy," Callie said without hesitation. Winning the window display award would make her happier. The plaque would be something physical to show her family. A way to prove how far she'd come since moving to Silver Falls and buying a business. "You realize happiness doesn't require a hot guy, right?"

"I do, but having one around wouldn't suck," Anna teased.

Callie connected another strand of lights to the last one. She appreciated her friend's concern and wanted to put Anna at ease. "I let that guy get to me, but I couldn't help myself. He reminded me so much of my brothers. I'm sorry for taking my frustrations out on you."

"You're forgiven." Anna ran her hands along a package of silver garland. "When you said the guy reminded you of your brothers, do you mean they're as physically hot as him?"

Gagging, Callie scrunched her nose. "Please don't say hot and my brothers in the same sentence. That's just…ew."

Anna laughed. "You didn't answer my question."

"You're dating someone."

She shrugged. "Call it curiosity."

"My brothers are easy on the eyes, but that's not what I meant." Callie fiddled with another light. "They love me, but sometimes…" *Most of the time.* "My family can be too much. That guy's I-know-better-than-you attitude is what I've been dealing with my entire life."

"No wonder you were aggravated." Anna set down the garland. "The next time you see him, you may feel differently."

"There won't be a next time." Callie brushed her hands on her jeans. "Whatever romantic scenario you're imagining isn't going to happen."

Anna's shoulders drooped. With a sigh, she stood.

"That's too bad because December *is* almost here." Anna usually faked innocence when she was planning—okay, scheming—something, but not this time. "You don't need to find a boyfriend, but the holidays won't be the same without a kiss under the mistletoe."

"Not the same for you. I haven't stood under the mistletoe in…a long time." Too long? Maybe. Callie couldn't remember the last time she'd kissed anyone, holidays or not. "Not that I'm a fan of the stuff. Mistletoe is poisonous. That's why I don't hang sprigs here and at home."

"So considerate, but…" Anna's concerned tone returned. "Promise me, at least once this holiday season, you'll do one thing without thinking about the dogs or anyone else but yourself."

"I am." Picking up a silver ball, Callie caught the reflection of her face in the glass. "The window display is my one thing this Christmas."

That was why she'd splurged on new decorations instead of using the old ones, drafted display designs until blisters formed on her fingers, and would decorate long past closing time to finish. Not that Callie considered this work. She enjoyed putting the window together as she much as she did working at the doggy daycare. Her job was so much more than a way to make a living. This was what she loved doing. Something her family didn't understand.

But that was okay.

Callie wasn't going to let anyone get to her again.

Not her family or friends...or handsome strangers.

BRANDT HADN'T TURNED around when he'd realized he was going the wrong direction but continued along First Avenue. That was better than being alone at his aunt's house. A few cars drove past, but the sidewalk was empty except for him. He didn't mind the snow or the cold, but he needed something to do besides thinking about the woman in the doggy daycare window. Seeing the bakery across the street gave him an idea.

Ten minutes later, he entered his aunt's quilt shop carrying a box full of scones. He'd debated between those, muffins, croissants, or doughnuts. Scones won because they would be less messy around the fabric. Yes, his aunt had taught him well when he'd stocked bolts and products for her as a teenager.

The layout had been redone, but the store was still as welcoming and comfortable as before. Underneath a tree were stacks of fat holiday fabric quarters tied with red or green ribbon. Instrumental Christmas music played at the perfect background volume for asking questions or shopping with friends.

"Good morning, everyone," he greeted the employees

and customers. He removed napkins from his jacket pocket. "In case you don't remember me or we haven't met yet, I'm Margot's nephew, Brandt. Please help yourself to a scone."

Staff and customers did. Some asked how he liked being back in Silver Falls. A few wanted to know how long he was staying. One wondered if he was returning for good. His answers became rote—he was happy to be with his aunt, he was staying until the new year, and he was only here for an extended vacation.

"I'm Lyndsey. I manage the store for your aunt." A tall woman with red hair took a blueberry scone. "Thanks for the snack. If you want to give one to your aunt, she's in the classroom setting up for this morning's workshop."

He picked up the box. "I'll bring these back in a minute."

The classroom hadn't changed since the last time he'd been here. Six long tables formed three rows where students sat. At the front was another table for the instructor. Corkboard covered three of the four walls. He remembered installing that with his dad. The built-in shelves and cubbies on the fourth wall, however, were new.

His aunt sat at the front table sorting items into plastic bins. She hummed along to the music playing in the retail area.

He moved toward her. "I like the wall unit."

Aunt Margot raised her head, her ever-present smile on her face. "Brandt? What are you doing here?"

"Thought I'd stop by to drop off a snack for everyone." He held out the bakery box. "Grab one or two before they're gone."

She removed a blueberry scone and then took a napkin. "This is so sweet of you."

"Least I can do. I told you I want to help you while I'm here."

"You are." She raised her scone. "I hope Angus and Sadie behaved."

"They had their moments, but we made it to the doggy daycare."

Finally.

He would speak to her about obedience classes after he researched the options. Asking for a recommendation at the doggy daycare would have been easiest, but he didn't want to go back there.

Aunt Margot bit into her scone. "Mmm."

Her obvious pleasure over the baked good widened his grin. "I'll have to do this again."

Nodding, she wiped her mouth with the napkin. "What did you think of the bakery?"

"The place hasn't changed." Which pleased him. Some things in Silver Falls shouldn't change, and the bakery was one of them. "The inside smells as wonderful as it always did. Everything in the display case looks delicious."

"Taryn took over from her parents a few years ago. She's become a fine baker in her own right."

He'd attended school with Taryn Lawson for thirteen years. Longer if he counted preschool. "I didn't see her. A guy was behind the counter serving customers."

"That must be the new person she hired. You'll have to stop by again to say hi to her."

Subtlety wasn't his aunt's strong suit, but he wouldn't fall for his aunt's meddling in his non-existent love life. "Maybe I'll see her when I bring you treats the next time."

"If you don't want to buy scones again, Taryn will help you figure out something else. She has a photographic memory when it comes to remembering her customers' favorites." Aunt Margot took another bite. "I may need another scone before you go."

He motioned to the box. "Help yourself.

She took another. "Did you see anyone you knew at Wags and Tails?"

"No." That was all he wanted to say about his visit there.

He sat on one of the tables in the first row. Based on the pattern hanging on the wall, a quilted table runner was today's project. His aunt had a similar one on her dining room table.

Aunt Margot set the scone on the napkin. "The owner and groomer are new to Silver Falls."

He assumed those must have been the two women who worked there. "Is the owner the bubbly blonde or the pretty brunette?"

His aunt's blue eyes twinkled with interest. She leaned forward over the table. "Pretty, huh?"

Uh-oh. That adjective had slipped out. Pretty, yes, but her personality was lacking. He didn't want to see her again, let alone be set up on a date. Which meant…

Time for damage control.

"Relatively speaking." Brandt attempted to sound nonchalant because he didn't want to fuel his aunt's misguided matchmaking efforts. "Your shop has a new layout. Have the changes increased sales?"

As Aunt Margot discussed her profits since the remodel, she forgot the brunette. Feeling as if he'd dodged a bullet, Brandt reached into the box for a scone—cranberry—his favorite.

One bite made everything right in his world. Now all he had to do was make sure his aunt's penchant for matchmaking didn't interfere with his vacation.

Chapter Seven

AFTER LUNCH, CALLIE stood behind the counter, relishing the stillness inside Wags and Tails. No barking. No paws running across the padded floor. The only sounds came from the grooming area.

Callie loved playing with the dogs during activity periods, but the lull was nice and gave her a chance to get caught up on work while Sam and Becca—one of the part-time employees—wrote updates on each dog's profile page for owners and supervised the dogs' rest time.

Answering clients' messages and replying to emails didn't take Callie long. She checked the calendar.

Yes!

Reservations for December would make this year her best profit-wise. Doubling the square footage and offering more daycare slots each day had been the right move. No—more than that. Expanding had been a game changer for the business.

Satisfaction flowed through her. She wiggled her toes. "It can only get better from here."

No finger crossing necessary.

The phone rang.

"Wags and Tails," she answered. "This is Callie. How may I help you?"

"Do you offer boarding services?" a female voice asked. "I need space the week between Christmas and New Year's. Two dogs. Small ones."

"We don't offer boarding." Callie pulled out her laminated recommendations list from the drawer underneath the counter. "But I recommend the following places."

She rattled off the names and numbers before hanging up.

Interesting. That was the second person who'd called today wanting boarding. Callie had the space and the plans drawn up, but she'd held off installing the dog suites. She hadn't wanted to expand too fast. Maybe boarding was something to consider in the new year. She'd add it to her to-do list.

A happy squeal erupted from the grooming area.

The sound pleased Callie. She wanted every dog to love being at Wags and Tails, including during their grooming sessions. Frieda, a pampered poodle, did. She loved being bathed, trimmed, and blown dry. She received the complete doggy spa treatment once a month. Too bad not all their dogs were more like Frieda.

The bell on the door jingled.

Margot Winslow entered the store. The woman had recommended Wags and Tails to her friends and quilt shop customers. Not only was she a valued client, but Callie also considered her a friend, even if that was only through their businesses.

Callie greeted her with a smile. “I hope it’s not too cold out there.”

“It’s warmed up a few degrees.” As Margot sashayed to the counter, her calf-length down coat brushed the tops of her snow boots. “I hope you’re having a lovely day.”

“I am.” Margot, who seemed ageless to Callie, was a ray of sunshine on this snowy day. “I was so focused on the window display this morning I didn’t see you drop off Angus and Sadie.”

To be honest, Callie hadn’t noticed anyone entering. Once she’d found her groove, nothing else mattered but positioning the lights.

“I wasn’t here earlier.” Margot glanced over her shoulder at the door. “My nephew brought them for me.”

Callie remembered hearing Margot talk about him. He was a computer programmer, or something technical like that, and had grown up in Silver Falls. “That was nice of him.”

“He’s a sweetheart. I’m so glad he’s spending his vacation with me.” The laugh lines on Margot’s face deepened. “He also delivered scones from the bakery this morning. I had two. A calorie splurge, but who cares? They hit the spot.”

“You deserve to be spoiled.”

Every December, Margot gave tins containing homemade cookies to the businesses on First Avenue. The cranberry and chocolate ones were Callie’s favorites. She couldn’t wait for this year’s batch to arrive in a couple of weeks.

The bell jingled again.

Callie looked over to see…

Him.

The guy from earlier.

Her stomach knotted.

Margot glanced over her shoulder. "Find a good parking spot?"

Callie couldn't believe the two knew each other.

"Close enough." He didn't meet Callie's gaze. If anything, he went out of his way to avoid looking at her. Not that she wanted to make eye contact, but could he be more blatant?

Using the shop's tablet, she sent a message to Sam and Becca that Margot was here. "Your fur babies will be right out."

"Did they behave today?" Margot asked, the way she did each time Angus and Sadie attended doggy daycare. The dogs were oh so loved and spoiled, which was how it should be. They'd hit the forever home jackpot when Margot adopted them.

Callie placed the tablet on the counter. "Perfect as always."

The guy straightened, disbelief crossing his face. Not that she was watching him. Well, not closely.

Margot turned toward the guy. "I told you they were good dogs."

He gave a slight nod as if being polite and not wanting to cause an argument.

Callie's jaw tensed. If he had issues with Angus and Sadie, something was seriously wrong with him. More than what she'd originally thought.

"Have you met my nephew?" The affection in Margot's voice matched her eyes. "Brandt Winslow, this is Callie Andrews. She owns Wags and Tails, and is the town's dog whisperer."

The hottie stranger was Margot's nephew? Callie's mouth hung open before she pressed her lips together. Of course, not saying anything would be rude. "Hello."

"Hi." He spoke sharply, still not meeting her gaze.

Their dislike of each other must be mutual. Knowing that didn't bother Callie in the slightest.

Margot's unwavering smile suggested she was oblivious to the tension simmering across the counter. "Brandt hasn't been back to Silver Falls for six years. He's curious to see how much has changed around town."

"We have plenty of time for that," Brandt said.

He might have been disinterested, but his rich voice washed over Callie like a warm breeze. No biggie. Lots of men had nice voices.

"I'm here through December," he added.

That long? Maybe this would be the last time she saw him. Lowering one hand beneath the counter, she crossed her fingers.

Margot tsked. "You'll be bored being alone at my house."

"I have work—"

"You're on vacation." Margot was acting more like a helicopter parent than a doting aunt. "A long one you've earned after working so hard for years."

Callie bit back a laugh. Margot could be a force of nature when she chose to be. She kept the First Avenue Business Association meetings running smoothly with a kind but firm hand.

"If the snow doesn't let up, I can show myself around," he said in a matter-of-fact tone. "It's not like I'll get lost in my hometown."

"I don't want you to miss any of the new things." Margot turned her attention to Callie. "I was planning to spend tomorrow showing Brandt around, but there's too much snow for me to do a proper walking tour. This old body isn't up for slipping and breaking a hip."

"You're not old." Callie and Brandt spoke at the same time.

Their gazes met for a nanosecond before his skittered away.

"I don't want to take any chances with the holidays coming up." Margot tapped her gloved finger against her chin. "Maybe you..."

Sam brought out Angus and Sadie from the back. The dogs' ears perked as soon as they saw their mommy. Angus wiggled his bottom.

Margot squealed. "Oh, my beautiful babies. Aren't they adorable?"

As Callie nodded, Brandt shook his head.

The guy definitely had a problem.

"Back to what I was saying." Margot smiled at Callie. "Perhaps you could show Brandt around tomorrow."

She flinched. "Me?"

"No," Brandt said at the same time.

Relief washed over her. After all the new customers Margot had brought into Wags and Tails, Callie didn't want to say no even if spending time with Brandt was the last thing she wanted to do. A good thing her nephew didn't have any trouble saying the word.

Margot bent over to pet her dogs. "I think this will work out for everyone involved."

Callie's gaze shot to Brandt's. Locked on.

She blinked, but whatever was going on—some connection—remained. No words were spoken, but none were needed. His eyes begged her to put an end to his aunt's plan.

She understood. He'd said no. Now it was her turn. Heaven help her, but she was willing to try.

But first she broke the contact. If not, she might drown in that sea of blue. Though what a way to go.

She focused her attention on Margot. "I'm happy you think I'm the right person for this, but others know more about Silver Falls. I'm sure Brandt has friends he'd rather catch up with than be stuck with someone he doesn't know."

His slight nod, barely perceptible, was another reminder of why she didn't want to spend time with Brandt. She didn't like him, but she'd done what he asked. He didn't need to be impolite—okay, rude—about not wanting to spend time with her.

She got that. He didn't have to remind her.

"Callie is a wonderful tour guide." Sam handed the two leashes to Margot, who appeared to have selective hearing and was ignoring her nephew and Callie. He brushed his bangs out of his eyes. "When my cousins visited, she showed them around while I took an exam I couldn't miss. They said Callie gave them a good feel for Silver Falls."

"Sam..." she warned. A glowing recommendation from one of her employees was only going to encourage Margot.

Sam merely nodded with a smile. His friendly nature made him a customer favorite, but it didn't make him any less of a troublemaker right now.

Anna led a prancing Frieda from the grooming area. The dog's sparkly pink and rhinestone collar glimmered like the lights in the window display. Candy cane ribbons were tied on her ears.

"Who's playing tour guide?" Anna asked.

"Callie," Sam and Margot said in unison.

As if on cue, Angus barked.

Sadie did, too.

Frieda remained silent, tilting her head and showing off her bows as if posing for a picture. Yes, the poodle was a diva.

Anna's wide grin made her look as if she'd eaten a canary, feathers and all. "Callie is perfect for the job. She's done the town's walking tour half a dozen times. Probably has the route memorized."

Callie had, but she didn't want to spend time with *him*. Not even if he was related to one of her favorite clients.

"Excellent because Brandt needs someone knowledgeable to show him the new construction and businesses," Margot said to Sam and Anna, as if this were a done deal.

Brandt's jaw jutted forward. "I don't—"

"Unfortunately, I have to work." Callie tried to speak slowly. Not easy to do when her rising anxiety level made her want a life preserver. "But, as Anna mentioned, a tour map is available at the library or city hall."

There. No reason to feel guilty. Callie had offered a solution to not being his tour guide, even.

"Mary Jo can probably work tomorrow morning," Sam offered, mentioning an employee who worked weekends only. "She's been hoping to pick up more hours with the holidays coming up. If she's here, we'll have enough people to handle things while you give Brandt a tour."

Anna nodded. "I don't have any grooming clients until eleven, so I can lend a hand, too."

Callie's muscles tensed. She was going to kill them both. Okay, not kill, because they were great employees and her friends, but she might give them the worst jobs on the checklist.

For a week.

Maybe a month.

"If Callie needs to work…" Brandt said.

"I do." Taking off another day would be wrong. She shouldn't do that. Rather, she didn't want to do that. "I was just away for four days. It's too soon—"

"The window display will be finished tonight." Anna didn't appear guilty for butting in. Then again, she never did. "Four days is nothing. You're here seven days a week. You need to have more fun."

Together, Brandt Winslow and fun were an oxymoron, but she couldn't say that aloud.

"Oh, Brandt needs to have more fun, too," Margot said.

"That makes the two of you the perfect pair."

Anna and Sam nodded, resembling bobblehead figures.

Callie opened her mouth to disagree.

"It's settled. Callie will show Brandt around tomorrow," Margot announced in the authoritative tone of a judge delivering a verdict. "What time do you want him here?"

A lump formed in Callie's throat. She didn't know how to answer.

Margot, Sam, and Anna glowed as if they'd won the lottery. Callie half-expected them to high five each other. Face flushed, Brandt appeared embarrassed or frustrated, maybe a combination of both. Callie assumed she looked shell-shocked given how she felt.

"Nine thirty or ten?" Her tone was indecisive, but this had blindsided her.

"Will that work, Brandt?" Margot asked.

"That's fine." He ground out the words between clenched teeth.

If his tone was a foreshadow of tomorrow, Callie might need another day off to recover from sightseeing. "We can meet here."

A nod was his only acknowledgment other than his lips thinning.

What had she gotten herself into?

Tomorrow would be the definition of not fun.

Callie didn't want to take time off from work to show him around, but Silver Falls was her home. She would do anything to help a client. Even if that meant playing tour guide to a visiting nephew who liked telling her what to do.

Chapter Eight

WHAT HAD AUNT Margot been thinking? The question had kept Brandt awake last night. Practically stomping along First Avenue this morning, he couldn't believe his aunt had successfully outmaneuvered him. He was on his way to Wags and Tails, which meant she'd won the first round. He'd have to step it up to make sure this didn't happen again.

A patch of blue sky peeked out from the clouds. Not what he wanted to see. He hoped a blizzard would hit even though one wasn't forecasted. He'd checked. Twice. A white-out was the only way to escape his aunt's plans for him.

Plans.

Yeah, right.

This was a blatant matchmaking attempt due to his unfortunate use of the adjective *pretty*.

One hundred percent his fault.

The mental lapse would cost him hours with the second-to-last person he wanted to spend time with in Silver Falls.

The worst part?

When Aunt Margot's attempt to pair him up turned into

an epic failure, she would be disappointed. And fail, it would. Neither he nor Callie Andrews wanted to be stuck together. Sightseeing was bad enough. Forget about them going on a date.

The four-letter word sent a shudder through him, but he knew why Aunt Margot was meddling.

Her end goal was to keep him in Silver Falls. Not until the new year, but forever. Finding him a date who would turn into a girlfriend—one who lived locally—would strengthen Aunt Margot's cause. That was the only reason behind this…madness.

But he had a plan to survive the next few hours—reply politely, feign interest, and return to his aunt's house ASAP.

When he reached Wags and Tails, he took a fortifying breath before opening the door. He went inside, each step bringing him closer to his doom. Okay, Callie wasn't *that* bad. Still, he'd rather face an army of zombies, super soldiers, or vampires in a video game and be destroyed every five seconds than spend the day with her.

The younger guy from yesterday stood behind the front counter. Once again, he wore the shop's standard uniform—a forest-green apron over a long-sleeved T-shirt and jeans. Long bangs fell over his eyes.

Brandt didn't see Callie. He released the breath he hadn't realized he was holding.

"Good morning." The guy acted perky. "Callie will be out in a minute. She's in the play area with the dogs."

"Thanks." Brandt had been sweating thinking about today, but the heat inside made him loosen his scarf, remove his gloves, and unzip his jacket before it got worse.

The guy pushed his bangs to the side. "I'm Sam."

"Brandt."

"I know." Sam rubbed his lips together as if hesitating.

"Have we met?"

"My dad, Dean Merrill, used to work at NiBrTech. I attended a few of the family events, but that was years ago."

The guy appeared to be in his late teens or early twenties. Something about his brown eyes were familiar. The image of a tall bald guy popped into Brandt's mind. "I remember your dad. Dean's one of the best IT guys I've worked with. How's he doing?"

"Good now." Sam's tone suggested a story with the emphasis on the *now*. He ran his finger along the edge of the tablet the staff used to check in dogs. "My dad's teaching math and computer science at the high school. He didn't want to leave Silver Falls, and that was the only job he could find after NiBrTech was sold."

A familiar ache formed in Brandt's stomach. He wished he hadn't eaten so many slices of his aunt's French toast. "I'm sorry."

He didn't know what else to say. Before leaving town, he'd written a letter to each employee, thanking them for their hard work and apologizing for what had happened. He hadn't known what else to do then, either.

Sam shrugged, but the young man didn't appear indifferent. "You're not the one who sold out the employees."

"No, I wasn't."

Everyone had received a severance package. Some who'd

had stock options ended up with a nice nest egg. Still...

He felt as if he should have done more, fought for himself and the employees, even though he hadn't had enough shares to overturn Nick and the investors who voted for the sale.

"How long have you worked here?" Brandt asked.

"Since Callie bought the place, coming up on three years now. I work full time, but she's great about scheduling my hours around classes. I try to take a class or two each semester."

"Going for a degree?"

"Trying. Doing it part time is going to take forever, but it's all I can afford."

Brandt's heart froze. He'd wanted to make sure this didn't happen to employees' kids so he'd set up a tuition program. "The NiBrTech Scholarship fund..."

"Was for graduating or rising high school seniors and students enrolled in college." Sam's mouth twisted. "Us younger kids didn't qualify."

Brandt swore to himself. He should have thought about all the kids, not just the ones immediately effected by the company's sale. That wasn't right or fair. He would call his investment manager and lawyer to see what could be done.

"Hey." Sam reached across the counter to touch Brandt's arm. "No one blames you. I sure don't."

Maybe not, but Brandt blamed himself. He'd established the scholarship fund, convinced Nick they should donate the NiBrTech building to the city, and then taken off.

Brandt hadn't looked back.

He hadn't wanted to.

That was on him.

"Thanks." Brandt shifted his gloves from one hand to the other. "Tell your dad hi for me."

A smile spread across Sam's face. "I'll do that."

As Sam returned his attention to the tablet, Brandt wondered what his life would be like had he stayed in Silver Falls. Unlike Sam's dad, Brandt wouldn't have been forced to take any job to remain in town. The company's sale had made him a wealthy man, but not working hadn't ever appealed to him. He would have been bored out of his mind if he'd retired at twenty-six.

The bell on the door rang.

A woman with a German Shepherd entered the shop. Ears straight, the dog eyed him warily.

Protector or a predator?

Brandt wasn't going to wait to find out. He moved quickly toward the window to leave a clear path to the counter.

Whoa.

Everything in the display was so…bright and silvery.

A little white was used for the fake snow that covered the platform, but that was it unless the waterfall's gray stones and crystal snowflakes counted—though some might call gray a muted silver tone. His mother, an interior designer, would. Probably his aunt, too.

He tried to make out the window's theme.

Blinked. Squinted. Tried again.

The display was bright and flashy like the neon lights in

Times Square, but beyond that…

Brandt hadn't a clue what the window was supposed to be or mean.

The waterfall appeared to function properly, so that was one positive.

Sam was still talking to the woman. No sign of Callie.

Was she blowing Brandt off?

His breath hitched.

Could he be that lucky?

He'd considered doing the same to her last night. If Silver Falls wasn't such a small town, he'd have cancelled the tour and spent the day working in the coffee shop, but the truth would have gotten back to Aunt Margot, who was a major spoke on Silver Falls' rumor wheel. Besides, he loved her too much not to go along with whatever she wanted, even if her meddling was…misguided.

But wasn't that why he was in Silver Falls this year?

To help her out this holiday season.

To make up for lost time.

To keep her smiling.

To be the best nephew she believed him to be.

That was why he hadn't shut down sightseeing with Callie. Oh, he'd called his aunt on making arrangements without his permission, but once she got something in her head, he'd have better luck changing the direction of an avalanche than her mind. His parents said he took after her in that regard, but…

No.

He shook his head as if to emphasize the point.

"Are you ready to see Silver Falls?"

The sound of Callie's voice startled him. He faced her. "Are you?"

She shrugged on her puffy red coat and then zipped it. "This is what Margot wants."

Guess they agreed about something—doing this for his aunt. "Yes."

And he was ready to begin.

The sooner the tour began, the sooner he could say goodbye.

As he followed Callie, Brandt redid his own parka. He pushed open the door. "After you."

"Thanks."

The word sounded forced, but he didn't care. Today was about his aunt's wishes, not his. One other good thing would come from today, too. Spending time with Callie would reaffirm he'd made the right decision leaving Silver Falls.

Forget his issues with Nick. Brandt could only imagine what his aunt's matchmaking efforts would have been like had he stayed in town.

He laughed.

Callie's face pinched. "Did I miss something?"

"I was thinking about my aunt." No way would Callie understand. "Thanks for playing tour guide. You were right about my aunt wanting this to happen. For whatever reason…"

He knew why, but he wasn't about to share. That would make things more uncomfortable between them.

"You mean a lot to her." Callie's words surprised him.

"Margot is one of my favorite people. I don't want to disappoint her."

He tugged on his gloves, glad they agreed on that. "I don't, either."

Callie motioned to her right. "Then let's get started."

Okay, wanting to make Aunt Margot happy gave them common ground. All they had to do was survive the next couple of hours.

How hard could that be?

Chapter Nine

As Callie walked next to Brandt on First Avenue, she inhaled, filling her lungs with the crisp, cool air. That helped ease her frustration at being here instead of working. At least the conditions were good for sightseeing.

Thanks to shovels and blowers, the snow had been removed from the sidewalk. The sun kept appearing from behind the clouds, so the temperature was warmer than yesterday. The nicer weather might make her time with Brandt go faster. She crossed her fingers.

So far, the tour was going well. She'd pointed out the new shops and some changes to old ones they passed. Maybe him not annoying her shouldn't surprise her so much. Although unspoken, he seemed to realize today was about Margot Winslow.

Nothing else mattered, including their dislike of each other.

They stood at the corner waiting to cross the street.

"How long have you lived in Silver Falls?" Brandt asked.

"It'll be three years in January." She'd started the new year in a new town with a new business. Every key on her paw-shaped key ring except the one for her car had been new. She'd moved to Silver Falls due to the business she'd wanted to buy, but her heart had known immediately this tiny town was her new home.

She stepped off the curb, and he did the same.

"How about you?" Callie shot him a sideward glance, taking in his profile. He was easy on the eyes from any angle. "Your aunt said you used to live here."

"I grew up in Silver Falls, went away to college, came back, and then moved away for good." He paused, as if he wasn't sure what to say next. "This is my first time back in six years."

There must be a reason for him to be gone so long when his aunt lived here, but that wasn't Callie's business. She accepted gossip was a part of small-town living, but she didn't participate. "There have been several changes, especially on this street, but overall towns like Silver Falls change slowly."

"Stuck in tradition." His tone wasn't harsh, but he didn't seem to miss his hometown.

She couldn't imagine not living here. "With some things, yes, but Silver Falls is moving forward thanks to the new mayor."

"A woman, right?"

Callie nodded. "Your aunt campaigned hard for Mayor Sellwood. Having others relocate to Silver Falls has also helped the town grow."

He raised a brow. "Others like you?"

At least he hadn't called her an outsider. Good, because that was the opposite of how she felt.

"Yes." She fiddled with the fringe on her scarf. "A perfect example is the new physician who joined the medical group a few months ago. Dr. Rosen is young, but he saw what the town needed. He opened an urgent care clinic on the weekends."

"That's a significant improvement."

"This is another." She motioned to the store on their right. "The ice cream parlor makes the summertime more enjoyable. Springtime, fall, and winter, too."

"Ice cream fan, huh?" His playful tone surprised her. She hadn't expected that.

His gaze held hers, a moment too long for her comfort level. Must be his magnetic blue eyes.

Wait. What was his question?

A glance at the shop reminded her. "I love ice cream, but I'm an equal opportunist when it comes to sweet treats."

"No wonder you and my aunt get along so well."

His rich, appealing laughter crashed into her, even though she was standing at his side. She fought the urge to fall back a step.

"I used to go to the one on the corner of First and D." He stopped in front of the ice cream parlor.

The window display contained snowmen made with T-Rex-sized scoops of fake snow, assorted colors of ice cream, and wearing hats that resembled large, upside-down cones.

"That store closed two years ago," she said. "This one has been open for over a year."

Brandt reached forward as if to touch the window but then pulled back his arm. "The other place had been around for as long as I can remember. I celebrated more than one birthday there."

"Good memories, I bet."

He nodded. His unfocused gaze made her think he was remembering the times he'd spent there. "Why did the original one close?"

"Mr. and Mrs. Muldoon were ready to retire, but none of their kids wanted to take over the business." That was how Callie had ended up buying the doggy daycare. The place had also needed a complete overhaul when she took over due to the owner not having the help he needed. "Small-town living doesn't appeal to many who grew up here. Most prefer living in the city, and they don't want to move back to run a family business."

"Not everyone is cut out for that kind of life."

Was he thinking about himself? "Your aunt doesn't expect you to take over the quilt shop."

"Which is a huge relief. Quilts are cool. I enjoyed helping her out at the shop so I could earn money when I was younger, but no way would I be interested in more." His honesty surprised her. "I remember the Muldoon kids. All of them worked at the ice cream parlor at some point growing up. A couple of them were always complaining about ice cream. I thought they were crazy."

"Maybe there is such a thing as too much ice cream, even though I can't imagine that."

"So what happened with the Muldoons?"

"They tried selling the ice cream shop, but no offers came. They shut down. Unfortunately, that's becoming a familiar story around here."

"I had no idea." Lowering his gaze, Brandt sounded almost guilty.

"Why would you? You moved away." Her words didn't lessen the deep lines on either side of his mouth.

He shoved his hands in his jacket pockets. "It's going to sound stupid, but I didn't think about things changing after I left."

"Not stupid." Callie understood because when she'd left LA, her focus had been on what she was moving toward—not what she'd left behind, even though she spoke to her family all the time. "Most people don't think about how a place might change or be different after they leave. They're too busy where they are now."

"Living their best life."

"Given we're millennials, yes."

A beat passed. And another.

His lips curved into a genuine smile.

Her mouth went dry.

"Thanks," he said.

She could play nice, too. First, she needed to swallow and did. "You're welcome."

"So how does this ice cream parlor compare to the old one?" he asked.

Callie looked around as if to see who was nearby. The closest person was on the other side of the street. "Better."

"Why is that?"

"This new place serves the same cones, bowls, sundaes, and milkshakes, but they also offer frozen yogurt where you pick the toppings. Oh, and ice cream cakes they'll decorate however you want."

"Not only a welcome addition to First Avenue but also an improvement."

"Yes, on both counts."

His rich laughter wrapped around her heart. That was the last place she wanted anything associated with him to be near, so she took a step to her left to put distance between them.

"You must be a connoisseur given how much you know about this place," he said.

"I pay close attention when sugar is involved, but I make a point to learn about each business in town."

Callie didn't tell him how she'd studied—okay, stalked—each business on First Avenue online before coming to Silver Falls to visit the doggy daycare in person. Buying Wags and Tails hadn't been a lark as her family thought. The shop hadn't been the first one she'd visited, either. She'd passed on two other dog-related businesses in other towns for various reasons.

"I stay on top of what's happening with our monthly First Avenue Business Association meetings," she continued. "There's a mixer with refreshments, and that's where I tasted one of the ice cream cakes for the first time. Delicious, and I've been buying them ever since."

"I forgot about those meetings." Brandt faced Callie. "Does my aunt attend?"

Guess he didn't know everything about Margot. Callie bit back a grin. "Always, because she's on the board."

"I had no idea, but I'm not surprised. My aunt likes being involved." A strange expression crossed Brandt's face. Not surprise, but almost…concern. "She's not working as many hours at the quilt shop, but she hasn't mentioned her plans for the future."

The way his voice trailed off ramped up the worry on his face. There might have been a twinge of guilt in there, too. From staying away so long? Callie shouldn't want to know, but she did.

"Having a full-time manager gives Margot flexibility with the quilt shop. Lyndsey is a perfect fit. Customers adore her. Not quite as much as they do your aunt, but a close second."

Margot had been cutting back for a couple of years now. If Lyndsey ended up buying the place, no one would be surprised, but maybe Brandt didn't know that yet.

Callie continued. "Margot doesn't need to teach any classes, but she enjoys passing on her love of quilting. Though if you ask her, she says she teaches to get Angus and Sadie out of the house so they can interact with other dogs."

That made him laugh. His entire body relaxed. "That sounds like Aunt Margot. Angus and Sadie are the children she never had."

Callie had a feeling Brandt was, too, but she kept that to herself. "Ready to keep going?"

He nodded.

As he fell in step next to her, he shortened his stride, which she appreciated. "Your aunt is a wonderful woman. I got to know her better when I took the Quilting 101 class."

His eyes widened. "You quilt?"

"I wouldn't call what I do quilting." Callie had struggled. Big time. "But I had fun, made friends, and learned the quilt shop is gossip central in Silver Falls. If everyone doesn't know your business there, then something is wrong."

Brandt grimaced. "When I lived here, I hated the lack of privacy."

She shrugged. "I must be getting used to it."

His hands burrowed deeper into his coat. "I never did."

People talking about others was unavoidable here. "Then it's a good thing you left, because that's part of small-town life."

He started to say something but then closed his mouth. Taking a few steps, he stopped and turned to her. His gaze appeared full of questions. "Why Silver Falls?"

She hadn't been expecting that one. "Excuse me?"

"Why did you move to Silver Falls? Wags and Tails?"

She nodded as they continued forward. "I wanted to work with animals, but I wasn't sure in what capacity." She kept quiet about all the jobs she'd tried—pet sitter, dog walker, obedience trainer, and rescue volunteer. That she'd been saving her money since her first job at sixteen, living frugally, and making sure she had strong credit to be able to qualify for a business loan. "I saw an ad online for a doggy daycare that was for sale. I'd never heard of Silver Falls, but I emailed the owner for more information. The rest, as they say, is history."

He jerked to a stop. "You just upped and moved here?"

His flippant tone bunched her muscles. Taking a breath, she counted back from ten.

"Far from it." She kept her voice calm, even though part of her wanted to yell. "I visited the town, met the owner, and shadowed him for three days. But as soon as I arrived, I knew."

"Knew what?" Brandt's breath hung on the air.

The temperature must be dropping again.

"That Silver Falls was home." Thinking about the day she arrived in town made her feel warm and fuzzy. "I made an offer on the business before I left."

He eyed her warily. "You were that certain?"

"Nervous, yes, but I had no doubt," she admitted. "Things haven't always gone as smoothly as I hoped. I have a great staff now, but getting to that point wasn't easy. Running a new business isn't, either. But I knew I was making the right decision from the beginning."

Despite what her family thought of her moving away and buying the doggy daycare.

"I had that same kind of certainty once." He moved at a slow pace, taking in each and every store window. "Gave up my personal life. Threw my heart and soul into making the start-up I'd founded with my best friend a success."

"That's what I've been doing. Must be one of the occupational hazards of owning a business."

"True, but I didn't realize that until everything was…gone."

Gone suggested he didn't have a choice in the matter. The way his jaw tensed was the second clue he hadn't.

A weight pressed down on Callie's chest. She hated being nosy, but she couldn't help herself. "What happened, if you don't mind me asking?"

He shrugged. "My partner didn't view the business the same as me. He wanted…out."

Callie waited to see if Brandt said more—like where this had happened or when. Margot had never mentioned anything other than saying she had a nephew who was into computers and used to live here.

He remained silent. Not something he wanted to share.

She understood, except…

Her throat thickened with emotion.

She'd been quick to lump Brandt into the same category as her family. Maybe she needed to reexamine her first impression of him, instead of assuming the worst when he'd offered her advice about the waterfall. He might have been trying to help—given what had happened at his apartment building—rather than telling her what to do.

"I'm sorry." Callie felt bad for his business and how she'd acted yesterday. "Hearing what happened to you, however, makes me relieved I didn't take on a partner when I purchased Wags and Tails."

Her brothers had offered to be silent partners. Her parents, too. But Callie had followed her gut. A good move, in hindsight. Sure, she worked longer hours and owed more to the bank, but not answering to anyone but herself was worth the extra time and loan payments.

Brandt's nostrils flared. "I wouldn't go into business with anyone again. I never want to be in another partnership."

His tone was firm but haunted. She wondered if he meant a business partner or a personal one, too. Whatever had happened still hurt him. Maybe that was why she wanted to bring back the light to his eyes and the smile to his lips.

Could she?

Worth a try.

"I wouldn't want a business partner." She imagined what she would feel like if that happened to Wags and Tails. Pain radiated from her heart, a deep hurt that sent her hand flying to her chest. Whatever he'd felt had to be a hundred times worse. "But from where I stand, your former partner doesn't sound like he was the right person to go into business with."

Brandt half-laughed.

He was too far away to touch, but her arm reached toward him anyway. "Are you okay?"

"Thanks to you, I am."

It was her turn to eye him warily. "I don't understand."

"People have made excuses for my ex-partner's behavior for years."

Years meant this hadn't happened recently. Still, she expected to hear bitterness not resignation given his reaction earlier. Maybe he had come to terms with the past more than she thought.

"No one has ever put what happened into such simple—such real—terms as you did." A closed-mouth smile spread across his face. "You're right. Best friend or not, he wasn't the right person to go into business with. There'd been signs, but I couldn't see them then. I do now."

"Glad I could help." Callie liked how the corners of his mouth curved upward instead of down. Maybe now they could go back to enjoying themselves. She had been.

"Stop," a feminine voice shouted.

Callie did, and so did Brandt.

Raine ran out of the coffee shop holding onto two takeaway cups with sleeves. Her face was flushed, but she couldn't be warm when she wasn't wearing a coat. "I thought I was going to miss you guys."

Callie had no idea what was going on. "Have you met Brandt?"

Raine nodded. "Yesterday. Well, sort of. I'm Raine Hanover."

"Brandt Winslow," he said.

The two exchanged smiles since Raine's hands were full.

"Nice to officially meet you." She handed a cup to Callie. "Margot phoned in an order. She wanted me to give you these as you passed by, so you wouldn't be too cold."

Brandt laughed. "My aunt never fails to surprise me."

Raine gave him the other cup. "This one is yours." She crossed her arms over her chest.

As Callie raised her cup, the vanilla and coffee scents tickled her nose. She sipped, the hot liquid warming her. "This is just what I needed."

Brandt drank, too. "Perfect."

"I need to get inside before I freeze." Raine's eyes twinkled with mischief. "Have fun sightseeing."

Callie hoped Brandt hadn't heard the innuendo in Raine's voice.

He stared over the lip of his coffee cup. "I wonder what else my aunt has planned."

"I guess we'll find out." Callie took another sip.

The coffees weren't the biggest surprise to her. Brandt was. He didn't seem as full of himself as she expected. The more she learned about him caused her curiosity to grow. About his life in Silver Falls and his world now. She wasn't sure what to make of any of that. Or…

Him.

Chapter Ten

SIPPING A CUP of delicious coffee—a dark blend that hit the spot—and strolling along First Avenue weren't the worst ways to spend a morning. Sure, Brandt could be coding, but spending time with Callie hadn't sucked the way he thought it would. Granted, the day was still young, but she was trying to get along. So was he. This sightseeing his aunt set up might turn out okay.

Another sip warmed him more. He wasn't used to the winter weather, but the only side effect was a runny nose. He could live with that.

The cold didn't seem to bother Callie. Her sips of coffee were slow and steady. The skin on her cheeks and nose was tinged red. Except…

There was a dab of foam above her mouth. The white dollop contrasted against her soft pink lips. Were both as sweet as they looked?

"Is something wrong?" she asked.

Uh-oh. Heat rushed up his neck. He'd been caught staring. If he didn't pay better attention to what he was supposed to be doing, he was going to fall and make a bigger fool of himself.

"You…" He cleared his throat. "Have something on your upper lip."

Their coffees hadn't come with napkins. His fingers itched to wipe off the foam. Using his tongue would be better since he was wearing gloves, but that might not go over so well.

Who was he kidding?

He'd deserve to be slapped and to have the police called if he did that.

Why had his mind gone there?

He hadn't given kissing more than a casual thought in weeks. Maybe months.

Yet…he wanted to lick Callie, a woman he barely knew, one he hadn't liked until today, who was tolerating him only for his aunt's sake.

Stupid.

But knowing that didn't make him lower his gaze. Even if he should.

The tip of her tongue darted out and then swiped across her upper lip. The foam disappeared, leaving a satisfied smile.

He nearly groaned.

She stared at him with an innocent expression. "All gone?"

He was.

He'd gone from stupid to complete moron.

With a deep breath, Brandt gave himself a mental shake. Aunt Margot was correct about him needing to date more. His lack of female company was playing mind games with him now that he was in close proximity to a beautiful woman.

He still hadn't answered her. "Yes."

Thank goodness. He loosened his grip on the cup before he destroyed the thing and splattered coffee all over himself.

"Thanks." She raised her coffee. "Vanilla lattes are my poison, so foam is a hazard."

It almost was one for him.

Stop thinking about her, foam, and licking.

Brandt sipped his drink to give himself more time to reply. "I've never been into fancy coffees."

Taking another sip, she closed her eyes, a slight hum escaping from her lips.

Just kill me now.

Her eyes opened. "You don't know what you're missing."

A kiss would give him a taste of hers.

Nope. Bad idea.

A police car drove past them. The officer behind the wheel waved. Callie raised her cup to him.

"Not everything has changed in Silver Falls." That comforted him. "People are still friendly to one another and the town's first responders."

"Always, and that was Officer Godfrey. His dog Peanut spends a day or two a week at Wags and Tails."

"Business is good?"

"Yes, we added to our space earlier this year, and that's helped." Callie lowered her cup. "Your aunt mentioned you worked with computers."

Brandt hadn't thought Callie listened to others. He was glad to be proved wrong.

"I'm a programmer, but I don't work for one company. I take contract positions. That way, I get to move around to different cities and states, wherever the work is."

The distance between them narrowed, but he didn't know if she'd moved closer or he had. The sidewalk wasn't sloped so gravity wasn't at play.

"Do you enjoy the flexibility of doing that?" she asked.

Did he? Brandt had to think before answering. "I like doing different things, so the variety of jobs keeps work interesting."

And he never had to worry about one day finding the company or position he'd poured himself into was no longer his. Didn't matter if he'd started the company or was simply an employee.

Working contract jobs was better. Safer.

She waved to someone on the other side of the street. "If you wanted variety, leaving Silver Falls was the right call."

Another nod, but that wasn't something he wanted to discuss. Now or ever.

"I'll have plenty of time to put down roots later." *Or not.* "Short-term leases work the best for my lifestyle."

"I'm the opposite of you. I wanted to put down roots as soon as I arrived in Silver Falls," she admitted. "That's why I have a lease-to-own option where I live. I've been building sweat equity by doing repairs and remodeling. That's the only way for me to afford a house and the business."

"I've moved so many times I have the process down to a science."

She shivered. "I never want to move again."

As they passed the quilt shop, Brandt waved in case his aunt was on the lookout.

He pointed to a tree skirt in the window display. "I used to make tree skirt patterns for her classes."

"You quilt?"

"No, but I can sew on a button and mend a rip." Thinking about the hours spent at Aunt Margot's dining room table brought a smile. "When I was a kid, my aunt used to try different teaching techniques on me. I was her guinea pig."

"You must love your aunt a lot to quilt."

"I do, but it wasn't that bad." He enjoyed spending the time with her even if they were in front of a sewing machine. "She baked cookies and gave me money to spend on the latest video game."

Callie laughed. The sweet, melodic sound brought to mind spring mornings and birds chirping.

"Sounds like Margot." Callie lowered her coffee. "She's able to figure out what motivates people, and she uses that to her advantage. Only for good, of course."

"Her good, at least."

They both laughed. His gaze held hers for a moment.

She motioned to the quilt shop's window. "Margot's Christmas displays have the perfect holiday homespun feel."

"They do, but my aunt's the one who came up with the idea for the annual holiday window display award, so she's been at this for many years."

Callie studied the window. "I didn't know the history,

but I'm not surprised Margot started the competition."

"A few businesses take the award seriously. Or at least, they used to."

"Some still do." Determination shone on her face. "Nothing wrong with wanting to win."

"Is that what you want?"

The steely glint in her eyes shouted *yes*. She nodded.

So the doggy daycare owner was competitive. That might explain her reaction over him mentioning the water feature.

He pictured her silver decorations and miniature white lights. The waterfall with faux rocks was a natural contrast to the overall bling feeling, but he still hadn't figured out her theme.

The bakery was up next. A midmorning snack would go well with their coffees, plus give them a chance to warm up for a few minutes. "Want to get something to eat?"

"There's only one answer to that question."

Given her self-proclaimed love of sweet treats, Brandt opened the bakery's door without hearing an official yes.

Callie went inside, and he followed.

"This is on me for your playing tour guide." He waited for her to say no or fight him.

"Thanks."

Okay, that was a surprise. A pleasant one. Maybe sight-seeing would work out.

She studied the pastries inside the glass display case.

He wanted the same thing he'd had yesterday.

"Look who finally decided to grace Silver Falls with his presence." Taryn Lawson grinned, complete with dimples on both sides of her face. She wore all white with a baker's cap on her net-covered hair. The same uniform her mom and dad had worn when they ran the bakery. "It's good to see you back, Brandt."

"Thanks." He appreciated the warm welcome, but he wasn't ready for a stroll down memory lane. "I'm assuming you know each other?"

"Blueberry muffin or bagel today?" Taryn asked Callie without any hesitation.

"Muffin," she said a beat later.

He half-laughed, feeling like an outsider instead of someone who'd lived most of his life in Silver Falls. "You *do* know each other."

"Callie's a regular. When I get a dog, I'll be one of hers." Taryn bagged a muffin. "What would you like, Brandt?"

"A cranberry scone." He pulled out his wallet.

"Put that away. These are on the house." The baker handed each of them a small white bag and a napkin. "Consider it a welcome-home greeting."

Silver Falls was still his hometown even if he didn't live here. As he gripped the bag, he crinkled the top. "Thanks."

"Yes, thank you," Callie added.

Taryn's gaze traveled from him to Callie and back again. "How do you two know each other?"

"Margot."

"My aunt."

Their words came out at the same time. Funny how that kept happening.

"My aunt didn't want to go out in the snow, so she asked

Callie to show me around," Brandt explained.

Taryn snickered. "You sure that was the real reason?"

Shrugging, Brandt hoped Callie hadn't heard about his aunt's matchmaking hobby. That might make things awkward if she thought this was a set-up. Even though he'd bet a thousand dollars that was his aunt's intention. "You know Aunt Margot."

Amusement gleamed in Taryn's gaze. "She likes to stick her nose in everyone's business."

That was an understatement. His aunt meddled, as much and as deep as she could, but that was part of what made her the woman she was.

"Thanks again, Taryn," he said. "We have to catch up. I'm here through December."

"An extended vacation?"

He nodded. "I finished a job. With the holidays, starting a new one didn't make sense."

"Good for you." Taryn pulled off her plastic gloves. "Stop by anytime. If I'm not working the counter, I'll be in the back."

Callie went to a table next to the front window. "This okay?"

"Perfect." Sitting, he stared at the bakery's display. "I'm impressed with Taryn's Christmas window."

Callie bit into her muffin.

Eating his scone, he examined the decorations.

A sign hung from the top of the window with *Visions of Sugar Plums* written in cursive on both sides, making it readable from inside and outside the bakery. Cakes, tortes, pies, and cookies, including gingerbread people, were used as decorations and characters. Almost everything appeared edible.

Talk about creative.

"It's fantastic." He pulled out his scone. "This display will be hard to beat."

She wiped her mouth with the napkin. "Taryn won last year."

"I'm not surprised if her window was anything like this one."

"The Nutcracker theme is festive, but not as elegant as last year's Christmas wedding display. No matter what she would have chosen, winning back to back is difficult to do." No emotion was in Callie's voice. Her expression had changed. If anything, she appeared detached. "Few have repeated as winners."

"That's because everyone is in it to win it." Brandt hoped to bring the smile back to her face. He waited and watched.

She ate more of her muffin.

He'd try again. "The judges will have their work cut out for them with all the incredible displays this year. All of them are great. Not just this one."

Callie fiddled with the sleeve on her cup. "Why do you like Taryn's window so much?"

"Branding."

"What do you mean?"

"Taryn uses bakery products for the decorations, so her brand is showcased," he explained. "That's a huge plus for them in drawing in customers—new and old. A competitive advantage so to speak."

"But this is a holiday window display contest. Not an advertisement or sales pitch."

"That's why her display works so well. It accomplishes both. The same as my aunt's."

Callie tore off a piece of her muffin. "You sound more like a marketer than a programmer."

"With a start-up, at least the one I was a part of, you wear different hats. In our early days, my cofounder and I divvyed up the tasks based on our strengths." Back then, NiBrTech had meant a never-ending workload. The late nights became routine, but he'd never found another job to be as fulfilling. "I'd taken business courses, so I did what I could marketing-wise until we had money to hire someone."

Eating the piece of muffin, she studied the back of the display, not as a casual observer, but as if taking mental notes and snapshots.

"Taryn used baked goods in her design last year," Callie said finally. "The ballet theme is clever."

"I hear a *but* coming."

"But…" She raised her gaze to his. "I prefer my theme."

Her steady confidence appealed to him on multiple levels. There was only one problem… "What's your theme?"

Her nose scrunched. "Silver Falls."

He imagined her window. The silver and the waterfall. "I get it now."

Her *duh* expression made him bite back a laugh. "I thought using a theme that reflects the town's name would be…"

"Clever," he finished before eating more of his scone.

"Creative," she countered.

He swallowed. "It is."

"I hear a *but* coming," she said, throwing his words back at him.

That made him laugh. "There's nothing wrong with your theme, but your display is something you'd see at a big-city department store."

As her mouth quirked, her gaze clouded. "That wasn't my intent, but I wanted to emphasize the silver."

"You succeeded in doing that."

"O-kay." Except she sounded anything but okay.

As she stared at her coffee cup, he felt like a jerk.

"Maybe I went overboard." She shrunk into herself as if someone had turned on a faucet and was draining every ounce of confidence that had been brimming moments before.

"There's nothing wrong with using silver." Making her feel bad hadn't been his intention. Far from it. "Nothing in the display, however, calls attention to what your business does. You don't have a dog—silver or otherwise. The competition doesn't have strict requirements, but brand matters whether you're a Fortune 500 corporation or a small-town shop."

Raising her chin, she stared directly at him. "Everyone around here knows what Wags and Tails is."

Okay, she had a point. "Maybe brand isn't all that, but the impression or *feels* a window leaves you with is. My mom decorated homes when they used to have the Silver Falls

Christmas Home Tour. The winning houses were never the fancy shimmery designs."

Callie's face fell.

Brandt hated she was taking this personally when all he wanted to do was help her. "Glitter and sparkles are popular during the holidays, but the traditionally decorated houses usually won."

She rubbed the back of her neck. "Why is that?"

"I asked my mom that question. She told me the shiny ones lacked the most important thing about Christmas."

Eyes full of interest, Callie leaned forward over the table. "What?"

"They lacked heart."

Her forehead creased. "Heart?"

"Heart," he repeated.

She tilted her head as if thinking. "You can't get more heartfelt than playing off our town's name."

"If you say so." The second the words left his mouth, he wished he could take them back.

Callie pushed back in her chair. "What's that supposed to mean?"

"Nothing bad." Brandt was being honest, but he didn't want to lose the progress they'd made this morning. "The silver in your window makes perfect sense with your theme, but adding a few traditionally colored elements wouldn't hurt."

"Traditionally colored?"

"Red and green. That's what my mom would do. My aunt, too." He'd helped decorate enough times he knew what changes might help. "All you have to do is replace the metallic tree with a green one and then use the same silver ornaments and garland. Add a dog figurine, silver or not, with a silver and red ribbon around its neck. It wouldn't change what you have if you added some..."

"Traditional colors."

"And heart."

Callie bit her lip. "Thanks for the suggestions."

"I'm happy to help."

Except he wasn't sure if he had, but she didn't sound as annoyed with him as she had yesterday. That gave Brandt the courage to continue.

"This is only my opinion." He wanted to keep things pleasant between them. "It's my first time decorating for the holidays in six years, so what do I know?"

She didn't say anything, only kept gnawing on her lip.

"I'm sure my aunt would be happy to help you if you wanted to make additions to your display," he continued.

Callie finished eating her muffin. "I appreciate the offer, but I'm happy with Wags and Tails' window as it is."

Of course she was. Which was why he should have kept quiet. But he'd never been good about keeping his mouth shut when he thought he could help. He'd tried. That was the best he could do. Except...

The silence increased the tension between them. Not to yesterday's levels, but they'd been getting along this morning.

Brandt needed to fix whatever was wrong or he had the feeling she'd be saying goodbye when they left the bakery.

He didn't care about sightseeing, but he wanted to spend more time with Callie and get to know her better. He only hoped he hadn't messed everything up by talking about her Christmas window.

That might be a subject to avoid in the future.

If they had one…

At this point, she might not want to see him again.

Was that a good thing or not?

Chapter Eleven

YOU CAN BE hypersensitive when people offer help.

Callie was ready to bolt from the bakery until she heard Anna's voice in her head. Two deep breaths kept Callie seated across the table from Brandt.

She shouldn't let him get to her. She'd told Anna she wouldn't, but what Brandt said hurt. Callie had worked so hard on her window display.

Don't take it personally.

She was trying.

Last year's winning theme had been elegant. She'd used that as a springboard to brainstorm and plan her Silver Falls theme. Her use of silver was meant to be tasteful, not whatever Brandt thought it was…tacky and overdone based on his tone.

He leaned forward. "Callie?"

Brandt wasn't trying to be a jerk. She got that. From what she'd seen today, he seemed like a decent guy, but his trying to help rubbed her the wrong way.

Maybe it was time to forget the tour. Seeing First Avenue wasn't much in the way of sightseeing, but she doubted he'd care if she wanted to return to Wags and Tails. That left her two choices—say goodbye or continue the tour as if he'd said nothing about her window display.

"Are you okay?" His voice was thick with concern.

"Yes." Both options had pros and cons. One would be easier to do than the other, but she'd never been a quitter. And if she were being hypersensitive…

She needed to get over that with her family coming for Christmas. This would be good practice.

Time to be strong. If need be, she could find an excuse to cut the tour short. Callie straightened. "Ready to keep going?"

Surprise flashed across his face. "Sure."

Had she let her hypersensitivity show? Probably, but she couldn't stop herself from reacting when he hadn't been able to make out her theme, gushed over Taryn's window display, and told Callie how to fix hers.

Jealousy?

Of course not.

Okay, maybe a little bit.

But winning this year was important to her.

As Brandt stood, she gathered the cups, napkins, and bags from the table and tossed them in the garbage. Before she could open the door, he did.

"Thanks." She brushed by him, shivered, and zipped up her jacket.

Brandt adjusted his beanie. "That hit the spot."

Callie nodded, not trusting her voice yet.

If only they hadn't discussed the window displays, but she couldn't dwell on what he'd said or allow someone to second-guess her efforts. Who was Brandt Winslow anyway?

Margot's nephew, yes, but also a computer programmer who hadn't been back to his hometown or decorated for years. He'd said so himself, so how would he know anything about the holidays or heart?

Bottom line—he wouldn't.

What he'd said was simply his opinion. She had one, too.

Her window display was fine.

Not fine. Perfect.

Rethinking wasn't necessary. The silver would stay. No red and green needed to be added. Putting in a dog wasn't a bad idea, but she wasn't in a rush to do that. Adding a sign like Taryn had, however, might make the theme clearer. Yes, Callie would do that.

With a plan in place, she smiled at him, hoping whatever tension remained disappeared. Now to figure out what stop was next on the tour. The art gallery had been opened only a couple of years, so Brandt wouldn't have been there. The library was newer and had a museum inside. But first…

"Was there anything in particular you wanted to see?" she asked.

"Not really." He pulled on his gloves. "This was…"

"Your aunt's idea," Callie finished for him.

Brandt nodded. "Not that you had any choice."

She shrugged, but at the same time she wondered if he took after Margot and felt compelled to butt into others' business. That would explain his *suggestions* about the Christmas window and the waterfall. "Well, we are the two who have the least amount of fun according to those who know us."

That brought a laugh. "Did you fire anyone for saying that?"

"No, but I may or may not have assigned extra clean-up duties." Callie headed toward the intersection that marked the end of the business blocks on First Avenue. "This isn't the first time they've said something similar. I have fun, but no one understands that work is fun for me."

He fell into step beside her. "That's how I feel when I'm coding. My aunt doesn't get it, even though she works long hours with her business and feels the same way about quilting."

Something in common. That was…nice. "When you love what you do, it's not really work."

"So true."

"Margot believes that, too, so she's probably just worried about you. She can't keep her nose out of other people's lives."

"Also true."

"On the flip side is my family." Callie shoved her hands in her pockets. "I work as much or more as my parents and brothers do, but they think all I do is play with dogs."

"Your family thinks you have too much fun, and your employees think you have no fun."

She laughed. "I can't win."

"I say we go to a place people associate with having a good time. We can appease my aunt and your staff that way."

Callie thought for a moment. "The park is nearby."

"A park, by definition, is fun."

"Let's go." They wouldn't have to change their direction. "But our definition of fun may be different. The thought of doing anything computer related would be a day of torture for me."

A sheepish grin formed on his face. "Spending all day surrounded by dogs would be mine."

She gasped. "You don't like dogs?"

"Dogs are okay."

Her jaw dropped. "Just okay?"

"I haven't spent much time around them." He didn't sound embarrassed or regretful. "I've never had any pets due to my mom's allergies."

As Callie led the way toward the park, she tried to make sense of what he'd said. Someone needed to make useful apps and software, but dogs were everything. He acted so indifferent. Unless…

"Do you still live with your mom?" she asked.

"Yes, and I spend my days playing video games in my parents' basement," he said in a matter-of-fact tone.

O-kay. She wasn't sure what to say to that.

"You should see your face." He burst out laughing. "That's a joke. I haven't lived at home since I graduated college."

If that was the case… "Then why don't you have a pet?"

"With the hours I work, leaving an animal alone for that long each day wouldn't be right. Plus, needing a pet-friendly apartment would add one more complication to moving."

"Those are good reasons, but having a pet can improve one's life. There are health benefits, too." She didn't want

Brandt missing out when he didn't have to. "A fish might work."

"Maybe." Amusement gleamed in his eyes. "The problem is I'm not good at remembering things when I dive into a project. I don't want a fish to go hungry."

"That wouldn't be good." Somehow, they'd ended up walking closer to each other. "Does that mean you're an absentminded-professor type?"

"Geeky computer nerd is more like it," he joked in reply. "My mom once gave me a houseplant. It was pretty and green. When I started a new job, I forgot to water it. The thing dried up and died. Lesson learned about caring for living things."

"In that case, I'd suggest silk plants and an aquarium video you can play on your TV." She hoped he understood she was joking. Based on his bemused grin, he did.

They stopped at the curb to let a minivan drive through the intersection.

"Do you have any pets?" he asked.

"Rex." Simply saying her dog's name warmed Callie's heart. "I adopted him two years ago from a local animal rescue. He'd been surrendered by his owners, but their loss was my gain. I lucked out."

"Sounds like Rex did."

"What do you mean?" she asked.

"The way you talk about Rex should be a relationship goal."

Heat rushed up her neck. "Thanks, I think."

"It's a compliment." Brandt cleared his throat. "I won't

be adopting any rescue animals in the near future, but I'm glad people like you and my aunt have."

"Thanks, but full disclosure. Rex rescued me."

"How so?"

"I never thought much about working seven days a week." As a car stopped to let them cross the street, she waved at the driver. "I enjoyed being at Wags and Tails, and someone needed to be there, but adopting Rex meant I needed to make time for him. He goes to work with me, but he needs time without the other dogs around. So now I work fewer hours on the weekends. Walks, one-on-one play time, and doing nothing are regular parts of our lives. I didn't realize how much I needed that. He's been great for me."

The space between her and Brandt lessened more. He'd also moved to the other side of her, so he was closest to oncoming traffic. She appreciated his gentlemanly manners.

"Sounds like it." Brandt watched the cars approaching the intersection as if he expected them to blow the stop sign. "I wonder if a fish video might do that for me."

Imagining Brandt sitting in front of a digital aquarium made her laugh. "You might want to upgrade to a dog or cat video."

His brows drew together. "Why is that?"

She gave him points for sounding so serious. "Fish are quiet. You'll forget to turn off the power if you were distracted by work. Don't want to waste electricity."

Brandt's brows furrowed. "How did you know I forget to turn off lights and other things?"

She stepped onto the curb, pointing the way to the park's

entrance where a statue of the city's founder welcomed visitors. That likely hadn't changed since he lived here, but she wanted to be a good tour guide. "It's a trait of plant killers."

The corners of his eyes crinkled. She forced herself not to stare.

"I didn't ask to be given that plant." He sounded like a kid who was in trouble. The way his lower lip jutted out was all kinds of adorable.

He was kidding around, but she fought the urge to reach out to him. A good thing her hands were in her pockets. "Not the strongest defense, but that might sway the jury."

"Will it sway you?" he asked with a hopeful tone.

Her heart bumped, something unexpected and unwelcome. She swallowed around the lump in her throat. "I'm on your side."

"Good to know."

She focused on her steps, so she didn't stumble. Being around Brandt made her lightheaded and off-kilter.

The smell of pine from a grove of trees lingered in the air. The aroma lifted her spirits. Once she had time to buy a Christmas tree, she'd have the fragrance throughout her house.

Snow covered the tree branches and the ground, but the paths had been cleared. The park was never crowded, but few were out today.

"I haven't been here since high school." Brandt surveyed the area, not appearing impressed. "Must admit the park was more fun when I was younger."

"Hey." She nudged him. "Give it more than a couple of minutes."

He held up his hands. "I was just saying…"

"Patience is a virtue." She gestured at a patch of untouched snow. "The fun is about to begin."

His mouth slanted. "That sounds almost ominous."

"Changing your mind?" she challenged.

He edged closer, stopping before he completely invaded her personal space. "Depends on what you have in mind?"

"When was the last time you built a snowman?"

❦

BRANDT HADN'T MADE a snowman since he was a kid and never in the park. He'd ridden his bike here, skateboarded, dipped his feet in the creek, slid down the slide, and hung from the monkey bars. But the park wasn't a place to go in winter.

Until now.

As Callie worked on the middle section, the tip of her tongue stuck out between her lips. She was taking this seriously.

She must have felt his gaze on her because she raised an eyebrow at him. "What?"

He continued to build the snowman's bottom. "Having fun?"

"Yes, are you?"

"I am." Which surprised him. "My aunt will be shocked but pleased at what you've pulled off."

Callie gave a mock bow. "Anna and Sam will be amazed

I'm doing this."

"Not a lot of snowman building in your past?"

"I grew up in Los Angeles, so not until I moved here."

She seemed to fit right into Silver Falls. Not all big-city types made the transition so smoothly. "Making up for lost time?"

"I love the snow." The enthusiasm in her gaze matched her voice. "I don't mind the rain. I enjoyed the SoCal sunshine, but having four seasons is the best."

"You're right." Except he hadn't experienced four seasons in a few years. Maybe that was why no place had felt like home. "People complain about the winter weather, but all that white is so…pristine."

She nodded. "Maybe it's because I never had snow until I moved here, but winter is my favorite. Even when the snow is melting and everything is more brown than white."

He wasn't surprised she felt that way. Images of Callie making a snow angel and catching snowflakes on her tongue formed in his mind. The only things missing were her dog and a kid…

Whoa. Where had that come from?

Rewind back to the dog. On second thought, all the way to the snow angel.

"Brandt?" Callie asked. "You okay?"

How long had he been lost in his thoughts? Too long if she'd noticed. "Sorry, I was just thinking."

"About coding?" she teased.

Distracting her would be better than telling the truth. He grabbed a handful of snow, made a ball, and tossed it at her.

Eyes widening, she darted behind a tree before peeking out. "What did I do to deserve that?"

Getting into my head. At least she wasn't under his skin. "Just having fun."

"But our snowman…"

"Isn't going anywhere." Brandt threw another snowball.

She ducked out from the tree. "It's so on."

The determination in her voice made him laugh, but he owed her a warning. "Remember, I grew up here. I wouldn't say I'm a snowball champion, but…"

Something pelted him in the arm. "Hey."

She cheered as if she were at a sporting event and her team had scored. "Direct hit. Not bad for a Cali girl."

"Lucky shot."

"Sorry, not sorry."

Another snowball hit his leg. "No fair."

"You started this." She dashed back behind the tree. "And you're the one standing out in the open."

She had a point. He ran behind the closest tree.

A snowball flew through the air and then exploded against the trunk. Back and forth they lofted the loosely packed missiles at each other. They zigzagged among the trees for a better position and to avoid being hit. Brandt had no idea how long they battled, but he hadn't laughed that hard in years. Nor had he been covered with so much snow. Not even after yesterday.

"Truce," he called.

"Does that mean you surrender?" she asked in a singsong voice.

She wasn't going to give up. He respected that. "It means I need a break."

"I could use a breather." Callie stepped out from behind a tree, brushing off the snow covering her.

Brandt did the same. "Let's call it a draw and finish up Mr. Frosty."

Trying to get the middle section on top of the bottom wasn't easy, but they managed using teamwork. The top went up easier.

He studied their efforts. "Almost finished."

She shook her head. "He's missing his face, and he has no arms."

Maybe he was out of snowman-building practice. Brandt found twigs and then stuck them into the middle section for the arms. Callie dug through the snow until she found rocks to use for his eyes and mouth. A fallen pinecone made the perfect nose.

"Not bad," he said.

"Mr. Frosty is great." She reached out her hand. "Give me your phone. I'll take a photo of you for your aunt."

"Oh, you're good." After he unlocked the screen, he handed her the cell phone. "Physical evidence of having fun."

She held up the phone. "Say cheese."

He did.

Callie returned his phone. "I'm used to taking photos of the dogs while they play so I can send them to their owners."

Brandt laughed. "So I'm like one of your doggy daycare charges."

"Except you have two legs and aren't covered in fur."

"As far as you know."

Her cheeks turned fire-engine red, something that had nothing to do with the chilly air.

A dog barked—make that two.

Saved by the barks.

Callie's head whipped toward the sound. "Oh, no. That's Jasper and Wrangler. They shouldn't be running around loose."

"You know the dogs?"

"Yes." The concern in her voice suggested she knew them well. Or maybe this was her being an animal lover.

The dogs sniffed what appeared to be a tree stump. Brandt squinted—golden retrievers.

She called someone on her cell phone. "Hey, I'm at the park. Jasper and Wrangler are here. Please bring me two leashes and call Beth to let her know. Thanks. See you soon."

Callie slipped her phone into her coat pocket. "Come on."

"What are you going to do?" he asked, following her.

"*We* are going to catch two dogs."

Feeling out of his element, he blew out a breath. "Okay."

"Follow my lead." She tossed a confident smile his way as if this was something she did every day. Maybe it was. "I'll tell you what to do."

Chapter Twelve

"STAY BEHIND ME, move slowly, and don't look the dogs directly in the eyes," Callie said to Brandt in a soft voice. She didn't want the dogs taking off.

Jasper and Wrangler weren't known runners—owners filled out a profile for dogs who went to Wags and Tails and she had most memorized—but Jasper knew how to open the front door, which was likely how he escaped. This wasn't the first time they'd been loose. At some point, their luck was going to run out.

"Got it," Brandt replied a notch above a whisper, which she appreciated. "But shouldn't we run after them?"

Her muscles tightened. "No."

Thank goodness he hadn't tried to help by taking off after the dogs. That would have been a disaster.

"Chasing dogs is a surefire way to make sure you don't catch them." She kept her voice low as she moved at a snail's pace. Thankfully, the dogs were more interested in what was around them than her and Brandt. "Many end up running into the middle of streets or getting into other dangerous situations because they're afraid of whoever is chasing them and they're trying to get away."

"I had no idea."

"You're not alone." She focused her attention on the dogs but kept her chin down toward her chest. The less intimidating she made herself, the better.

Jasper held his tail still and at body level, which suggested he was alert and fine. Wrangler's tail was tucked between his legs, a sure sign the poor baby was nervous or scared. Maybe both.

Her heart hurt for the sweet boy, whose brother kept getting him into trouble. In April, Jasper had jumped out the window of Beth's SUV when she stopped for gas. Wrangler had followed him. Thanks to an animal-loving sheriff's deputy from nearby Summit Ridge, the dogs had been found safe. Callie hoped this story had a similar happy ending.

"If they come toward us," Callie said. "Run away so they chase us."

"They'll chase us?" he asked with disbelief.

"It has worked in the past."

He sighed, a drawn-out exhale that must have used up whatever air had been in his lungs.

"You okay?" she asked.

"I'm glad you know what you're doing because if I was on my own, those dogs would be long gone."

Brandt didn't sound nervous, more hesitant. That made sense given his lack of experience with pets.

"You're doing great, but we need to get closer." She wanted the dogs to come to them. That would be the safest way to recover them, especially without leashes. "We're moving slowly so we don't spook them."

As she stepped, something crunched beneath her boot.

Jasper's nose swung in her direction.

She froze. Brandt crashed into her backside, pushing her forward.

Oh… She tumbled face-first, seemingly falling in slow motion, the snow rushing up to greet her as gravity pulled her down.

Arms reached around her, grabbing her waist, spinning her so she was now staring at the sky.

Someone grunted.

Not her.

She landed against something. Hard.

Air rushed from her lungs. She struggled to breathe.

Her hips and lower back hurt as if she'd twisted the wrong way, but other than that…

Gloved hands held onto her.

Not any hands.

Brandt.

He was lying under her, his legs tangled in hers. Jackets and damp clothing separated them, but their position was close.

Intimate.

The hard muscles of his thighs kept her bottom off the snow. The cold air felt warmer as if the temperature had shot up twenty degrees in the last five seconds. Or maybe the way hot blood raced through her veins was the reason.

The pair of strong arms that kept her from landing on her face continued to hold her, offering an unfamiliar feeling of security.

Of safety.

Of belonging.

His gloves were wet, but she imagined his bare hands holding her. Touching her.

Her heart thudded.

"Are you hurt?" Concern rang out in his question.

"I'm okay." Her voice was husky. Probably shock over falling and ending up where she had. "Are you?"

"Fine." His warm breath blew against her ear, sending a pleasurable shiver through her. "I'm sorry for bumping into you."

"I'm the one who stopped without warning." Callie couldn't believe he'd saved her from hitting the ground. She wasn't overweight, but no one would call her thin. "Thanks for breaking my fall. You have to be hurting."

"Not much." He didn't sound like he was in pain or annoyed, but his body language would tell her more.

Callie tried to scoot off him, but his arms didn't loosen. She liked the comfort of being close to someone, but she was worried he was injured.

When she turned her head toward Brandt's, her face ended up inches from his. Their mouths were nearly at the same level.

As her pulse kicked up, her mouth went dry.

If she leaned forward slightly, her lips would be against his.

Desire shot through her. Imagining their mouths together and their hands in each other's hair sent her heart pounding. His seemed to be beating as fast as hers.

Oh, no. She wanted to kiss him.

Not a peck.

A full-on movie-worthy kiss.

Flutters erupted in her stomach—an aviary worth of butterflies with huge wings. Her body trembled with anticipation.

His eyes were dark, full of questions and longing. The same yearning she felt staring at him.

She swallowed. Hard.

"Callie?" he asked.

Move back.

A hundred and three reasons to do that screamed inside as if she were listening to a podcast about self-preservation on the highest volume setting, but Callie stayed where she was. She didn't want to move. Didn't want this moment to end.

Not yet.

Something about Brandt called to her in a way she'd never experienced before. Sure, he'd annoyed her. More than once. Did she dare…

His gaze left hers, and he stared over her shoulder. "The dogs."

His voice shook her from whatever trance he'd cast on her. She'd forgotten about Jasper and Wrangler.

How had that happened?

Okay, the fall, and then Brandt, but still…

"They're coming toward us," he whispered.

His breath sent goose bumps prickling across her skin. His woodsy, mint scent surrounded her. She wanted to wrap herself in his essence.

"What do we do now?" he asked, finally loosening his arms.

"Stay still." Too bad she couldn't move off him now. This wasn't far from the position she'd planned to drop into when she'd stopped. Lying down was the best way not to intimidate the dogs, but she hadn't planned to be mostly on top of him.

Snow seeped through the calves of her jeans that were against the ground. Brandt had to be soaking wet, but they needed to get the dogs first.

Jasper trotted over. He sniffed their feet before moving up their legs. If only she had a dog treat with her…

The dog backed away from Brandt. Not surprising given he was a stranger. Jasper came over to Callie's side, nudging her with his muzzle as if trying to see what was going on.

She held out her hand, wishing she'd thought to remove her glove. She'd hit Brandt, not the ground, but her head was fuzzy as if not all her brain synapses were firing correctly.

Barking, Jasper rolled over on his back to expose his belly. He enjoyed belly rubs almost as much as treats.

As she reached for his tummy, Callie slid off Brandt. Her bottom hit the cold ground. She pressed her lips together to keep from crying out. She missed his warmth.

Focus on the dogs.

Not that she had a choice with Jasper pawing at her.

"You silly boy." She rubbed his belly, ignoring how the cold was taking hold of her. "Running away is never the answer."

Jasper wiggled to reposition closer to her.

Wrangler edged toward them, but each step was tentative as if he couldn't make up his mind which way to go or what to do. He kept his distance from Brandt. Not surprising given Wrangler didn't know the guy.

"Do you want your belly rubbed, too?" she asked Wrangler, trying to keep her teeth from chattering. Her wet clothes and the freezing temperatures were not the best combination.

"Reach out your hand," she instructed Brandt.

He did, but his cautious movement reminded him of the way Wrangler was approaching.

Even now, the dog stayed next to Callie to sniff Brandt's hand before ignoring him and shimmying between her and Jasper.

She rubbed both dogs. "Jealous of your brother?"

Wrangler's paw waved in the air as Jasper's had.

Brandt laughed.

Okay, maybe the guy wasn't a lost cause when it came to dogs.

"You must want more rubs." She glanced at Brandt. "We need to hold them by their collars until someone arrives with leashes. I'm going to get Jasper. He's the feistier of the two. Can you hold onto Wrangler?"

"Yes," Brandt said without any hesitation.

She respected his willingness to help. "I'll pet both. As I scoot down, come toward Wrangler and rub him. If we're careful, they might not notice we're holding onto them."

As she moved, he shifted behind her. The rubs kept the

dogs relaxed. She placed her left hand on Jasper's collar while petting his stomach with her right.

"I've got this one," Callie said, thankful the plan had worked for Jasper.

"It's okay, Wrangler." Brandt's singsong voice made her grin despite being chilled to the bone. "I've got you."

Callie blew out a breath. Wrangler wouldn't go anywhere without Jasper, but knowing Brandt had the dog brought a rush of relief.

He touched her arm. "You're shivering."

She was, but they needed to take care of the dogs first. "Someone will be here soon."

As if on cue, Beth Owens hurried toward them with two leashes in hand. Tears gleamed in her eyes. The dogs' owner clipped a lead to each collar. If the dogs ran, they could only go the length of their leashes. Though neither moved while they were being rubbed.

"I can't believe Jasper opened the front door again." Beth sniffled. "I was in the laundry room, switching the clothes to the dryer. It only took a minute, but they were gone when I came out. Thank goodness Sam called when he did. I'd searched the neighborhood by foot and was about to hop in the car."

Both dogs were napping, so sweet and calm, nothing like adventurous runaways. Callie hoped they didn't do this again. "I'm sure they didn't look back once they were off."

"I don't want to know what they've been up to or how they made it all the way to the park." Beth touched each of the dogs as if to assure herself Jasper and Wrangler were fine.

"Thank you for finding them."

"They found us." Callie remembered her manners. "Brandt helped me with the dogs. Beth Owens, meet Brandt Winslow."

Beth bit her lip. "Winslow?"

"I'm Margot's nephew," Brandt replied.

"No wonder I recognized your last name. Thanks for your help." Beth's gaze bounced between her dogs, Brandt, and Callie. "Your aunt is the best. She was so helpful when we moved from Denver to open our restaurant."

"Another new business owner," Brandt said.

Nodding, Beth's gaze narrowed. "Oh my goodness, you're both soaking wet. What did my ungrateful beasts do to you?"

Callie forced the corners of her lips upward even though doing so hurt her frozen mouth. "That wasn't the dogs' fault."

"It wasn't, but we should get off the cold ground now that they're on leashes." Brandt stood, reaching out his arm to her.

Taking his hand, she rose to her feet.

Beth gave each of the leashes a tug. "I'm going to take these two home. As soon as I get them settled, I'm calling a locksmith to install a new doorknob. I've been meaning to do that."

"A deadbolt might help," Brandt suggested.

"It would if I remembered to use it," Beth admitted. "But good idea, thanks."

"You're welcome," he said.

Maybe Brandt was simply a good guy who liked to help people. He'd done it twice with Callie. Three times if she counted him breaking her fall and now with Beth.

"Thanks again for your help." Beth gave each dog a pat on their sides. "I'd like to show my appreciation by treating the two of you to dinner at the café. Say Saturday night at seven?"

"That's not necessary," Callie answered quickly.

Brandt agreed. "We're happy to have helped."

"You saved my fur babies today." Beth gazed affectionately at her dogs. "Dinner is the least I can do. What do you say?"

Callie glanced at Brandt, who gave a slight shrug. She knew how much the dogs meant to Beth and her husband. "Okay. Thanks."

"Great." Beth beamed. "I hope you enjoy your date night."

Date night? A tightness formed in Callie's chest. She didn't know what to say.

Brandt raised an eyebrow, but he smiled at Beth. "Thanks."

"Be there at seven. I'll take care of everything." Beth pulled on the leashes until both dogs stood. "Now get yourselves inside so you can dry off and warm up."

With that, she tugged Jasper and Wrangler on their way.

As Callie and Brandt hurried back toward First Avenue, she thought he'd say something about dinner. The fact he hadn't made her wonder. Was he having second thoughts now that Beth had called it a date night? Did he care? Should

Callie ask him? Was she overthinking this?

Probably.

A breeze sent a chill ripping through her. She crossed her arms over her chest, but that didn't lessen the cold biting into her like a rabid Jack Frost.

Brandt unzipped his jacket. "Take my coat."

She put a hand on his. "Thanks, but you're wetter than I am. The shop is only a couple of minutes away." Still, she appreciated the offer. "You have to be freezing."

"Not freezing."

If she weren't so cold, she would have laughed. "You sound like my brothers again."

Brandt tilted his head. "Again?"

Oops. Busted. No problem. "A guy who's never cold, never lost, and never wears sunscreen."

That was true even if that hadn't been what she meant.

"Yes to the first two, but I always wear sunscreen." Amusement rang out in his voice. "Lobster red isn't a good color for me."

Eager to get inside, she quickened her pace. "Does that mean your use is a vanity issue and not a health concern?"

"A combination."

"That's honest." Maybe he'd tell her how he felt about their upcoming dinner, but first they needed to warm up.

He pushed open the door to Wags and Tails.

The instant she crossed the threshold, the heat surrounded her like a hug from a long-lost friend. She pulled off her coat, gloves, and shoes.

Brandt removed his outerwear. The dark color of his

jeans showed how wet he'd gotten. Way worse than her.

"We keep spare clothes here." He was about the same size as Sam. Maybe a little taller. "Might not be a perfect fit, but you can't walk back to Margot's all wet."

"Anything dry would be great," Brandt said. "I don't care if it fits or not."

That meant he *was* cold, but she wasn't going to call him on it. "We have coffee in the office, too."

"Dry clothes and a hot drink." He counted off the items on his fingers. "Free coffee earlier, a free pastry, and a free dinner. Not bad for a Wednesday morning."

He didn't sound upset, more amused. "Are you okay going out to dinner at the café?"

"More than okay." His smile wavered. "Are you?"

Yeah, surprisingly she was. "It'll be nice."

And that had nothing to do with the dinner being free. She wanted to spend more time with Brandt. And that gave her an idea. Maybe they could find another time to continue their sightseeing tour.

Chapter Thirteen

"DO YOU WANT to pick up Angus and Sadie today?"

As Brandt pushed the shopping cart through the market's produce section with his aunt on Friday, he fought the urge to shout *no* as he'd done when she'd asked a similar question yesterday. Instead, he focused on the acorn squash.

"Or do you need to code more?" Aunt Margot asked from the display of onions.

Brandt had used working on his game as an excuse. Not a lie because he'd been fiddling with it yesterday, but he hadn't wanted to tell her the real reason he'd said no. That he hadn't been able to stop thinking about Callie, seeing the desire in her gaze, and reliving the way she'd almost kissed him at the park on Wednesday morning. He'd hoped distance would put an end to those thoughts. So far, it hadn't.

Brandt placed a squash in the basket. His aunt used to make a baked squash with brown sugar, maple syrup, apples, butter, and walnuts. He would gather the ingredients, so she'd be set.

"Do you need me to pick up the dogs?" he asked.

"I can do it unless you want to." Aunt Margot sounded

disappointed, which he didn't like, but if she found out he wanted to see Callie, his aunt would be unstoppable. He couldn't allow that to happen even though he wanted to drop off *and* pick up the dogs each day. Truth was, he would spend the day at Wags and Tails if it meant more time with Callie.

The display of red and green apples shouted Christmas. Had Callie added anything new to her display window?

Stop. Now. He had to forget about her.

At least until their dinner on Saturday night.

"I have more work to do." Not a lie, but not the entire truth.

"Your mobile game. I know." Aunt Margot placed a bag of garlic cloves into the cart. "If I didn't know better, I'd think you were avoiding Callie. You haven't mentioned her. I hope nothing happened during your tour."

His aunt knew him well. Always had.

"Nothing happened other than having to cut the sightseeing short due to finding the two dogs." He bagged four large red apples. "I'm seeing Callie on Saturday night."

For dinner.

A free meal. A thank you.

Not a date night.

Aunt Margot's gaze narrowed, making him wonder what she saw that he didn't. "You could see Callie in an hour or so if you went to Wags and Tails, instead of having to wait until tomorrow."

Had Aunt Margot been moonlighting for the devil? He was oh-so-tempted to say yes. "Not today."

"You said you enjoyed being with her."

"I did." Brandt avoided saying *fun* because he didn't want to give his aunt any ideas. Canceling the dinner before things got out of hand might be the best move, except he wanted to spend time with Callie.

"Why haven't you seen her again?" Frustration colored her voice and face.

"Callie owns and runs a business. You know how time consuming that is."

"I do." Aunt Margot scooped walnuts from a bin and then dumped them into a bag. "But Callie is competent, understands time management, and is a good boss."

"She's so much more than that." The words slipped out of his mouth. "I've never seen anyone with such empathy and passion for animals."

He added the apples and a container of caramel dip to the other groceries.

His aunt held the walnuts over the cart as if frozen. "Those are strong opinions about someone you say you barely know."

"Watching her with Jasper and Wrangler showed me that." He tried to sound casual. "I'm sure she would have reacted the same even if she hadn't recognized the dogs."

Callie's worry over the runaways had been palpable, and she'd come up with a plan on the fly. Falling had been the only glitch, one he hadn't minded when she'd landed on him.

"She knew what to do," he continued. "She kept them calm so they wouldn't bolt and told me what I needed to do to help her."

"She's good with dogs."

"And people," he said quickly. "The dogs' owner was upset. Beth said she'd get a new doorknob, but Callie didn't judge or criticize her for not doing it sooner."

With a smile as bright as the Las Vegas Strip, Aunt Margot tossed the walnuts into the cart as if she were shooting a basketball at a net. "That's the kind of person Callie is. She'll go out of her way to help anyone, whether they have two legs or four. She's special."

He agreed, but something about Callie still bugged him. "Too bad she's also stubborn. She offers help, but why doesn't she accept it in return?"

"Callie Andrews is an independent and self-reliant woman. If she has a stubborn side, so what? There's nothing wrong with that." Aunt Margot's respect for the doggy daycare owner was clear in her voice. "She's a bit like I was when I was younger."

He laughed. "You're still that way."

"Which means you should be used to it." Aunt Margot moved toward the bagged salads on the back wall. "Spinach or romaine?"

"Romaine." Brandt pushed the cart. Callie reminded him of Aunt Margot in some ways, but not all. His aunt didn't date. Did Callie? Her face had paled when Beth mentioned a date night. He hadn't heard a boyfriend or an ex mentioned about Callie when his aunt talked about Anna, the groomer, dating a contractor.

Aunt Margot dropped the bag of romaine and one of

shredded cabbage on top of the other produce. "Do you know what you're wearing tomorrow night?"

"This isn't a date." He spoke fast with an edge to his voice. "If it were, I wouldn't be meeting Callie at the café. I'd pick her up."

Only he didn't remember telling Callie to meet him there. That meant he would have to firm up their plans before tomorrow night.

His aunt picked up a jar of blue cheese dressing. "There would be nothing wrong if tomorrow night was a date."

"But it's not." He didn't want to hurt his aunt, but she needed to be realistic about what was happening on Saturday. "Please don't get your hopes up that the dinner might turn into more than a free meal."

"Christmas is a time for hope and wishes coming true."

He'd tried. "If that's the case, then I'm wishing for a delicious dessert after we eat. Something chocolaty."

Callie might like that.

He imagined himself feeding her a bite.

Nope, not going to happen.

"Callie likes chocolate."

Aunt Margot wasn't going to give up. He managed not to roll his eyes. "Most people do."

Brandt waited for his aunt to say more, but she didn't. Good because he didn't want her or anyone else trying to push them together. He wasn't in the market for a girlfriend or a vacation romance, but if he were…

He wouldn't hesitate to ask out a woman like Callie Andrews.

❦

ON FRIDAY EVENING, Callie ran over the checklist for closing. Becca had left early to attend a basketball game at the university with a boy she liked. Sam, too, was on a date with a classmate who he described as supermodel gorgeous with dark skin and warm brown eyes that sent his heart racing. Anna was still here, but she was going out, too.

Love was in the air this holiday season.

For everyone except her.

Your choice.

Callie didn't have time to date because she needed to keep her business growing. She also couldn't afford the distraction of a new romance with her family coming. Except these past two days, those reasons hadn't stopped her from thinking about Brandt.

Pulling out a disinfectant sheet from the container, she thought about his call two hours ago. A short, awkward conversation where he told Callie he'd meet her at the café at seven before hanging up.

She scrubbed the counter.

The call had been unexpected and weird. No pleasantries. Not even a hello. He couldn't get off the phone fast enough.

Callie's stomach knotted.

Has she misread them getting along on Wednesday? If so, having dinner on Saturday would be awkward.

Lying next to Rex, Milo whined on the dog pillow. The way his back leg twitched suggesting he was dreaming. Not surprising after a long day of playing. He and Rex were the only dogs who remained, but they were always the last to go home.

As Anna exited the grooming area, she untied her apron. "Are you excited about your date tomorrow?"

"It's not a date." Callie tossed the disinfectant cloth into the garbage can. "The dinner is a thank you for finding Jasper and Wrangler."

Callie had to stop thinking about Brandt, of having fun with him and imagining her lips against his. Using another wipe, she scrubbed the counter again.

Anna tossed her apron into the laundry basket. "Are you sure about that?"

"Yes." But Callie couldn't hide her feelings from Anna. "I thought we were getting along, but I was wrong. He doesn't like me."

Anna picked up her purse and jacket from the floor. She'd dropped them off there before checking the grooming area. "You like Brandt."

"I barely know him."

"You want to get to know him better." The certainty in her voice suggested she'd been thinking about this.

"Maybe."

Anna didn't appear surprised. "That's why you've been disappointed each time Margot has shown up the past two days."

"Not disappointed." The day after their tour, Margot had delivered the freshly laundered sweats and socks Brandt had borrowed from Sam when she dropped off the dogs. No reason to be disappointed or care Brandt hadn't brought the dogs or picked them up, either day. He wasn't a dog person. "I enjoy seeing Margot."

Anna put on her coat. "You wanted to see Brandt more."

It wasn't a question, but Callie answered anyway. "A part of me wanted to know if the fun we'd had together had been a one-time thing."

Anna bounced toward the counter as if she were riding a pogo stick. "This is huge."

"Huge?"

"You haven't wanted anything from a guy since you moved here. Not even a phone number. Wanting to know anything about him is great."

Callie wasn't so sure about that. "Thinking about Brandt..."

"Makes you want to kiss him," Anna finished for her.

Yes, but admitting that to herself was hard enough. No way could Callie tell anyone else. "Leaves me feeling conflicted."

"Kissing is way better than being conflicted."

She'd take conflicted. "Brandt didn't want to talk to me for more than twenty seconds earlier. He doesn't want to kiss me."

Anna touched Callie's shoulder. "He has you rattled."

"It's stupid."

"Not at all. You had fun with him, and you want to have more. Nothing wrong with that."

"I guess." Callie wasn't sure of anything right now. "But dinner—"

"Whatever you do, no matter how nervous or unsure you

get, please don't cancel." Anna spoke in the voice she used to coax dogs onto the grooming table. "Go. Eat. Have fun. Promise?"

So much for getting out of tomorrow night. "Okay, I won't cancel."

Even if that was the smartest thing Callie could do.

"You never know what might happen with Brandt." Anna leaned against the counter. "Tonight is my third date with Davis this week. Not that I'm counting. Okay, I totally am."

Three dates? Wow. Callie had no idea. Things had changed since Monday morning. "Why didn't you say anything?"

Anna shrugged. "Still not wanting to jinx it."

Callie knew how badly Anna wanted to be in a committed relationship. "I'm happy for you."

"I like him." Anna blew out a breath. "More than I've liked anyone in a long time. I'm hoping he feels the same way about me."

"The guy would be stupid if he doesn't. Besides, no one spends that much time with someone unless they like them."

Anna straightened. "I hope you're right."

"I am."

Which was why Callie knew Brandt didn't like her. Romantically at least. His aunt had forced him to go sightseeing. Beth had made their dinner plans. Not once had Brandt chosen to see her.

Dread slinked down Callie's spine. Tomorrow was going to be bad.

The bell on the door jingled. Davis Tucker entered wearing heavy work boots, faded jeans, and a black puffy jacket. He was handsome with rugged features and hazel eyes. Strands of blond hair stuck out from his cap. Tall with wide shoulders, Davis's athletic build screamed former football player and beef-fed Midwesterner.

"Hey." When he saw Anna, his smile widened. "Ready to go?"

Anna clipped a leash to Milo's collar. "I am now."

"Have a wonderful time." Callie had two more things to do before heading home with Rex. Another night eating dinner and watching television together, her and her dog. Not that she minded. "I'll see you on Monday."

A beat passed before Anna focused on her with a confused expression as if she'd forgotten Callie was there.

She bit back a smile. Anna had it bad for Davis.

"Oh, right." Pink tinged Anna's cheeks. "I'm off tomorrow. I forgot."

Easy to do when making heart eyes at her date.

Callie pressed her lips together, so she wouldn't laugh and embarrass her friend. "A good thing I said something, so you didn't wake up early tomorrow for no reason."

Anna and Milo went toward Davis. The little white dog kept his distance from the guy. Not surprising given Davis's height. Anna waved. "Don't work too late."

After she and Davis left the store, Callie went to Rex. "I wonder if Davis is Anna's one. I hope he's what she's been searching for."

Rex stretched out now that Milo wasn't there.

"I can tell you're bored." She leaned over to give him a

pat. "I'll finish up the checklist, so we can head home."

She had dinner to heat up, boxes of decorations to bring in, and an outfit to figure out to wear for her dinner with Brandt.

Casual, semi-casual, or Christmassy?

Callie hadn't a clue what to wear. Not that it mattered if this wasn't a date, right? Still, she'd never eaten dinner at the café, only lunch. No reason to go overboard with her clothing choice, but she would wear something nicer than her usual jeans and long-sleeved shirt.

Not for Brandt.

For herself.

Chapter Fourteen

SATURDAY NIGHT, BRANDT sat across from Callie at the jam-packed Falls Café. The high-backed booth offered privacy. Though the overall atmosphere, in spite of the full tables, shouted intimate given the dim lighting, romantic instrumental music, white linens, flickering votive candle, and a white rose in a small vase.

Not at all what he was expecting when he was used to the diner down the block that served burgers, fries, and milkshakes with a 1950s décor.

This café had been designed for long, slow dinners with booths along the sides and tables in the center. The perfect place for a date, and other couples seemed to agree given how crowded the place was.

Too bad he and Callie were acting more like strangers. Sure, they'd said hello and exchanged the requisite pleasantries when they'd arrived, but the silence at the table was unexpected given how well they got along on Wednesday.

He didn't think he imagined them getting along. Or maybe his idiotic phone call had caused the problem. Though call was a relative term. He hadn't let her speak other than when she answered the phone. He might as well have left her a voice mail.

Stupid.

As he studied the menu, his knee bounced under the table. He needed to settle down. "I thought this place would be more like the diner."

"They serve the best onion rings, but Silver Falls needed a restaurant like this." Her gaze darted around as if she were trying to take in everything but him. "It's good to see a menu whose main function isn't to contribute to heart disease. Not that I mind greasy foods sometimes."

"And sweet treats more than often."

Her lips parted forming a perfect o. "You remembered?"

Oh, yeah. Callie and dessert had become synonymous to him. "That stuck with me."

So had other things, but Brandt didn't want to creep her out. His brain stored conversations almost verbatim. That didn't make him a stalker.

She studied her menu as if the secret of the universe was written on the sheet of cardstock. Deciding what to order should be his priority, but his gaze kept straying to Callie.

He wanted to take a better look at her. Something he should have done when they met at the hostess stand a few minutes ago, but he'd been more concerned with not saying the wrong thing or too much or not enough.

He'd been guilty of the latter. The brief call yesterday had seemed the safest, most prudent option. Now he wasn't sure because of her strained voice tonight. He hadn't been this nervous in…

Brandt couldn't remember the last time.

Or when he'd felt so off-balance, but that was due to Callie. Her purple sweater brought out the green of her eyes, making their color appear more vivid. She'd piled her hair on her head in a casual style that gave him an unobstructed view of her neck—graceful like a dancer. Tendrils framed her face, accentuating her high cheekbones. Gloss made her lips shine and hint at the sweetness of how they'd taste.

Beautiful.

He wanted to tuck a few of the strands behind her ear. Not because they were out of place, but because he wanted to touch her without wet gloves on his hands. If his fingers happened to brush her soft skin, so be it.

On that inappropriate thought, he raised his menu, if only to have something to do with his hands. The entrees, however, didn't interest him as much as Callie.

"You look lovely tonight." He spoke without thinking.

"Thanks." She raised her gaze to his. "So do you."

"My aunt told me to wear a tie."

Brandt wasn't sure why he said that, but he liked the smile she gave him. The first of the evening. He wanted there to be more.

"Margot is an interesting mix of days gone by and current trends." Callie wiped the side of her water glass and then dried her fingers on her napkin. "She was right about the tie, though. Makes a statement."

He'd packed one tie in his suitcase—a Christmas-inspired one his aunt had given him—for the church service they'd attended as a family when he lived here.

"What kind of statement does a nutcracker tie make?" he asked.

As she studied him, Callie rubbed her chin. "That you know the first day of December is the perfect time to break out your holiday accessories. The tie suggests you're not a Scrooge or Grinch who hates the holidays. Rather you embrace them and aren't afraid to let others know it. The tie also shows you're confident."

Sitting straighter, he pushed back his shoulders. "All that from a tie, huh?"

"You asked," she answered with a playful grin. "Not many men under the age of fifty wear them around town these days unless they're going to work or church. Impressive."

"Leave it to Aunt Margot to also be a personal stylist extraordinaire." He was only half-joking. The tie had broken the silence between him and Callie. Eased the tension, too. "I guess that means Silver Falls has adopted the casual Friday mentality."

She nodded, placing her menu on the table. "Not only on Fridays. Monday, Tuesday, Wednesday, and Thursday, too. This isn't a fancy town, so how people dress doesn't matter, but it's nice to see someone making an effort."

"Even if that effort was due to his aunt?" Brandt hated how much he wanted to know the answer to that.

Flecks of gold lit up like tiny sparks in Callie's eyes. "Especially then, because you wanted to please someone you care about."

Luck had been on his side, as well as Aunt Margot, for meeting Callie Andrews. He laughed.

She leaned forward. "What?"

"If the doggy daycare doesn't work out for some reason, you could make a killing as a life coach or everyday cheerleader. You know how to make someone feel good. Important."

With a shrug, she sat back. "That's called being nice."

"Not everyone is *that* nice."

"They should be." Her matter-of-fact tone told him to change the subject.

He scanned his menu. "There's so much to choose from I may have to come back."

"Mmm-hmm." She flipped over hers. "I've only eaten lunch here, so dinner will be a new experience."

For him, too.

He drank a sip of ice water. "I'm ordering the prime rib. Know what you want?"

"I'm trying to decide between one of the specials."

"Don't feel guilty if you want to splurge," he said. "Dinner is on the house, but I plan to tip well."

"Me, too." She lowered her voice. "I haven't forgotten we owe Jasper and Wrangler for this meal. I gave them extra treats when they were at Wags and Tails on Thursday. Whatever I eat here will beat the leftovers or microwaveable meals I usually have."

He had to laugh. "The joys of cooking for one."

"You, too?" She didn't sound surprised.

"Sometimes," he admitted. "Depends on what employee extras a company offers. Some only have a breakroom, if that, but others have cafeterias. The top ones even hire chefs who serve three meals a day."

"Must be nice."

"One of the perks of working in high tech."

"Have you always worked as a programmer?" she asked.

"I was coding in high school and working before I graduated college."

Lines formed above the bridge of her nose. "I thought you lived in Silver Falls at some point, but there aren't tech companies here."

"There used to be." This was the perfect time to tell her about NiBrTech, but Brandt didn't want to ruin the evening. "The company was sold."

"That's too bad." Her sincerity didn't surprise him. "Not many technical jobs available in the area unless you work at the university."

That was in Summit Ridge.

He thought about Sam's dad, Dean. At least he'd found a position in town.

A waiter dressed in black took their order. The prime rib for Brandt and bacon-wrapped scallops for Callie. No wine since she was opening Wags and Tails in the morning.

She sipped her water. "Have you toured the rest of the town?"

"No." He hadn't wanted to do that without her. "I've been working on my mobile game."

"Don't you mean having fun?" she joked.

"Right. Fun." Except being with her was redefining the definition.

"Me, too, at Wags and Tails."

Asking if she'd done more with her window display

flashed in his mind, but was quickly dismissed. Not going there tonight. Maybe not ever.

The waiter delivered a basket of bread, small plates, and a concoction of olive oil topped with balsamic vinegar and fresh herbs.

Brandt's mouth watered. "If our main courses are half as delicious as the bread, Jasper and Wrangler are going to need more treats."

She grabbed a slice of bread, tore the piece in half, and dipped it in the oil. "I was thinking the same thing."

His gaze locked on her. Whatever connection he'd felt on Wednesday returned like a lightning-bolt strike. He'd be happy to sit here and stare at Callie all night. Longer if the café's staff let them stay.

He forced the piece of bread into his mouth and chewed.

A perfect starter for the evening.

Brandt had the feeling this might be the best non-date he'd been on. "So, what's Rex doing tonight while you're here with me?"

AS THE SERVER removed the dinner plates, Callie fought the urge to pat her belly. The delicious meal and enjoyable conversation had left her feeling full and satisfied. The first she'd expected. The second, not so much, but she wasn't ready for the night to end. Surprising, but true. "Amazing dinner."

"Ready for dessert?" Brandt asked.

She raised her hands. "I can't. Everything was to die for.

I'm so full."

"Get it to go," he said. "I don't want you to miss out."

Warmth settled in the center of her chest. He was so sweet. Handsome in his button-down shirt and tie, too, but she'd been trying not to notice that or how appealing the slightly messy hairstyle was on him. "I'll be fine. I promise."

"When we finish the sightseeing tour, let's end at the bakery for dessert."

When, *not* if. She wasn't sure why that pleased her so much. Or to know he wanted to spend more time with her. "Sounds like a plan."

"I don't believe it. Brandt Winslow." Mr. Jones, the hardware store owner, approached the table and shook Brandt's hand. He wore a dress shirt with his slacks but no tie. His lumberjack coat had been replaced by a wool jacket. "I never expected to see you back in Silver Falls after all this time."

"I'm spending the holidays with my aunt."

"Margot must be thrilled to have you home."

Brandt nodded, but he appeared uncomfortable.

"How do you know Callie?" Mr. Jones asked.

"Margot," they said at the same time.

"Oh, my. Wait until I tell the missus." Mr. Jones let loose a deep belly laugh. "You two better watch yourselves or Margot will be planning your wedding the next time you go out on a date."

Uh-oh. Callie's heart sank to her feet. Everyone in Silver Falls knew about Margot's matchmaking, but Callie had been upfront when she moved to town about not dating until her business was stronger. She hoped Margot hadn't forgotten, but that would explain why she'd wanted Callie to show Brandt around.

"We haven't had a first one," he said.

Okay, so he hadn't thought of this as a date. Her, either. She should be relieved they agreed, but a heavy feeling overtook her, one that had nothing to do with how much she'd eaten.

Weird because she didn't want a date. Having a good time with Brandt must be messing with her brain.

"I wish the two of you the best of luck. Once Margot sets her mind to something…" Mr. Jones tipped his head. "I'd better get back to the table before the missus thinks I'm locked in a bathroom stall or lost."

As soon as Mr. Jones was out of earshot, Callie zeroed in on Brandt. "Is your aunt playing matchmaker with us?"

The dim lighting didn't keep her from seeing the color on his cheeks darken. He cleared his throat. "Aunt Margot mentioned me dating while I was here. I said no. But sometimes that doesn't deter her."

"Her matchmaking is legendary, but I told her no when we met, and she's left me alone. I don't want that to change."

"It hasn't." The words spilled out. "Won't. I'll make sure of it. It's just…"

Callie leaned forward. "What?"

"I get the feeling my aunt thinks if I end up with a girlfriend in Silver Falls I'll stay here."

Curiosity made Callie ask. "Would you?"

"No idea, but I forgot how everyone sticks their noses into other people's lives."

She understood. "There are no secrets in Silver Falls, but I wouldn't want to live anywhere else."

"I lived here for twenty-six years. Four of those I was in college, but leaving town was the right decision."

Callie appreciated his honesty. "What was it like growing up here?"

"The best childhood a kid could ask for." A wide smile spread across his face. "Summers were awesome. We'd go from house to house gathering everyone for whatever it was we were doing that day. Riding bikes, scooters, skateboards. We considered ourselves a pack of marauders, but we were more gaming geeks than bad boys."

"I can't imagine you as a bad boy." She pictured a younger version of Brandt. He must have been a cutie. "You could pass as a frat boy if you popped your collar and used product in your hair."

Rich laughter filled the booth. "Cool or not, we'd buy sandwiches, chips, and a soda at the deli and then eat in the park before hanging out at the creek."

"Those days must have been so carefree." She hadn't been allowed to walk to her friends' houses without supervision, but LA was a different galaxy from Silver Falls.

He nodded. "We thought we were so grown-up being unsupervised during the day, but we weren't. If anyone thought we were about to get in trouble, they were on us. Fast. Didn't matter if they were our parents or not."

"It takes a village."

"Or in this case, a town of busybodies." He shook his head. "One time, my foot got caught in the spokes of my bike. It hurt so bad. People showed up before my friends could get help. The police and fire department, too."

"Were you okay?" she asked.

"I fractured my ankle."

"Ouch."

"It happens." Brandt appeared completely relaxed, palms down on the table and shoulders loose. More attractive than ever.

She fought the urge to cover his hand with hers. That was what people did on a date. Not a dinner between…

Whatever they were.

"The best times were snow days," he continued.

"I have zero experience with snow days as a kid." She liked hearing him talk about Silver Falls. "Tell me why they were so great."

"Because the anticipation was almost as good as having school cancelled." Tilting his head, he sighed. "We'd wear our pajamas inside out thinking that would make it snow more. When we woke up, we'd wait to hear on the radio or TV if there would be school or not. No one slept in. As soon as our moms let us outside, we'd trudge through the snow to the hill with our sleds and stay until we got too cold."

"What a wonderful place to grow up." If she had a family, she wanted her children to have memories like his.

"I see why people move here and want to stay." A thoughtful expression crossed his face. "Communities like Silver Falls are rare."

"I hear the infamous *but* coming."

"But I don't know if I'd consider Silver Falls home again."

She had to ask. "Why?"

"Being here after college wasn't the same as growing up. Not bad, but the gossip mill seemed worse and not many people my age lived here. Only a few of my high school friends were around, so making new ones was difficult with my work schedule. I had to drive to Summit Ridge if I wanted any kind of a social life."

Callie understood. "When I moved here, I was so busy working I didn't pay much attention to making friends. The ones I have met through work, the business association, and that quilting class, but I see how that would be an issue coming straight from college."

"Things might be different now that I'm older, but I enjoy the freedom I have." He wasn't apologetic, just truthful. "If I feel stuck or unsatisfied, I find a new position. It's easy."

He'd mentioned working contract jobs. She would hate that lifestyle, but some people would love it. Brandt was one of them. "I'm sure Margot only wants you to be happy."

"I am," he said without a doubt. "But I'll remind her that neither of us wants a relationship. Okay?"

"Thanks." Callie appreciated him going to bat for them. Well, him and her. "I won't say anything to make her believe she's succeeding in her efforts."

"Good thinking."

Yes, it was. She needed to be careful around Margot and her nephew. Best not to let either know how a goodnight kiss from Brandt would make up for the dessert Callie had turned down tonight. Or how she couldn't help thinking what might happen if he decided to stay in Silver Falls.

Not for his aunt or some mythical girlfriend, but for himself.

Those would remain her secrets.

No one would know.

Well, except for Rex.

She planned to tell him everything when she got home.

Chapter Fifteen

STANDING BEHIND THE counter on Thursday afternoon, Callie turned the knob on the bottom of the Christmas tree figurine. "We Wish You a Merry Christmas" played.

As she sang along, she had no doubt this would be the merriest of holidays. Business was booming, the week was passing in a blur, and things with Brandt were okay.

Okay sounded good to her. Much better than where they'd started over a week ago not liking each other.

She wasn't sure what to call him—friend, acquaintance, no longer a stranger? Their not-a-date had ended with a goodnight after they'd left the café. No handshake or hug.

Forget a kiss.

She'd been a tad disappointed until realizing she was better off with a new friend than a potential…whatever. They'd kept in touch via text since Saturday. She'd seen him each morning when he dropped off Angus and Sadie. When he'd picked up the dogs, she'd given him pointers to make walking them easier.

That was enough.

Callie didn't need or want more, even if she occasionally daydreamed about hanging out with a certain hottie computer programmer after work.

She double-checked reservations for this weekend. She wanted to make sure she had the staff she needed for the number of dogs on Sunday.

Mr. Hurley, who ran the Christmas tree lot, was getting another shipment this weekend. She wanted to purchase a tree on Sunday. Her family had only had artificial trees because her mom and dad considered those the safest option.

Not this year.

Callie wiggled her toes.

Based on the number of dogs scheduled for Sunday, she wouldn't need to bring in extra help when she left at lunchtime. That would make her life easier.

A text notification buzzed. No customers were in the lobby, so she pulled her phone from the apron's front pocket.

One of her brothers, the youngest of the three, had replied to the group chat she'd sent to her family telling them they would be having a real Christmas tree this year.

She unlocked her phone and read his text.

Bro #3: *Get a noble fir. You can see the ornaments better. Be sure to pick a good one. No holes. Ask about bugs. I've heard nightmare stories about infestations from real trees.*

She typed a reply.

Callie: *My tree. My choice, but ick on the bugs. They are not invited for the holidays. No crashers allowed.*

Bro #3: *You tell them, sis. But I'll bring bug spray just in* *case. Unless you reconsider and get an artificial tree. Mom and Dad would prefer that.*

Of course their parents would, but this was Callie's tree. She also hadn't asked for opinions about what type of Christmas tree to get, yet she'd received Keaton's. Maybe he would be the only one to reply.

Anna led a basset hound named Stinky from the grooming area. The dog lived up to his name so received a weekly bath. "Texting Brandt again?"

"One of my brothers." Though Callie would love to hear from Brandt today. "Keaton."

"Oh, the brainy professor." Anna had never met any of Callie's family, but she'd made up names for each brother based on what she'd heard. Funny, but she wasn't that far off with each one.

"Yes." Which meant Keaton had likely researched Christmas trees and bugs. She shivered. "How's Davis?"

Anna shrugged. "He's been busy with work, so I haven't seen him this week."

"But you saw him three times last week and both days this weekend."

"I know." She sighed. "I thought construction jobs would slow down in December, but he has more work than before. Even over the weekend, so he can't attend the Holiday Open House at the animal rescue."

"That event means so much to you." Families who adopted animals through the rescue, where Anna volunteered her services as a groomer, returned to have their pet's photo taken with Santa. Entertainers performed, refreshments were served, and a holiday craft fair benefited the rescue. "Maybe he can come after work."

"He doesn't think he'll be finished in time." Anna sounded resigned to going alone. "I'm disappointed, but his job is important. I'm inviting him to have dinner at my house and go to my church's Christmas play next weekend."

"That will be fun."

She nodded. "Do you and Brandt have any plans?"

Of course Anna would ask. She did every day. "I mentioned I was going to the Winter Concert at the elementary school tonight, but he never said he was going."

Anna laughed. "You and your Christmas music."

"It's one of my favorite parts of the season."

"Which is why you play it nonstop," Anna teased. "Come on, Stinky. You're clean enough to play all the reindeer games with the other pups now."

Anna led the dog toward the play room.

The front door opened with a jingle of the bells. Mrs. Sellwood, a retired schoolteacher and the mother of Silver Fall's mayor, entered with a blast of cold air. "Your Christmas window is very bright, dear. Clever play on words, though I never knew so many decorations came in silver."

The sentiment was nice enough, but the woman's underlying snooty tone told her true opinion about the display. "Thank you. Is there something you needed?"

"I'm out of those organic dog biscuits. I'd like another box."

Callie went to the shelf, grabbed a package, and returned to the counter. "I'm happy Madden liked them."

"He loves them."

She rang up the treats. As the woman paid with her debit card, Callie bagged the purchase. "Will there be anything else?"

"No." Mrs. Sellwood took the bag before glancing over her shoulder at the window. "But I'm excited to see what other items you're going to add to your display to wow the judging committee."

The woman left the store, leaving a trail of her heavy floral perfume in her wake.

Callie stared at the closed door.

To wow the judging committee?

The words poked at her heart like pine needles.

Anna returned to the lobby. "Who was that?"

"Mrs. Sellwood." Callie sighed. "She doesn't like the window display."

Anna grimaced. "Mrs. Sellwood doesn't like anything or anybody. Not even her own daughter, our illustrious mayor."

That made Callie laugh. "She likes Madden."

Anna snickered. "Only because other people's dogs are horrible monsters without manners. No matter that hers is well known for peeing on people's feet."

Madden was one of the reasons they kept extra clothes and shoes in their lockers.

"Don't let that old woman get to you." Anna hugged Callie. "The window is pretty."

"My goal was spectacular."

Anna waved her hand in the air. "Same thing."

Was it? Callie wished she knew. "Mrs. Sellwood thinks

I'm adding more items."

"Are you rethinking things?" Anna asked.

Callie wished she knew the answer. She was torn.

"I have faith in the design, but I'm wondering if I should add more." She had confidence in herself. The window was good. Good enough to win. But others weren't as convinced. "I believe in what I put together and don't want to make any big changes, but it's hard when I hear comments like Mrs. Sellwood's. Even Brandt had ideas."

Anna raised a brow. "Brandt who is a computer nerd?"

"His mom is an interior designer and his aunt owns a quilt shop," Callie explained. "He's the only son and nephew so he helped them out. He knows more than you'd think a guy like him would."

"If you want to do more to the display, then go for it. But only because you want to or are up for the challenge. Not because Mrs. Sellwood or Brandt or anyone else said so." Anna glanced toward the window. "I've seen the other displays on First Avenue. We have a good shot this year, so don't second-guess yourself."

Warmth flowed through Callie. Making a few changes or additions could be good as long as she stuck with her original vision. No matter what she decided, she appreciated Anna's support. "Thanks, you made my day."

"That's what friends are for, but it's the truth in this case."

Callie's text notification went off again.

Bro #1: *Get a Douglas fir. That is the quintessential Christmas tree. No others will do.*

Callie: *I haven't decided.*

Bro #1: *Buy a Douglas fir. Trust me on this one.*

Bro #1: *Be sure someone else chops down the tree. You don't want to hurt yourself or lose an arm.*

Her mouth hung open. Lose an arm? "Unbelievable."

"Brandt?" Anna asked.

If only… Callie put her phone in her pocket. "My oldest brother, Flynn."

"The arrogant surgeon," Anna said.

The adjective fits him today. Callie nodded. "Being overprotective as usual."

"I wonder what the egotistical lawyer will say."

"Garrett's in court for a big case, so it may take him a few days to text."

She could only imagine what he might reply, but that didn't matter.

Callie knew what she was doing. With her business, her life, and…

The Christmas window.

She didn't need to be swayed by others' opinions. What she'd done with the theme wasn't good. It was perfect. No reason to make changes or add anything. She had confidence, so she would stick with the original design.

And win.

THE LAST PLACE Brandt expected to spend his Thursday night was at his former elementary school, but when Aunt Margot told him she was watching her favorite reality TV show with friends, he decided to get out of the house before his aunt's guests arrived.

That hadn't been his only reason. He wanted to see Callie.

He only wished he'd had time to tell her that he was going so they could have met ahead of time. Now, he would have to search for her.

The hallways had been painted, and the carpet was different, but the displays were familiar. Hard-to-read writing. Hand-cut snowflakes. Red and green garland made from inch-thick construction paper strung everywhere.

Brandt followed the crowd into the auditorium but didn't see Callie. She had to be here somewhere.

A baby cried. Someone sneezed. Another person coughed.

Ahead of him, Brandt recognized a beanie on a head of flowing brown hair. "Callie."

Turning slightly, she scanned the crowd. As he worked his way toward her, her pretty face brightened. "You made it."

"My aunt had other plans, so I decided to come to the concert at the last minute." He spoke fast, the way he did whenever he was around her. "That's why I didn't get back to you. Sorry."

"That's okay. I was going either way." Her smile matched her cheery tone. "We should grab seats before they are all gone. This is the ticket to have in Silver Falls."

He stiffened. "You need a ticket?"

She nudged her shoulder against his arm. "I'm kidding."

Brandt liked her being close. When he'd dropped off the dogs this morning after successfully walking them without the same issues as before, she'd stood on the opposite side of the counter. The only thing separating them tonight would be the seat arm.

He followed her to two empty seats on the right side of the stage, where they both sat and tried to get comfortable. "Have you been to this before?"

"Every year." She held onto the program printed on light green paper. "I love Christmas music. Doesn't matter what kind."

Before Brandt could ask more, the lights dimmed.

As a group of children dressed as snowflakes converged to the center of the stage, the audience applauded. Brandt stared in amazement. Not at the performers, but at the number of cell phones recording at the same time.

The kids sang "Let It Snow."

Halfway through the song, two snowflakes cartwheeled across the stage. Cheers erupted. More clapping.

Reindeers with glowing red noses came next. A group with jingle bells followed. A choir of snowmen then took the stage.

When he leaned close to Callie, the vanilla scent of her hair tickled his nose. He wanted another sniff. "Mr. Frosty would fit right in with that group."

She laughed. "Except he'd be in puddles with those hot stage lights."

The concert continued. Kids went to the wrong spot or flubbed lyrics, but that made the performance more memorable. As the children came out to take a final bow, the audience gave them a standing ovation. No wonder Callie attended each year. Seeing the joy on the young faces at the end was the best part.

"Thanks for telling me about the concert." As the crowd exited the auditorium, Brandt placed his hand at the small of Callie's back. He didn't want to lose her, but that was only part of the reason. He liked touching her even though she wore a thick coat. "I enjoyed it."

"You never know what might happen on stage, but the kids look like they're having so much fun up there."

"I see why you come each year."

They followed the crowd into the hallway outside the auditorium. People waited in line to get out the front doors.

"Brandt," a man yelled.

A chill shot through Brandt. Every muscle bunched. Breathing became a struggle.

Callie waved. "Nick."

Pressure built at Brandt's temples. He forced air into his lungs. How did she know Nick Baxter?

Callie hugged Nick as if they were close. "Savannah did great tonight."

"She did." Nick's gaze kept drifting to Brandt. "Robin made me video the entire show."

Callie shook her head. "That's what you're supposed to do when your kid is on stage."

"I guess so." Nick's voice was shaky as if he were nervous.

Brandt didn't care. He couldn't.

Nick focused on Callie, clearly avoiding Brandt's gaze.

"How do you two know each other?"

"Margot." Callie's grin widened, which Brandt didn't understand. "How do you guys know each other?"

Brandt pressed his lips together, shoving his hands into his jacket pocket. He was tempted to walk away, but he didn't want to leave Callie with Nick. Brandt didn't trust the guy.

"We grew up together," Nick explained. "Best friends."

He sounded like they still were friends, close as brothers. Brandt doubted they'd ever been that close. Childhood memories that kept coming back to him suggested he'd been blind to Nick's true personality.

Brandt's hand clenched. He'd never hit anyone in his life, but he wanted to punch Nick. Hard.

Six years was a long time to carry a grudge. Yeah, Brandt should be over feeling this way. If he'd stuck with therapy he might be, but each new job and move meant starting over with a new therapist.

But that didn't matter.

Nick's actions did.

The guy was a jerk. His selfish behavior and need to be in control had ruined lives. That was unforgiveable.

Brandt's blood pressure spiraled, so he took a breath. And another. "Former best friends and former business partners."

He wanted to tell Callie how Nick had sold their company behind Brandt's back, but he couldn't.

Nick's face paled. He stared at Brandt. "I have to pick up my daughter, but I'd like to get together while you're in town."

"No."

Nick flinched. Not surprising given how harsh Brandt had spoken.

Callie touched his arm. He forced himself to stand straight and not lean against her for support.

"Thanks for coming tonight." Nick's voice trembled. "Maybe I'll see you around town before you leave."

Brandt hoped not. Nothing Nick said would make a difference. He'd been offered help, a way to step back so he could put his family first, but Nick's ego wouldn't let him give up control.

Callie's hand remained on Brandt. "Tell Savannah she did great."

As Nick turned away, his shoulders hunched.

"Are you okay?" she asked Brandt.

"I'm not sure."

Bumping into Nick while in town had been in the back of Brandt's mind, but he hadn't expected to feel so much resentment. The sale had given Nick enough money to retire and live comfortably for the rest of his life, but Brandt wasn't sure how the guy had remained in town after what he'd done. Silver Falls was his and Robin's hometown. She'd sworn never to live anywhere else due to her large extended family, which was why Nick had wanted NiBrTech here, but after selling out so many people…

Had Nick thought about the cost of what he'd done?

Probably not.

Callie rubbed her hands over the arms of Brandt's jacket. "You're shivering."

He needed a hug, but her touch comforted him.

"Raine stays open late on performance nights." Callie kept her hands on him. "We should head over there for a hot chocolate. That'll warm you up."

He needed more than a hot drink to chase away the cold, but being with Callie was better than going back to his aunt's house.

"I'd like that." Holding onto her hand, he squeezed. "Thank you."

"Thanks aren't necessary." Her gaze held no judgement, only compassion. "Let's go."

At that moment, he'd follow her anywhere. Maybe Aunt Margot knew something he didn't.

Chapter Sixteen

AT TEA LEAVES & Coffee Beans, a fire burned in the gas fireplace. Christmas carols played. But Callie had a tough time enjoying the pleasant atmosphere after seeing how distraught Brandt had been at the school. She tucked her gloves into a pocket and then placed the jacket on the back of a chair at a corner table before heading to order.

As she stood in line, she tried to make sense of what had happened. Her heart hurt for Brandt. Callie wanted to wipe the pain from his eyes.

She stepped up to the counter. "I'll take two of Raine's special hot cocoas."

The blue-haired barista named Timmy winked. "Splurging tonight, Callie?"

The drinks came in double-portion mugs with chocolate shavings and a swirl of fudge sauce over the whipped cream. One of those might help Brandt feel better.

"I always splurge when I come here." After she paid, she stuck a tip in the jar. "Thanks."

As she returned to her table, a family of five entered the shop. The three girls, dressed in fancy holiday dresses, giggled and pranced around on their tiptoes as if pretending to be ballerinas.

Cute.

Callie sat, waiting for Brandt. Snippets of their conversation from Wednesday made more sense now.

Threw my heart and soul into making the start-up I'd founded with my best friend a success.

My business partner didn't see our business the same as I did. He wanted... out.

Best friend or not, he wasn't the right person to go into business with.

Brandt had been talking about Nick Baxter. She'd never heard much about Nick's old company—Brandt's name had never been mentioned—only bits and pieces that hadn't made a lot of sense without knowing the whole story, because even in a town known for gossip, people kept quiet about that subject. Given Margot was Brandt's aunt, Callie was beginning to understand why.

More families entered the coffee shop. Kids ran around saying hello to friends. Tired parents held sleepy toddlers and babies while standing in line to order.

A text notification buzzed.

She grabbed her cell phone, but it wasn't Brandt. Garrett, her middle brother, was weighing in with his Christmas tree opinion.

Bro #2: *Long day in court. Buy the proper size of tree. You said you live in a cottage, so don't fill up half the living room with a large tree trying to impress us.*

Callie: *Will make sure tree doesn't dwarf my tiny house.*

Ugh! Were all lawyers as pompous as Garrett? Her dad was. Her blood boiling, Callie placed the phone in her purse before taking several deep breaths.

She should have known a simple text would lead to her brothers dissing her in some way. Maybe not on purpose, but they always had to get some jab in. Some families joked around over stuff like this, but her brothers hadn't added emojis. No *LOLs* or *hahas*, either. They'd meant what they said.

Yes, they loved her, but...

Flynn assumed she'd hurt herself.

Garrett believed she couldn't be practical.

Keaton wanted her to go along with their parents, so there wouldn't be any conflict at Christmastime.

Let it go.

That was what she needed to do.

She didn't want to be upset when Brandt arrived. He was the one who needed comfort and support. Not her.

She concentrated on her breathing. One breath after another.

The tension seeped from her muscles, slowly with each exhale. Her muscles relaxed more and more until she no longer needed to think about each breath.

Laughter from a nearby table soothed whatever stress remained.

Much better.

Brandt entered the coffee shop. Shoulders slumped, he wasn't smiling. When she waved, he made his way to her, pulling off his jacket and gloves.

"Sorry it took me so long." Deep lines were etched around his mouth and forehead. "I never knew there could be traffic on a weeknight in Silver Falls."

"Half the town attended tonight's performance." Callie motioned to the chair across from her when all she wanted to do was hug him. "I ordered hot chocolate. Have you had one here?"

He sat. "No."

"Get ready to be amazed."

"I'm ready." Except he didn't look it.

Brandt sat forward on the chair, ready to bolt at a moment's notice. One hand rested on top of the small table. The other gripped his car keys as if they were a lifeline. He glanced around the coffee shop.

Searching for Nick.

That was what Brandt was doing.

Her chest tightened.

Do something.

Callie covered his hand with hers. She waited to see if he pulled his away. He didn't.

Good.

"I always come here following a performance." His skin was cold even though he'd been wearing gloves, but she wasn't surprised after the way he'd trembled at the school. Her thumb rubbed the side of his hand. Maybe that would distract him. Allow him to relax. "I've never seen Nick and Robin in here after one."

Callie prayed tonight wouldn't be the first time.

Brandt exhaled before leaning back against the chair. He

loosened his grip on his keys. "I don't want to see him again."

His raw, jagged hurt hit hard. Callie kept her hand on his to let him know she wasn't going anywhere. She needed to be here for him, however he needed.

"I'm not going to ask if you're okay." The time for subtlety had ended when Brandt reacted to Nick calling his name. "It's obvious you're not."

"I..." Brandt's gaze darted to the door. "I wasn't expecting to see him. I knew I might sometime, but not tonight."

"That had to be a shock."

Brandt nodded. "How do you know him?"

Him. Not Nick. "His dog comes to Wags and Tails. He's also a friend."

Brandt lowered his chin to his chest, but he didn't say anything. She hadn't wanted to add to his hurt.

"Robin and I met during the quilting class at your aunt's shop." Callie wanted to explain her relationship with the Baxters. "I met Nick through his wife. We've done things socially. Dinners and parties."

As Brandt placed his car keys in his jacket pocket, the metal clanged. "He was my best friend and business partner until he sold our company without telling me. I found out when the other employees did."

Callie tried to reconcile the Nick Baxter she knew—a caring husband and father who'd made his money in high tech and invested in companies these days—with what Brandt had told her. Tried and failed.

"Tonight was the first time seeing him in over six years,"

Brandt continued. "I'm sorry for reacting the way I did."

"You have nothing to apologize for." The words ran out of her mouth. She needed to talk slower or he might not be able to understand her. "Seeing Nick must have been a shock."

"It was."

"Two cocoas for Callie," Luca, the other barista who worked the night shift, called out.

"I'll be right back."

She hurried to the counter, grabbed the two large mugs, and returned to the table without spilling a drop. She set one of the hot cocoas in front of Brandt. The chocolate sauce and shavings were arranged almost like artwork in the heaping servings of whipped cream.

She placed the napkins in between them. "These aren't the easiest to drink but worth the mess."

The corners of his mouth curved upward. Not quite a smile, but a hint of one. She'd take it.

"Thanks. This *is* amazing." He sounded more like himself. "And exactly what I need."

She sat. His hand was no longer on the table, and she missed touching him. "If you'd rather not talk about Nick…"

"I've spent years not talking, but that hasn't helped me. I'm not sure what will work." Brandt sipped the cocoa. "This must be what heaven tastes like."

"You're a chocoholic."

"I prefer to call myself a connoisseur of chocolate."

She drank hers.

He wiped his mouth with a napkin. "Nick and I were born in Silver Falls. I don't remember a time we weren't best friends. Nick was the one who wanted to be the center of attention…the star. I didn't care about that, so I was happy to let him shine. We decided to attend the same college and be roommates."

"Didn't you get tired of each other?" she asked.

"Not once." Brandt sipped his hot cocoa. "We were both only children. He was the closest thing I had to a brother."

That must have made whatever happened between them a hundred times worse. Callie took another drink, hoping he'd continue.

"My sophomore year of college, I had an idea for an app. We decided to work on it over the summer. That project led us to found NiBrTech."

"Nick Brandt Technologies?" she asked.

Brandt nodded. "He wanted his name first, and it didn't matter to me. We worked all summer and then continued when we went back to school. We realized what started out as a social media app had a broader use due to the algorithms I created. By the time we graduated college, we had investors and more contracts than the two of us could handle on our own."

"Wow." She'd read about people like this, yet Brandt was one of them. "Sounds like a dream come true."

"It was." He half-laughed. "Until it wasn't."

Callie wanted to comfort him, but she didn't know how.

"Nick…" Saying the name brought a grimace to Brandt's face. "He'd been dating Robin off and on since high school, but they got serious our senior year of college. That's why he wanted to build the company in Silver Falls because her family was here, and she wouldn't move away."

Not surprising. Robin loved this town and had a big family who lived here. "What did you want?"

"A city made more sense for hiring a technical staff, but Nick was adamant about being in Silver Falls for Robin, so that's what we did. The cost of living was cheaper than most of the high-tech centers, so that worked in our favor."

"That was one of the draws of Silver Falls for me, too."

Brandt drank his hot chocolate. "Those early years, there was always too much work to do. We were growing fast. Nick got married a year after we returned to Silver Falls. A few years later, Robin got pregnant. Things changed after that."

"Changed how?" Callie hadn't meant to push, but she wanted to know.

"The long hours Nick worked bothered Robin, and she wanted him home more. Nick didn't want his role at the company to change. Cofounders are often known to get into battles, but we'd never had any issues because I didn't want to be in control. Nick, however, wanted to rule over everything like a king. He shut down discussions about hiring a CEO to take over so he could lessen his responsibilities, nor would he add another assistant or more executive-level staff to offload some of his workload. He never dealt with pressure well, but he claimed to have it under control. He didn't."

Unease coiled inside her. "What happened?"

"Robin gave Nick an ultimatum—the company or her. He'd never told me that. He was biding his time while he searched for a buyer. He no longer wanted to run NiBrTech, but he didn't want anyone else to do it, either."

Something didn't make sense to Callie. "But you were cofounders."

"Yes, we had equal shares in the company, but I was never interested in the business side, so I let Nick handle that." Brandt shook his head. "I trusted him and gave him power of attorney, so I could focus on my responsibilities. For the first five years, it worked."

Until it didn't.

The words were implied but unspoken.

"Nick controlled your shares."

Another nod. "We'd taken angel investor capital at the beginning, and then a venture capital group also invested in us, so others had equity stakes. When Nick found an eager buyer, who made a jaw-dropping offer, the investors couldn't sign on fast enough. They'd be getting their money sooner and for more than expected, so Nick had a majority of shares even without mine. The only problem was the buyer didn't want the company, only the assets."

"Assets?"

"Usually companies want to acquire the employees along with everything else, but not this time. The buyer wanted to kill their competition—us—by taking our algorithms and technology and putting us out of business." The raw hurt in his eyes spoke volumes. "By the time I found out about the sale, there was nothing I could do."

His company and hard work had been sold by the friend he considered a brother. After that kind of betrayal, seeing Nick tonight had to have been a nightmare.

She squeezed Brandt's hand. "I'm so sorry that happened."

"Thanks." He stared into his hot chocolate. "I made enough money from the sale to never have to work again, but coding was never about getting rich to me."

Her heart ached for him. "Is this why you left Silver Falls?"

He nodded. "Even though my aunt and parents lived here, I couldn't stay. Too many memories and reminders of what happened. Before I left, I tried to help our employees, but there are only so many jobs in a town this size. Few that paid what we did with full benefits. The worst part was having people side with either me or Nick. I couldn't let Silver Falls become divided. I left, so it wouldn't be."

His words sank in. Angered her. "You did nothing wrong."

He shrugged. "I shouldn't have turned a blind eye to the business side, so I could focus on what I preferred doing. Nick believed what he did was right."

The guy hadn't appeared happy tonight. "He sounded remorseful."

"Maybe, but I don't care. Nick Baxter wasn't the man I thought he was back then. I have zero interest in finding out who he is today." Brandt took a sip of his hot chocolate. "So that's my woeful tale. Do you have one?"

Her story was nothing compared to his, but maybe telling him about her family would distract him. Worth a shot. "Not woeful, and nothing as painful as yours, more...aggravating."

"That sounds like a crazy ex."

She laughed. "No, nothing like that. It's my family."

"In LA?"

Callie nodded. "We're not estranged. We get along. My parents and three brothers will be here for Christmas."

"I hear a *but* coming."

"But none of them accept me for who I am. That must sound like whining after everything you've been through."

"No one can stop you from feeling the way you do."

"They sure make me feel...stuff." She toyed with the napkin on her lap. "Owning a business isn't good enough, according to them. My parents know I like working with animals, so they keep pushing me toward vet school even though I've told them for years I don't want to do that. And no matter what I do or how well things are going, they treat me like I'm still the baby of the family and can't do anything on my own."

"That must suck."

She nodded.

"If your parents are anything like my parents, they only want what's best for you. Even if they're wrong."

"Dead wrong." She blew out a breath, but he had a point. "My parents pushed education on me and my brothers from an early age. There was never a question we'd go to college, but graduate school was also assumed."

"You have a master's degree?" Brandt sounded surprised,

but not in a bad way.

"No." She wasn't ashamed by that fact. "A bachelor's degree, but my parents and brothers... My dad and Garrett are lawyers. My mom and Flynn are doctors. Keaton is a professor."

"That's impressive."

"And intimidating when I didn't want to go to college for more than four years."

"Advanced degrees aren't for everyone."

She appreciated Brandt's support. "I'm proud of them for what they've accomplished, but more schooling and working a high-pressure job isn't me. Owning a business has its own stresses, but I love what I do. I'm successful, but they can't see it."

"Maybe they don't want to see." He raised his cup. "They might not be ready to admit to themselves you're grown up and doing well on your own."

"That could be." She ripped the edges of the napkin. "But it raises a lot of questions. Ones I've struggled with for years. Do my parents believe I could be as successful as my brothers if I became a vet? Or is it that they think they know better than me, or even see me as a failure?"

"No way it's the last one," he said with no hesitation.

She'd needed to hear him say that. "When I told my family I was moving to Silver Falls to buy Wags and Tails, the five of them staged an intervention. As if loving dogs and wanting to work with them was an addiction or something negative in my life that would destroy me. That told me I was making the right choice leaving. I needed to get away from them."

Brandt closed his eyes, covering his mouth with his hand.

"It's okay if you want to laugh," she said.

He did. "I'm sorry. But thinking about having an intervention over this..."

"It was crazy. Embarrassing." She shook her head as if that could vanquish the memory. "Maybe we need to go to family counseling when they're here."

"I tried therapy." He didn't sound impressed. "It didn't help."

She laughed. "We're a pair."

Brandt nodded. "But you found what you were looking for by coming to Silver Falls."

"And you got what you needed by leaving."

He had a faraway expression in his eyes. "Sometimes taking off is the best, the only, option."

It was her turn to nod. "Being back in Silver Falls could help put what happened with Nick behind you. Give you closure."

"Closure would be good. Better than pretending it doesn't matter."

"Pretending delays the inevitable." His not wanting to be emotionally invested in his work or putting down roots made sense now. If he had closure, maybe he wouldn't feel the need to change jobs and move around so much.

He reached across the table, took the shredded napkin from her fingers, and held her hand. "You don't need to keep ripping that apart. Hold on to me instead."

Her heart melted. A pile of goo must be pooling at her feet.

He squeezed her hand. "Having your family here for the holidays will be the perfect opportunity to show them what an incredible woman and business owner you are. Because that's exactly who Callie Andrews is. If they can't see that, then they've wasted a lot of money on their degrees."

He was giving her a much-needed boost of confidence. Heat rushed through her. "Thanks."

"Thank you for suggesting we come here. I didn't want to be alone."

"You can hold on to me, too." Callie had no idea what was happening between them. She didn't care. "I mean it."

"I do, too. Whatever you need."

That gave her an idea. A fun one. Something they needed after tonight's discussion. Excited, she wiggled her toes.

This would be good for him—the perfect distraction so he could forget the past and lose himself in the holidays. All she needed was for him to say yes. Crossing her fingers, she hoped he would. "Does that mean you'd be up for Christmas tree shopping with me this weekend?"

Chapter Seventeen

SUNDAY AFTERNOON, BRANDT stood in the tree lot on the edge of town where an inflatable Santa greeted visitors and speakers piped in Christmas music. The snow flurries provided an extra dose of holiday spirit. Not that any was needed with the jingle bells sounding each time someone bought a tree.

He shook Mr. Hurley's hand. "Still in the same place."

"Buying this lot thirty years ago was my best investment." Pride filled the local tree farmer's voice. The man was bundled up in a thick coat, hat, and gloves. "Well, next to convincing Sharon to marry me. Though she didn't fare too badly in that deal."

Brandt laughed. Other than more gray hair in the man's beard, Mr. Hurley and his tree lot hadn't changed.

"Business going well?" Brandt asked.

"Nearly sold out of my first load, so I brought in another batch yesterday." Mr. Hurley pointed to a few trees still wrapped up after being delivered. "The last few years have been hit or miss. Some people prefer the pre-lighted trees because they're easier to set up and take down, but only a real tree will do for the Christmas die-hards and city folks who've moved to Silver Falls like Callie."

Wherever she might be.

She'd said hello to Mr. Hurley before disappearing down a row and out of Brandt's sight. He had a feeling she took picking out a tree seriously. That meant they might be here all afternoon. He didn't mind. Seeing her when he dropped off the dogs wasn't enough, and texting wasn't as good as spending time with her.

Her colorful striped hat caught his eyes. "She doesn't act like a city girl to me."

"Three years makes a significant difference. It helps that Callie has found her place here. She's good people," Mr. Hurley said. "Is your aunt playing matchmaker yet?"

No secrets in Silver Falls.

"Trying." His aunt had been dancing around the house like a crazy woman, when she'd heard he was going to get a tree with Callie. Telling his aunt they were only friends and he hadn't kissed Callie had brought up one question.

What was he waiting for?

He didn't know, except taking things day by day, moving in slow motion, felt right. Callie had her business, and he was only in town until New Year's. This couldn't go anywhere.

"Whatever she's doing is working." Mr. Hurley laughed. "You're here together."

Brandt placed a finger at his lips. "Please keep that on the down low."

"Not a problem." Mr. Hurley slapped his hand on Brandt's shoulder. "Us fellows have to stick together."

"Yes, we do."

Amusement gleamed in Mr. Hurley's eyes. "You'd better catch up to your girl before she picks out a tree without you."

Your girl.

Warmth spread through Brandt. A bit caveman and sexist, but he liked hearing Callie called his.

He found her two rows over examining a tree as if it were a rare sculpture. "Having any luck?"

"Not yet, though this one has potential."

His mom used to study each tree from every angle. Sometimes twice. "My mom told me that we had to take our time picking out a tree. But when we found the right one, we'd know."

"She sounds like a smart woman."

"She is." Like Aunt Margot. Thinking of the two most important women in his life sent warmth flooding through him. "You want a noble fir?"

"Yes, that's my favorite, though not all my family agrees," Callie explained. "We've never had a live tree. One brother wants a noble like me. The other said only a Douglas fir would do. The third was more concerned with the size."

"What about your parents?"

"They want me to get an artificial tree, but that's not what I want."

Brandt ran his gloved hand down one of the branches of a nearby tree. No needles came off. Not surprising since Mr. Hurley was known for his fresh trees. "Not that it matters, but I prefer nobles, too."

She moved down the row, eyeing each tree she passed. "White or colored lights?"

"White," he said without hesitation. "They remind me of stars when it's dark in the house."

"I never thought about lights that way, but they do."

"How about you?" he asked.

"White, but no reason other than aesthetic."

"What kind of tree topper?"

She blushed, though he had no idea why. "An angel or a star."

"Both?"

Callie nodded. "I have one of each that I love, so I alternate each year."

Picturing her with a topper in each hand and a loving gaze in her eyes was easy to do, but the idea of her decorating a home for the holidays sent tingles shooting to his stomach. Unexpected ones he couldn't explain. "That's a sweet tradition."

She shrugged. "Some people think it's weird or a waste to have two."

"It's not." He didn't want her to feel bad for figuring out how to make use of two tree toppers that she liked. "Which will top the tree this year?"

"The angel." Excitement shone in her eyes. Callie held her hands, one above the other, about a foot apart. "She's about this tall. Her gown is white silk. Her halo and wings are gold."

"Sounds pretty." He circled around a tree to see if it had bare spots. "My parents use a pretty blown-glass finial topper."

"I've seen those on decorating shows. I'd be afraid of breaking one."

"They are fragile."

She looked over. "What do you put on your tree?"

"I've been too busy to put up a tree." He pointed out a bald spot. "If I celebrate, I'm with my parents. This year, I'm here with my aunt so there's no need to have a tree of my own."

The corners of Callie's mouth turned down. "If?"

Her tone and face were so sad, and he realized her reaction was for him.

"Hey." He touched her arm. "I don't work every holiday. When I had to, I didn't mind. Not everybody is crazy for Christmas."

As her mouth quirked, questions filled her gaze. "You act like Mr. Christmas with your advice, helping decorate your aunt's house, and coming here with me."

He shrugged, trying to downplay his role when normally he'd be ignoring the holidays if he were alone. "Spreading Christmas cheer is contagious within the city limits of Silver Falls. There's no vaccine or cure. I can't help myself, but who knows how I'll feel next year if I'm not here."

"Maybe you'll spend the holidays with your aunt again."

He wouldn't mind that, especially if he had another reason to return to Silver Falls—Callie.

Uh-oh. He was playing right into Aunt Margot's hands. "Maybe. You never know."

"Oh, this is a nice one." Callie studied the tree like a doctor examining a patient. "Not that tall. Garrett would like that. But other than making sure my arm isn't cut off chopping down a tree, I'm ignoring my brothers' advice."

Brandt laughed. "Given Mr. Hurley took care of the chopping at his farm, no one will be cutting off any appendages today."

"I think my brother Flynn assumed I was going into the forest to get a tree. I…" She gasped.

He followed her line of sight to a tree that was around six and a half feet tall. The tree was fatter at the bottom but had a nice shape. "Is that…?"

"The one," Callie said with certainty. "I thought I wanted a taller one, but this is it. Your mom was right. You do know which one."

Brandt moved closer to the tree. "I'll carry it to Mr. Hurley."

"We'll carry it together."

Mr. Hurley had called Callie good people. Aunt Margot had said Callie was special. Both were correct, but Brandt sensed there was even more to her.

Brandt picked up the bottom of the tree. "I've got this part."

Callie held onto the top. "I have mine."

As they carried it toward the checkout stand, contentment washed over Brandt. Tree hunting with Callie was fun. She wasn't a perfectionist when it came to trees, but she knew what she wanted. He would be happy to do this again with her next year.

If he was here.

He might not be.

Probably wouldn't.

Except a part of him wanted to return.

Because of Callie.

He let that thought sink in.

Weird given they hadn't kissed. Holding hands didn't count as touching because that had been a way to offer comfort. But something about her…

With each step they took, working in unison to carry the tree, a question grew louder in his mind. Had his mom only meant Christmas trees when she said a person would know when they'd found the one?

❦

AT HER HOUSE, Callie met Brandt at the back of her pickup truck. She was happy he'd come with her to find a tree. The time had been almost magical with the light snowfall. The flurries had turned into larger snowflakes, adding to the Christmassy feel of the day.

She shimmied with excitement. "We bought the best tree on the lot."

"I agree." Brandt waited for her to lower the tailgate. "Is everything ready inside?"

"The stand is in place." She opened the back so they could remove the tree. "I'll take care of the door if you don't mind holding the bottom part again."

"You had this planned out when you invited me to come," he joked, helping carry the tree to her front porch.

"Maybe." Callie had been more interested in them having a good time. Truth was, she was used to getting a tree on her own. Sometimes that meant finding creative ways to get the tree from her truck to the stand in the living room. The past two years, she'd managed, but having Brandt here made things easier. Not to mention fun. "But we make a good team."

His gaze met hers. The blue of his eyes seemed sharper, and something inside her softened. "We do."

She unlocked the front door. "It's a straight shot to the stand."

Mr. Hurley had put the tree into the shaker to get rid of anything loose. She hoped that included bugs. Any water from the snowflakes clinging to the branches would dry quickly thanks to forced-air heating and her fireplace. She'd be able to decorate tonight.

Kneeling on the hardwood floor, Brandt positioned the trunk into the tree stand. A few minutes of her telling him which screws to tighten and then loosen led to a straight tree.

He stood. "Ta da."

She placed her hand over her heart. "It's perfect."

"I agree." He moved closer, taking in not only the tree but also the entire living room. "This is a nice house. Your family will be impressed."

"Thanks." Callie appreciated him saying that but also crossed her fingers. She didn't want to take any chances. "The kitchen and bathrooms were renovated before I moved in. I've been going room by room through the rest of the house."

His gaze met hers, and a connection grabbed hold of

Callie. Whatever was passing between them felt real, almost as if she could reach out and touch the energy flowing between them.

"Sweat equity," he said.

That surprised her. "You remembered."

He nodded. "I see why you'd want to put down roots here."

"That's a lot coming from a nomad like you," she joked, receiving a wink in reply.

"It's charming."

"Thanks. That was part of the appeal."

The chair rails, molding, and hardwood floors had needed repairs and paint, but the cosmetic work was nothing she couldn't handle after watching a few DIY shows and videos.

Brandt broke the contact, continuing to the unlit fireplace. The bricks were back to their original red after she'd stripped the white paint off them. "It's a decent-sized house."

"Three bedrooms and two bathrooms. Bigger than I need for Rex and me, but I'll end up using the space."

"When your family is here."

"Yes, and in the future."

"For your own family."

It wasn't a question, but she nodded anyway. She could picture what she wanted and didn't mind sharing that even if Brandt—aka Mr. Anti-Roots—probably thought she was crazy. "Husband, kids, and more dogs."

"More dogs are a given."

His laughter filled the living room. She hoped to hear more of that sound before he left town.

"This house will be perfect for what you want," he added. "Where's Rex?"

"At Wags and Tails. I'll pick him up before closing time. I didn't want him to be lonely at home while I got the tree."

"You're lucky you can bring him to work."

"I am, but several of the shop owners have dogs or cats in their stores. None of them serve food, of course."

"Makes sense." He stared at the photographs sitting on the mantle. "Is this your family?"

"Yes."

"You and one of your brothers resemble each other."

"That's Garrett. The lawyer. He used to say I was his pink mini-me."

"Pink?"

Heat stole up her neck and then settled in her cheeks. "That was the only color I'd wear for a few years. Or so I've been told."

"Stubborn?" The mischievous gleam in his eyes suggested he knew the answer.

She raised her chin. "I can be."

Brandt strode toward her. His steps were slow, but his eyes locked on her.

Her pulse skittered, matching the increase in her breaths. She had no idea what he was thinking…doing, but…

The tree was set up. She'd moved the boxes of decorations inside last night. All she needed was to wait for the tree to dry before stringing lights. That meant Brandt didn't need to stay. Too bad she didn't want him to go.

Uh-oh. That meant he should leave. Now.

She cleared her dry throat. "Thanks for helping me with my tree."

"It was fun." He came closer, his gaze still on hers. "I like spending time with you."

"Me, too. With you." Callie's tongue felt too big for her mouth. Her heart pounded. "What are we doing?"

Brandt touched the side of her face. "I have no idea, but I want to kiss you. If you want…"

Rising on her tiptoes, she pressed her mouth against his. His soft lips met hers, and everything she hadn't known she was missing was suddenly found.

This kiss…this man was what she needed.

Her hands found their way to his chest. One of his arms slipped around her back, pulling her closer.

The scent of him surrounded her. His warmth, too. She wanted to soak both up so she never forgot this moment.

He increased the pressure against her mouth before backing away. His unsteady breathing matched hers. "I guess that means you wanted to kiss me."

"Good guess." Callie wasn't sure of anything at the moment, except how quiet her voice was and how much she wanted another kiss.

Standing in front of Brandt, her palms against his chest, Callie felt the rapid beat of his heart. It matched hers.

His arm remained around her waist. His other hand was in her hair. Somehow during the kiss she'd missed that happening, but not surprising given the pleasurable sensations she'd been feeling.

She willed her pulse and heart rate to slow, taking two

deep breaths before daring to open her eyes.

So handsome.

Her pulse sped up. What was happening? "I don't know what this is between us."

"We don't have to label this."

"No, we don't." Callie wished she sounded more certain.

"You said you weren't interested in dating. I'm assuming that means you don't want a boyfriend."

She lifted her chin. "I don't."

He ran his hand over her hair, the strands sifting through his fingers. "I'm not trying to find a girlfriend."

Neither of them wanted a relationship, but something was happening between them. Friendship, yes, but the kiss showed her there was chemistry, too.

"I'm only in town until New Year's," he added.

She did a quick calculation. That was a little over three weeks away. "Not that long."

As he cupped the back of her head, she fought the urge to lean into him.

"Let's take things day by day," he said. "See what happens."

Having a limit on their time together would keep their feelings under check. An expiration date would keep their hearts safe.

What was the worst thing that could happen?

His fingers traveled along the side of her head to her jawline. "What do you say?"

Yes. There was only one answer to his question.

Callie took a steadying breath. "Okay."

"Fantastic." He kissed the tip of her nose.

She would enjoy their time together. When the new year arrived and he had to leave, she would say goodbye with no regrets. Yes, she could do that.

Until then, she wanted to make the most of the time they had.

And would.

Chapter Eighteen

On Tuesday evening, Brandt stood on First Avenue waiting for Callie. During their walk last night with Rex, she'd told him she wanted to continue their tour. He didn't know how much he could see now that the sun had set, but he only cared about spending more time with Callie, so here he was.

Brandt hoped the sightseeing included a kiss or two. Having Callie kiss him on Sunday had been the best thing that had happened to him in…he didn't know how long. Yes, he wanted her lips on his, but he also wanted to make the most of his vacation with her and his aunt. He was juggling his time between the two and likely wouldn't finish his game this month, but he was surprisingly okay with that.

"Hey." Callie was double-parked on the street. She had the passenger window rolled down. Christmas music played. "Ready to see more of Silver Falls?"

"Yes." Except he'd be happy staring at her for the rest of the night. Her hair was tucked into a bright red knit hat that matched the scarf wrapped around her neck.

"Hop in."

He did. "I didn't expect you to be driving."

"It's too cold to walk." She pulled away from the curb. "I hope Margot doesn't mind me stealing you away again."

"She's teaching a workshop at the shop, so I wouldn't be seeing her tonight. I also didn't tell her what I was doing. I don't want her to think…"

"Her matchmaking is working."

He nodded, even though he couldn't deny his aunt pushing him toward Callie had led them to wanting to spend more time together. "Thought that was for the best."

"Smart move knowing Margot."

"Walking Rex last night was helpful, but I'm still having a few issues with Angus and Sadie not listening to me."

"Why don't you and the dogs come over to Wags and Tails on Thursday night? We can have you work with Rex a little and then the other two."

"That would be great." They hadn't finished this outing, and he already had plans to see her again. He tapped his foot to the beat of the song on the radio. "Thanks."

As she turned into a familiar parking lot, Brandt's heart slammed against his rib cage. "Where are we?"

"The library." She parked. "It opened between the time you left, and the time I moved here."

Staring at what used to be NiBrTech, he forced himself to breathe.

"For a small town, Silver Falls has an amazing public library." Callie pulled the key from the ignition. "There's a museum, a career center, classrooms, and a multipurpose room that can be rented for events. It's one of my favorite places to go when I have time."

He opened his mouth, but he couldn't speak. At least something good came out of the sale for the community. That had been his hope.

Her nose scrunched. "Brandt?"

He cleared his dry throat. "This used to be NiBrTech."

Her face dropped. "I'm so sorry. If I knew that, I didn't remember."

"It's okay. You didn't know."

"I should have." Callie's hands trembled, and she fumbled to put the key back in the ignition. "We'll go somewhere else."

He touched her hand to stop her. "I want to go inside."

Her gaze jerked to his. "Are you sure?"

Brandt nodded. "Positive."

He opened the door, slid out of the truck, and stood straight. His pulse hadn't slowed, but he needed to do this if only to bring him one step closer to the closure Callie had mentioned the other night at the coffee shop.

She met him around the back. Her hand reached for his.

Brandt laced his fingers with hers, grateful for her company. "Let's do this."

As they approached the entrance, Callie gave him an encouraging smile.

The building looked the same from the outside, though the signage now read Silver Falls Public Library. Convincing Nick to donate the building had been Brandt's final effort to do something for the town before he'd left.

The double glass doors opened automatically, the heat mixing with the wintry air. He hesitated but then stepped inside.

Just a building.

The doors closed behind them.

He released the breath he'd been holding. The smell was different. So was the paint. Two plaques caught his eyes.

The first noted the building's dedication in July of 2014.

The second was to show the town of Silver Falls' gratitude to Nick and Robin Baxter for their donation of the building.

Brandt huffed out an unamused laugh.

Typical Nick.

Robin's name had never been on the title. The land and building had belonged to both Nick and Brandt. Leasing hadn't made sense when they weren't planning to leave Silver Falls.

Was this Nick's mea culpa to the town? His way of saving face since he was planning to stay?

No matter.

Brandt had never wanted recognition or notoriety. Not the way Nick craved it.

But seeing this put what happened into better perspective. This was additional proof Nick Baxter wasn't the man Brandt thought he was.

Callie squeezed his hand. "Everything okay?"

"Yes."

Brandt could make trouble for Nick by telling the truth about the building donation, but that wouldn't be fair to Robin and their kids. Besides, Brandt bore responsibility for giving Nick the means to deceive everyone. Brandt was the one who'd left town before everything settled. If he'd wanted the credit, he should have stuck around and made sure things happened the right way.

Not Nick's way.

Brandt faced Callie. "I'm curious to see what they've done with the place."

"Let's start with the first floor," she said.

Each of the library sections were clearly defined by nonfiction or fiction labels and subcategories. A bank of computers sat in the middle available for use by patrons.

"This is the children's area." Callie led him into an area where the human resources and accounting departments used to be. Bookshelves, small tables, and more computers occupied the space. "They hold story time in there. And the room with the tables is used for activities."

With each step, a weight lifted from Brandt. The building might be the same, but any hint of NiBrTech was long gone. He needed to put everything in the past behind him, too.

No more lip service that he had.

"This is amazing." He touched a chair that resembled something from a Dr. Seuss book. "I would have loved to have a library like this when I was a kid."

"Me, too. But it's great to have it now, too." She glanced around. "The library has won awards."

"I'm not surprised." Seeing this not only put the past into perspective, but it also filled him with pride. Having contributed to something so beneficial for kids and the community felt good. Took away the sting of regret for not being able to save NiBrTech. "Thanks for bringing me here."

She pulled his hand. "There's more to see."

A feeling of contentment washed over him. The urge to go somewhere else that had kept him on edge for the last six years was gone. At least for now.

The library played a role in that, but the bigger part belonged to Callie. She was making a difference with him dealing with the past and making him think about his future. He liked the way he felt around her, and he didn't want the feeling to end.

He grinned. "Lead the way."

❦

LYING IN BED that evening, Callie glanced at the digital clock on her nightstand. Not quite eleven. Rex was sprawled out across the foot of her bed. He'd fallen asleep an hour ago while she'd been watching a movie. That had ended thirty minutes ago, but she wasn't ready for sleep.

Not when she couldn't stop thinking about Brandt.

The visit to the library could have ended up a disaster, but she'd never seen Brandt so carefree after exploring the building. His steps, his posture, appeared…lighter. He'd thanked her for bringing him there, and he said he wanted to go back to spend more time at the museum to learn more about the history of Silver Falls.

But on Wednesday morning, he didn't drop off the dogs—or pick them up in the afternoon. Margot hadn't mentioned Brandt, either time. That was a first.

Callie reread texts from earlier.

Brandt: *Thanks again for last night. Just what I needed.*

Callie: *So glad. See you later?*

Brandt: *Have plans with my aunt tonight. Will call.*

Except he hadn't called. Or texted.

He was an adult. If anything had happened, news would spread like wildfire through town. So why was her stomach churning?

You like Brandt.

Anna's voice was in Callie's head again. And yes, she did like him. More than she thought possible after knowing him for so short a time.

She'd fit Rex into her life. She was making time for Brandt while he was in Silver Falls. After he left, would there be a void?

Callie didn't want to know the answer.

Later that night, her phone rang. Brandt's name flashed on her screen.

She took the call and then held the phone to her ear. "Did you have fun with your aunt?"

"Depends on your definition of fun. We went to a paint night in Summit Ridge with a few of her friends." He laughed. "The subject was a poinsettia plant. Most everyone nailed it, but mine resembled a red-and-green alien."

"I thought anyone could make a masterpiece at paint night."

"Me, too." He laughed again. "Guess I'm the one who'll ruin their perfect record. A good thing I wasn't planning on quitting my day job to become an artist."

Callie liked how he joked around. "You're exaggerating."

"I wish I were, but my aunt agreed I had zero painting talent."

"Ouch."

"I know, right." Brandt's voice sounded distant as if he was shifting the phone to his other ear. "What did you do tonight?"

"Boring stuff." She snuggled under the blanket, wishing she was cuddling against Brandt. "Cleaned and then watched a movie."

"A Christmas movie?" he asked.

Callie thought about the happily ever after ending with a romantic marriage proposal in the snow. For some reason that scene had brought happy tears to her eyes. She usually wasn't so sappy. "Of course, it's December. If I'm not listening to Christmas music…"

"You're watching a holiday movie."

"You have me figured out already," she teased.

"Not quite, but I'm working on it." He sounded serious. "My aunt has an event at the quilt shop tomorrow night. If you're in the mood to watch another, I can come over after we work with the dogs."

She'd missed seeing and hearing from him today. "I'd like that."

He yawned. "Guess I should say goodnight."

"You sound tired."

Each evening, their goodbyes lasted forever because no one wanted to be the first to hang up, but she didn't mind if the calls cut into her sleep time. An extra yawn or two the next day was a small price to pay if she could talk longer to Brandt.

"I'm okay."

"You need sleep, and we'll see each other tomorrow night."

"Maybe I'll see you in my dreams."

Her pulse speeded up. "As long as it's not a nightmare."

He laughed. "Never with you."

Callie hadn't wanted a boyfriend, but she was feeling like she might have found one. At least for the next couple of weeks. And she liked the idea. More than she imagined she would.

❦

ON THURSDAY, BRANDT sat at his aunt's dining room table. It was where he'd been working each day on his game. Only work wasn't on his mind. He was considering extending his stay into the new year.

Was he being stupid for wanting to stay or dumb if he didn't?

As the idea circled in his brain, he closed his laptop and stood. Once he started thinking about Callie, his brain shut down to any other subject.

Brandt had no idea what to do, but taking things day by day was getting harder each time he glanced at the calendar. January was fast approaching. The idea of leaving Silver Falls made his insides twist and turn.

Whatever was happening between Callie and him felt right.

Maybe the newness of being together was driving him to want to stay. They hadn't put a label or name on what they were doing—hanging out, spending time together, dating. Even though Callie had work and he had his aunt to consider, they were making the most of what time they had. Brandt had seen Callie almost every day. Later tonight, they would watch *Elf* at her house, cuddling under a blanket while sharing popcorn and drinking peppermint hot chocolate.

And to think he had once thought Callie reminded him of Nick.

Brandt laughed.

Callie Andrews was independent, but he liked that about her. She preferred to help others than accept help herself, but given her family situation, he understood her need to be self-reliant. Leaving her parents and brothers in Los Angeles to move to a new town in a different state couldn't have been easy, but she'd done it, made a success of her business, and created a home.

The front door opened. Aunt Margot entered the house with an envelope in hand. For once, she wasn't smiling. "Nick Baxter dropped this off at the quilt shop. He asked me to give the letter to you."

Brandt's shoulders tensed, but he took it if only so his aunt could say she'd done her part.

"I don't know why he didn't text or call you." Aunt Margot rolled her eyes. "You've had the same number forever."

"I blocked him six years ago."

He slid his finger underneath the envelope flap, hesitated, and then pulled out a folded piece of paper.

Brandt,

It's been six years. Don't you think it's time we talked? Please call me. My number's the same as before.

Nick

"What does he want?" Aunt Margot asked.

Brandt balled the note to toss in the recycle bin. "To talk."

Concern clouded his aunt's eyes. "Do you think that's a good idea?"

"My gut says no, but…" He thought back to what had happened at the school and then being at the library. "Callie says I need closure so I can move on, but I'm not sure talking to Nick is the way to get it. What do you think?"

"Listen to Callie." Aunt Margot's expression softened. "It's been six years, sweetie, but you're still wandering around trying to find what you lost."

He stiffened. "Nothing's lost. I like what I've been doing."

Aunt Margot gave him a pointed look. "Have you ever thought about why you like working contract jobs and moving so much?"

Brandt counted off the reasons with his fingers. "I never get bored. I can travel and live in various places."

"All true, but taking one job after another also means you don't have to commit to a company, sign a long-term lease, or make lasting friendships. You can avoid making deep connections with others using the excuse you won't be there long. As soon as you feel yourself getting attached to anything, you quit and move on to the next thing."

"I don't quit." He raised his chin. "I take a new job.

"Semantics, dear." She flashed a knowing smile. "What you're doing—how you're living—is safe. There's no risking any part of yourself, professionally or personally."

"I…" Brandt wanted to disagree, except he wasn't one hundred percent sure he could. "If I've been trying to feel safe, it wasn't something I did consciously. I embraced the idea of having freedom. I didn't look beyond that."

"And now?" she asked.

After talking to Callie, what his aunt said made sense, even if he wished it hadn't. He rubbed the back of his neck. "I should have paid to talk to you instead of those overpriced therapists."

"Yes, you should have." Aunt Margot's eyes lit with laughter. "I would have given you homemade cookies while we talked."

He had to laugh, but that was cut short when he remembered the scrunched-up letter. "Does this mean you think I should talk to Nick?"

"You're the one who has to decide that, but this isn't all about Nick. It's about getting what you need to put the past behind you. Otherwise, you're going to be stuck in the pattern of going from job to job and town to town. That won't be good for you in the long run."

"Maybe." *Probably.*

"Think about it."

"I will. It's just… He's had six years to contact me. He could have used any number of social media sites to find me.

Why now?" Brandt wouldn't put it past the guy to have a hidden agenda. "I don't trust Nick. I doubt I'll be able to trust him again."

"Talking to a person doesn't mean you have to trust them, dear," Aunt Margot said in her wise-woman tone. The same one that had convinced him to spend this Christmas in Silver Falls. "If you choose to hear him out, you're the one who'll decide if he's being sincere or not. For all you know, he's the same bottom feeder he was. And if so, then you can kick him to the curb."

Brandt flinched. He wasn't used to hearing her talk like that, though her advice went right along with Callie's. "Aunt Margot."

"I don't trust Nick Baxter, either. Not many do." His aunt's gaze hardened. "There's a reason his and Robin's only friends are people who moved to Silver Falls after Nick sold NiBrTech. He donated the library and took credit for it, but everyone knows that building belonged to the both of you. Robin's a sweetheart, but no one respects Nick and for good reasons."

Brandt had thought the guy had gotten everything he wanted. He'd never considered Nick might have faced any consequences or repercussions for his actions.

"I'll think about everything you said before I make a decision."

Aunt Margot seemed to be holding back a smile. "Seeing Callie again tonight?"

He nodded—the less he said, the better.

"Invite her to come over on Saturday night to help us

bake cookies for the First Avenue tins," Aunt Margot said. "More hands make less work."

"I will."

"What are the two of you doing?" she asked.

He loved his aunt but sometimes… Might as well tell her or she would keep asking, though he wasn't mentioning watching a movie. "Callie's going to work with me again so walking the dogs isn't such a chore."

"I thought Angus and Sadie were behaving better?"

Busted. "More training never hurts."

Aunt Margo laughed. "Not a bad excuse to use to get a date."

"It's not a—"

"You may be fooling yourself and Callie, but I see what's going on between you two." His aunt beamed as if she'd been asked to plan their wedding. "And I couldn't be happier."

Brandt was happy, too.

But a part of him kept waiting for something to go wrong.

Nothing this good ever lasted.

Chapter Nineteen

WAGS AND TAILS was closed on Thursday night, but three dogs remained—Rex, Angus, and Sadie. Callie sat on the floor in the large play area with Margot's two dogs. Brandt circled with Rex on a leash.

Angus and Sadie stared up at her. Callie knew what they wanted—rubs. But she was having a tough time keeping her attention off Brandt. He'd surprised her tonight by saying he was going to talk to Nick tomorrow. That after visiting the library, Brandt wanted closure, and this might be the best way for him to get it. She'd offered her support and a kiss. He'd taken both.

Then Brandt had invited her over on Saturday night to bake cookies with his aunt. The invitation surprised her due to Margot and how they were trying to keep a low-profile around her, but Callie said yes. There was no other place she'd rather be than with him.

"Sit," Brandt ordered.

Rex glanced up at him but remained standing. As if not having a care in the world, the dog scratched himself, slid his eyes toward Callie, and sat.

Oh, Rex. You smart dog. You've got Brandt's number.

She tried to hide her amusement. "Don't be afraid to use a firmer tone if you think Rex isn't listening."

He rubbed the dog's side. "He knows what he's doing."

"Sometimes he does," Callie admitted. "But you're the one in charge."

Brandt shot her a cheeky grin. "The alpha dog."

Shaking her head, she petted Angus and Sadie. "The human."

Brandt was doing better than the first time he'd held Rex's leash. He appeared more comfortable. Tonight when he'd arrived, he'd reached out to Rex before the dog nudged him to get attention.

Seeing that had made her want to dance a jig.

Silly, but true.

She was giddy around the guy.

And she owed Anna an apology for teasing her about being gaga over Davis. Callie had never understood wanting to be with someone so much until Brandt.

"Sit." Shaking his head, he focused on her. "That wasn't right."

She rubbed Sadie. "Good job figuring that out yourself."

Head tilted, Rex stared at Brandt as if waiting to see what he would do next.

The two were so cute together. Brandt kept letting Rex lead even though this was the second time they'd practiced. No wonder he had trouble getting Angus and Sadie to and from Wags and Tails. Those dogs were likely taking *him* for a walk.

"Try a firmer voice," she instructed. "You don't have to

raise the volume and yell, but you want Rex—or any dog—to do what you tell them."

"Sit, Rex." Brandt's head turned to Callie as if to see how he did.

Knowing he wanted her approval made her tummy cartwheel.

"Better." She flashed him a thumbs-up sign. Angus and Sadie needed a firmer hand, so she wanted to perfect Brandt's tone before he worked with the other two dogs. "I want you to lead him to the end of the mat, then try again."

Brandt did. "Sit."

Rex sat and then cocked his head at Brandt.

Pride for both her boys burst through Callie. "That's it."

"Yes." Brandt's smile was brighter than the Christmas lights on First Avenue. Squatting so he was at eye level with the dog, he rubbed Rex's neck the way she'd showed him earlier in the week. "That's my good boy. We did it."

Tail wagging, Rex panted.

Her chest squeezed tight watching the two bond. She gave them a few moments to celebrate.

"Now it's time to try it with Angus or Sadie," Callie said finally. "Your choice."

"Sadie." Brandt laughed. "I have a feeling Angus is part gremlin and wanting to cause trouble."

"Be careful." With a wink, Callie took Rex's leash and gave Sadie's to Brandt. "What you say might come true."

He winked back. "It has where you're concerned, and I couldn't be happier."

Her mouth parted. "How am I supposed to respond to

that?"

"A kiss would suffice."

Callie kissed his cheek. That was all she would allow herself now. But later, she wanted more. "Let's see how you do with Sadie."

❦

ON FRIDAY AFTERNOON at the bakery, Brandt sat across from Nick. Maybe talking would give Brandt the closure he wanted. A public meeting seemed a better idea than a private one. No matter how things went down with Nick, Brandt could enjoy a cup of coffee and a cranberry scone.

He'd dressed casually, jeans and a hoodie, but Nick showed up in a suit and tie as if he were going for an interview. Brandt hoped Nick's clothing choice wouldn't set the tone for today.

Silence added to the tension at the table. Brandt sipped his coffee. Nick was the one who'd wanted to talk. No way was Brandt starting this conversation.

Childish, maybe, but at least he'd shown up. That had to count for something.

"Thanks for meeting me." Nick's shoulders hunched as if he was trying to hide with his bad posture. An untouched cup of coffee sat in front of him. "It's been too long."

So it begins… "You could have contacted me if you'd wanted to talk."

"You needed time."

Yeah, right. Brandt may have snorted. He wanted to get this over with. "What did you want to talk about?"

Nick picked up his coffee and sipped. As he set the cup on the table, his hand trembled. "I'm sorry."

Finally. Brandt's tense muscles loosened.

After all these years, Nick was going to apologize. Brandt leaned forward. "It's good to hear you say that."

"It's true." Nick released a shaky laugh. "I shouldn't have let six years go by without contacting you."

Waiting for Nick to continue, Brandt bit into his scone.

Nick stared at him, mouth closed, not talking.

That couldn't be his entire apology, could it?

Brandt picked up his cup and then sipped his coffee.

Still nothing.

He had to ask. "Is that all you have to say?"

"No."

Okay, good. "Go on."

"I have a fantastic opportunity for you."

A stone settled in Brandt's stomach. "For me?"

He had no idea why he'd responded. Shock, maybe.

"There's a company in Raleigh who could use your talent in app development. You have the ultimate skillset for what they need." Nick's pitch would make a car salesman proud. "You'll get an equity share. Your salary is negotiable, and there's a full benefits package including medical, dental, vacation, and an eight-week sabbatical every six years."

Brandt didn't have to think about the offer. "I'm not interested."

"If this takes off, you'll be rich."

"I already am. What's in it for you?"

Nick moved the handle of the coffee cup back and forth.

His hands shook. "A piece of the pie, too."

Realization dawned. Nick wasn't here to apologize because he'd destroyed NiBrTech and their friendship. He was here for himself. Six years and nothing had changed.

"You're running out of money." There was no judgement in Brandt's voice, only disgust.

"Money is tied up in investments."

Must be a lot because only desperation could cause a man who'd betrayed a friend to come to that person with a job offer. Brandt shouldn't be surprised, not after everything else Nick had pulled, but...

"What did you do? Angel money? High-risk investments?"

"I'm not broke."

"I hope not since you had enough money for you and Robin, your kids, and your grandkids never to have to work."

Nick rolled his eyes. "There's never enough. Don't tell me you haven't blown through yours."

Brandt gripped his coffee mug, mainly so he didn't smack the guy sitting across from him. Other than the NiBrTech building, he'd used his proceeds from the sale to pay off his aunt's mortgage, buy his parents' retirement home, and establish the scholarship fund—one that now would provide funds for any younger kids who needed help, too. A reputable investment manager had invested the rest of his money. His returns more than covered the amount he'd spent.

"Okay, I won't tell you." Brandt didn't care if he sounded flippant.

Nick Baxter was a tool. A user. A loser.

The same old Nick who'd thrown a tantrum when Brandt suggested they hire a new CEO reappeared. The Nick who'd bought into the hype he alone was the driving force behind NiBrTech's success, not the technology—the algorithms and code.

Brandt stared over his coffee cup. "Do you want to tell me why your and Robin's names are on the plaque in the library and mine isn't?"

Nick's face paled. "You never cared about that kind of thing. People hated me. It was so hard on Robin because she wouldn't consider moving away. I had to do something."

"So you lied and took credit for something that wasn't even your suggestion?"

"You have no idea what I was going through. I had to regain my status. Improve my reputation."

It was all about Nick. As usual. "You're unbelievable."

"I'm the reason for our success. Without me, you'd never have had a building you could donate."

Nick's egotistical tone had gotten worse over the years. Once upon a time, Brandt had thought Nick was only brimming with confidence, but that was nothing more than arrogance.

Brandt set his cup on the table. "I thought we were partners. A team."

Nick snarled. "You're just a computer nerd who likes his nose pressed against his monitor."

"I'm proud of what I do." Brandt wasn't about to back

down. "Did."

"Me, too." Nick squared his shoulders. "Except you wouldn't have had any idea how to sell what you created. Without me, you'd be nothing."

Liar. Brandt could see the lie in Nick's gaze. The guy was pathetic, and Brandt had been a fool to trust him, but he wouldn't make that mistake again. Still, he wanted answers.

"Do you ever think about what you did?" The question had weighed on Brandt for years. "Calling all the employees together, even the ones out on maternity and sick leave, to tell them the company was being sold and they would soon be unemployed?"

"Everyone received a generous severance package."

As if that made up for losing the stability of a regular paycheck and a job in the town where they lived.

"I have no regrets," Nick added in a snobbish tone.

And that clarified everything. Nick had blamed his wife and Brandt and everyone else except himself. Yet, Nick was the only one responsible for the destruction of NiBrTech. No one else.

Brandt had been carrying around the past for too long. Nick Baxter wasn't worth the trouble. "If I hadn't returned to Silver Falls, who would you have asked—tried to use—to bail yourself out of whatever current mess you're in?"

"It's just another job, Brandt." Sweat coated Nick's hairline and forehead. "You go through them like bubble gum."

"That's how contract positions work."

"This will be better, if it hits—"

"I don't need anything to hit."

"I need you to do this." Nick's voice cracked. "I promised—"

"I don't owe you anything." Brandt stared at his former friend and cofounder feeling nothing but pity. "Do you even realize how many families you crushed when you sold the company? How many lives were torn apart when people had to move away to find a job?"

"It was a business decision."

"No." Brandt had been holding his anger and hurt for too long. "NiBrTech was never just business."

He stared at Nick's confused face. Brandt wondered if the friend he thought he'd known for most of his life had ever existed. Probably not.

"NiBrTech was ours, Nick. Yours and mine," Brandt continued. "Our dream. One we shared with our employees. Each person who worked for NiBrTech contributed to its success from the cafeteria staff—who would stay late to make sure the technical team had food when we were on deadlines—to those engineers and programmers who kept our technology from becoming obsolete."

Nick wouldn't meet Brandt's gaze.

That wasn't going to stop him.

"You not only betrayed me by taking advantage of our friendship and my trust, but you also betrayed every single employee who helped make the company successful." The words poured out. "If you'd truly understood what we'd built with NiBrTech, you would have never sold us out. You would have realized we had barely scratched our potential, that we were poised to be a billion-dollar company someday.

But you didn't, and you know what? That's not my problem."

Nick regarded Brandt as if he had lost his mind, but that wasn't the case. Brandt finally knew what was missing and what he needed to find.

Peace.

Peace with the past.

Peace with himself.

He wasn't there yet, but he would be. Soon.

"I've been carrying around a ton of guilt thinking I could have saved our company, but I was wrong." *So wrong.* "You never thought of NiBrTech as ours. For me, the company was everything, but it was nothing more than a stepping stone to you, even though you were stuck in Silver Falls because Robin didn't want to live anywhere else."

Nick was still doing the same thing. Focused on what would help him out. That was why he'd wanted to see Brandt today.

The guy didn't care about him or their friendship. There would never be an apology, but Brandt no longer needed one.

"Goodbye, Nick." Brandt stood. He didn't wish Nick ill, and he wasn't going to kick the guy to the curb as his aunt had suggested because the man wasn't worth the effort. "I hope you figure things out."

"There's nothing to figure out." Nick's face reddened. "My life is perfect. I live like a king, and I raise my kids near family in a custom-built estate with a runway and hangar. I sit on several boards of directors. The Raleigh deal is only one of many. I have investment opportunities you could only imagine. You'll never have my kind of success."

"No, because I've never wanted that."

Brandt headed to the door. Whatever anger, resentment, and regret he'd entered the bakery with was no longer a part of him when he left.

Was this what closure felt like?

If so, it felt really good. He was ready to see what came next.

Brandt thought about Callie. He wasn't sure what he wanted, where he wanted his future to be, but he saw her as part of it.

Would she want to be?

Chapter Twenty

ON SATURDAY NIGHT, Callie arrived at Margot Winslow's house. Multicolored lights graced the eaves of the second story. An illuminated plastic snowman sat on the porch waiting to welcome guests. Big ornaments hung from the branches of the leafless trees. The decorations were bright and cheery, not the over-the-top displays that would cost a homeowner a mortgage-sized electricity bill. She'd been excited when Brandt asked her to come over, but nerves threatened to get the best of her now.

Standing on the porch, she clutched a bottle of Merlot. Her mother had taught her to never show up at someone's house without a gift. Callie had no idea what was appropriate for cookie making, but red wine went with chocolate so that seemed good enough. Now she wasn't sure.

Callie had been friends with Margot for almost three years, but the woman adored her nephew. Matchmaking hobby aside, what if Margot didn't like Callie being more than a friend to Brandt? Thinking about the possible answers made her want to turn around and drive home.

Stop worrying and ring the doorbell.

She did.

Two familiar barks sounded from inside.

"Get back." When Brandt cracked open the door, Angus and Sadie tried to squeeze through, but he kept them back so Callie could enter.

"You used your firm voice." She kissed his cheek. "Good job handling the dogs."

"I had an excellent teacher."

He took the bottle of wine and then helped her out of her coat. As his hand brushed her shoulder, heat exploded at the point of contact. The flash of attraction in his eyes told Callie he'd felt something, too.

Brandt hung her jacket on the coat tree next to the front door before kissing her on the forehead.

They were acting like middle-schoolers, but they'd only been together around dogs—café and library aside—so tonight would be different with Margot here. She also wasn't sure what he'd told his aunt about them.

When he stepped back, Callie noticed the Santa apron he wore over his black Henley and faded jeans.

"Nice outfit," she said.

"Glad you approve because Aunt Margot has an apron for you. I believe it's Mrs. Claus. My aunt doesn't know the meaning of subtle."

Okay, maybe Callie didn't need to be nervous.

Both Angus and Sadie sat patiently.

"Such good dogs." She kneeled to pat each one before glancing up at Brandt. "You've got these dogs behaving so well. I should charge for lessons."

"Would you accept kisses as payments?"

She tapped her chin with her fingertip. "Kisses and cookies."

"You're on." His lopsided grin caused her heart to stumble.

Callie couldn't wait to be paid. She stood.

The crackling fire provided a welcome warmth to a comfortable living room. The sharp scent of pine mixed with the aroma of cookies baking. Her mouth watered even though she'd eaten before coming over.

One-of-a-kind ornaments hung from the branches of an artificial tree. Smiling snowmen lined the fireplace mantel. She couldn't help but think of Mr. Frosty—the snowman she and Brandt had made in the park. A patchwork-quilted bear sat on a kid-size rocking chair. Christmas carols played.

"How was your day?" he asked.

"Quiet for once, though…"

"What?"

"I'm worried about Anna. Her boyfriend has so much work. She's hardly seen him this month, and she's so sad. I'm thinking of seeing if she wants to do something tomorrow night since you'll be with your aunt."

"Do," he encouraged.

"I will." Callie couldn't wait to make Anna feel better. "How was your day?"

"Cookies, cookies, and more cookies." His big smile suggested he hadn't minded. He curled strands of her hair with his fingertip. "I've been taste-testing batches, so no complaints."

"I had no idea Margot's famous cookie tins took an entire weekend to make."

"She's done it for as long as I can remember." He let go of Callie's hair. "This isn't my first rodeo, but I'm happy you're here. Come see what we've been up to."

He led her into the dining room where an extra folding table was covered with cooling racks containing dozens upon dozens of cookies.

"Wow." She stared in disbelief. "That's a lot of cookies."

"We've put some in the tins."

Homemade baked goods and Brandt. A tasty combination. She wiggled her toes. "One of your aunt's tins will be mine."

He slid his arm around her. "Don't forget I helped."

"I won't." Leaning into him, she enjoyed the feel of being close. "I'll even share."

"Lucky me." Affection filled his voice.

She stared longingly at him. "Lucky us."

"Enough flirting and making goo-goo eyes at each other," Margot said from the doorway of the kitchen. "I need your help."

"We're on our way." He winked at Callie. "You have no idea what you've gotten yourself into."

"You're the one who invited me," she said, nerves shooting through her once more.

"I invited you," Margot yelled. "He was only the messenger."

Brandt kissed the top of Callie's hand. "Forgive me."

"Of course," she said without hesitation. "Cookies are involved. How bad can it be?"

When she entered the kitchen, she froze. The kitchen was as homey as the rest of the house with an island and plenty of counter space, but every surface—including the windowsills—were covered with bowls, rolls of parchment paper, and cookie sheets. Flour was on the floor. Enough so she could see her footprints.

Uh-oh. This was bad. A complete mess.

"Don't look so shocked, dear." Margot ripped a piece of parchment paper from a roll. "There is a method to the madness."

"An assembly line of sorts," Brandt offered.

Callie didn't know what to say, so she nodded.

"Relax and wash your hands because I'm sure you touched my dogs."

Callie did, using plenty of soap.

Margot hugged her and then handed her an apron. "This is to protect your clothes since we're not being neat and tidy about making cookies."

Callie put on the Mrs. Claus apron that matched Brandt's. Guess he was correct about Margot's intentions. He tied the back for her.

"Tonight, we're making drop cookies," Margot explained.

Callie rubbed her damp palms over her apron. "I've never made those before."

"I'll show you what to do." And Margot did.

The dogs stayed out of the kitchen, but that didn't stop them from lying in the doorway staring at the cookies being made, patiently waiting for one to fall onto the floor.

By the time the first six dozen were made, Callie's face hurt from laughing so much. Margot kept them entertained with stories about Brandt when he was a kid.

"And you should have seen Brandt when he'd run away from home and come to my house." Margot laughed. "One time, he dragged a suitcase with him."

"How often did this happen?" Callie asked.

Face red, Brandt shrugged.

"Every few weeks or so." Margot turned on the oven light to check the current batch. "I finally told him to leave clothes here, so he wouldn't have to bother packing."

"That made things easier." Brandt shoved a cookie into his mouth.

Margot gave his arm a playful tap. "You're eating more than you're making."

"Cookies belong in my mouth," he countered.

"These belong in the tins." Margot released a dramatic sigh. "But I suppose one more won't make a difference."

Brandt beamed. "This is why she's my favorite aunt."

An exaggerated eye roll from Margot followed. "I'm your only aunt."

Seeing the interaction between aunt and nephew warmed Callie's heart. Their affection for each other was palpable.

Margot searched the countertop. "What did I do with the parchment paper?"

Brandt handed over the roll with a flourish, like a page giving the queen an important scroll. "Here you go, milady."

"I'm no lady," Margot shot back.

The two burst into laughter.

Things weren't perfect with Callie's family, but she knew they loved her in their own way and she missed them. A lump burned in the back of her throat.

Brandt put his arm around her. "You okay?"

"Thinking about my parents and brothers."

"Good thoughts?" he asked.

She nodded. "They drive me crazy, but it's hard not to miss them during the holidays."

He brushed his lips over her hair. "The twenty-fourth will be here soon."

That meant New Year's would arrive the week after that. Callie's stomach hurt. She didn't like thinking about Brandt leaving.

"Does your family bake?" Margot asked.

"Not like this." Callie couldn't imagine her mother wearing an apron or knowing how to use a fancy mixer. That was what personal chefs were for. "We don't have a baking day during the holidays, more like a baking hour. We use the refrigerated sugar cookie dough that comes in little squares. We dip those in candy sprinkles and colored sugars and then bake them. Santa no longer stops by our house, but I still leave cookies and milk out, along with celery and carrots for the reindeer."

"You poor child. It's no wonder Santa gave up on your family." Margot made a face—a cross between *ick* and horrified. "Those aren't Christmas cookies. Those are an atrocity."

Brandt shook his head. "Not that my aunt has a strong opinion about this or anything."

Callie laughed. "It's okay, because that's all we knew. It was still fun. Our Christmases are the evergreen, sunny-sky kind, but we had our own traditions."

"Like what?" Brandt asked.

She thought back. "My mom couldn't take off time at the holidays since people still get sick, but my brothers always took me to see Santa. We'd do a serious pose for our parents and a silly one for us. It never failed that my dad would have a case, so they'd also drive me around to see the lights at night. When my parents didn't have to work, they would go with us. On Christmas Eve, we'd each open one present. It was always pajamas. We'd put those on and play board games all night. That was the only time my brothers wouldn't cheat so I could win."

"When your parents and brothers are in town, let's start a new tradition," Margot offered. "I'll come over to show you and your family how to make real Christmas cookies."

Callie's breath hitched. "The cranberry-chocolate ones?"

"Along with a few others." Margot smiled.

"That will be great." Anticipation made Callie's toes curl. "Do you want to join us?"

He nodded. "I'd love to."

"Get more jelly for the next batch," Margot told her.

Callie reached for the strawberry jelly at the same time as Brandt. Their fingers tangled. As heat burned where their hands touched, tingles spread from the spot.

Sparks.

She could get used to this.

Well, until he left.

Margot tsked. "Are you two going to stand here staring at each other or are we baking more cookies?"

"Cookies," Callie and Brandt said at the same time.

The time flew by until she stifled a yawn.

"Time for you to go home before you fall asleep standing up." Brandt untied her apron. "I'm going to see Callie out."

"Thanks for your help." Margot hugged her. "We'll talk about the best time for your family's cookie day."

That was when Callie remembered. "They don't arrive until the twenty-fourth."

"There are twelve days of Christmas so plenty of time to do this after the twenty-fifth," Margot said.

"Sounds great." And it did.

In the living room, the two dogs slept next to each other on the couch. Brandt held her coat while she put it on.

"My aunt likes you." He pulled out her hair from the back of her jacket.

A ball of warmth settled in her chest. "Good, because I like her."

He outlined her lips with his fingertip. "You're going to be invited back to hang out with us."

Yay. Callie leaned forward to be closer to him, wanting his lips to take the place of his finger. Who was she kidding? She wished the night wouldn't have to end. "I can't wait."

"Me, either." His tone was soft, and the emotion in his eyes romantic. "You're always so calm even when I can see the excitement in your gaze."

She was the reason his eyes shone like the lights on the tree. Knowing that made her feel beautiful, desirable, and strong. "I was never a drama princess. My parents forbid that kind of behavior before I was born."

Laughing, he cut the distance between them in half. Once again sparks flowed between them, connecting them, bringing them closer. "Does anything faze you besides your family?"

Callie shrugged because she wanted him to stop talking and kiss her. "I work with animals, most who have a mind of their own, so you learn fast how much control you don't have."

He leaned in closer. "I wish I could see you tomorrow."

The longing in his voice matched how she was feeling, too. "You're spending the day with your aunt. She's excited about going to the city to shop."

He smoothed her hair with his hand. "And you get to have fun with Anna."

Callie nodded. "I'll see you on Monday."

Though that sounded far away at the moment.

He opened the door and then followed her outside. She pressed the key fob. Her car lights blinked, and the door locks clicked open.

"Thanks for coming over." He lowered his mouth until his lips gently touched hers. This time, he tasted like cookies. Sweet, chocolatey, and all kinds of yummy. He didn't press harder, but his lips lingered.

She enjoyed the feel of them against hers.

Brandt straightened much too soon, breaking the contact, but her lips continued to tingle. He didn't step back. The heat from his breath fanned her face. "You need to get home."

She would rather keep kissing him, but he was right. "I do. Rex is waiting for me."

"Drive safe." Brandt's hand cupped her face. He didn't seem to want to let go of her. That was fine by Callie. "Text or call me when you get home."

"I will." Her feet didn't want to move toward the car. She wanted another kiss. "Goodnight."

He lowered his arm to his side, and she missed his touch. "Goodnight to you."

A minute later, she backed out of the driveway. As soon as she could no longer see Brandt in her rearview mirror, she touched her lips.

Heat. Tingles. Brandt.

His kisses were better than cookies.

Callie couldn't wait for another taste.

On Monday.

Chapter Twenty-One

AFTER THE LAST dog had been picked up from Wags and Tails on Sunday afternoon, Callie checked her inbox. Not many emails had arrived, but the one from the First Avenue Business Association caught her attention. She clicked on it.

Judging of the holiday windows for the annual award will take place on December twenty-third.

That was a week away.

Flutters of anticipation exploded in her stomach. She could taste victory. "It's as good as ours, Rex."

Her dog lounged on his pillow. His eyelids drifted closed.

"Don't fall asleep. Your cousin Milo and Aunt Anna will be here soon, then we'll go home."

The bell on the door jingled. She expected to see Anna and Milo, not…

"Nick." Brandt hadn't told her specifics of their meeting—other than he was glad he'd talked to Nick and had gotten the closure he needed to move on. She hadn't pushed, figuring Brandt would tell her more when he was ready. "What are you doing here?"

"Robin spent the day Christmas shopping. She's tired, so

she sent me out to pick up dinner." He shifted his weight between his feet. "I saw your lights on."

Nick had dropped by before, but Callie hadn't been seeing Brandt then. He hadn't brought up her friendship with Nick and Robin, and Callie hadn't asked. Maybe she should have.

"Anna is meeting me here in a few minutes," Callie replied. "We're having a girls' night in."

"I won't tell Robin, or she'll sneak over and leave me with both homework and bedtime duty," he joked. "I'm ready for a break after spending all day decorating gingerbread houses and watching every animated Christmas cartoon known to man."

This was the easygoing Nick she'd gotten to know, the one who'd delivered a hot meal and taken Rex for a walk when she'd been sick last winter. That put Callie at ease.

"Robin mentioned you're dating Brandt Winslow," Nick added.

"Not dating."

Saying that aloud left a bitter taste in Callie's mouth. She'd agreed to not using labels, but now that they were going out more, enough that others noticed, explaining their relationship was difficult.

"We're spending time together while he's in town," she clarified, not liking the way that sounded when they were becoming closer, holding hands, and kissing.

You wanted this.

Callie had, but a part of her didn't want that any longer.

"Spending time together." Nick laughed. "That sounds

like Brandt."

Her eyes narrowed. "What do you mean by that?"

Nick dragged his upper teeth across his lower lips. "We've been friends for almost three years, right?"

She nodded. "Both you and Robin are my friends."

Relief flashed in his eyes. "I'm assuming Brandt told you about me selling NiBrTech."

Another nod. "You sold the company without his knowledge."

"I did, but I'm guessing he didn't tell you why."

"He said a few things." She wasn't sure what Brandt would want her to share, especially when Nick seemed to be more of a nemesis or archvillain than friend.

"Did he mention that commitment is a four-letter word to him?"

She crossed her arms over her chest. "Not really."

"It's as true as it was then as now," Nick said in a resigned tone. "Six years ago, Brandt was waiting for the right opportunity, so he could leave NiBrTech and Silver Falls."

No way. Brandt had offered solutions. Unease tightened her shoulders. Was Nick trying to cause trouble? But that made no sense. He was her friend. "Brandt didn't say that."

"I didn't think so." Nick scratched his cheek. "Brandt was all about coding. He didn't care about the business."

"Brandt mentioned he wasn't interested in the business side of the company, so you handled that."

"Not interested. That's a good one." Nick rolled his eyes. "Brandt dumped anything non-technical into my lap, so he could concentrate on what he liked to do. I wouldn't have been able to handle the company without him, so I sold. And you're correct. I did it without his knowledge since the investors agreed with the sale."

"Why?"

"I couldn't allow the value of the company to decrease if he'd found out and quit before we sold."

That sort of made sense, but Nick was painting Brandt in such a negative light. Though Brandt had done the same with his former friend. She tried to mesh the stories both men had told her, but something was off. Either she didn't have all the information, or someone wasn't telling the truth. Nick wasn't nearly as emotional as Brandt while talking about NiBrTech.

"Based on your expression, Brandt must have left out a few details. I'm sorry about that." Nick sounded sincere. "But that's why I stopped by. Robin and I are worried about you because Brandt's known for running away. He's been running since he was a kid."

Callie remembered what Margot had said about Brandt showing up at her house with his suitcase, but that had been a childish reaction, not something ingrained in him.

"He ran after NiBrTech was sold. And he continues to do so. He rarely stays more than a few months at a job. He's lived all over the country, but he never lasts long in one place. Robin and I care about you, and we don't want to see you hurt."

"Brandt and I… It's not serious." As soon as Callie spoke, she knew that was no longer true. Somehow through all of this, she was falling for Brandt Winslow. Falling hard.

"A lot can happen in a brief period. Be careful," Nick warned. "It's not a matter of *if* Brandt will take off again—it's a question of *when*. You don't want to end up heartbroken."

Callie stiffened. His tone was too familiar. Like her family. She didn't need one more person—two if she counted Robin—telling her what to do or, rather, warning her, as if she couldn't take care of herself. She didn't want to be rude, but this had to stop.

She stared down her nose. "Look, Nick, there's no need for you and Robin to worry. I'm not a starstruck teenager. I can handle what happens."

He shrugged. "If you say so."

"I do."

"Have fun tonight." Nick left.

Callie watched the door close. She didn't understand why this kept happening. Her family was bad enough. Were the words *Can't take care of myself* tattooed on her forehead?

She wanted to talk to Brandt about Nick's visit, but he was out with Margot. Besides, Callie had plans with Anna. Maybe they could talk later or tomorrow.

Anna entered with Milo, who wore a Christmas sweater. "Ready for takeout from the Red Dragon and a chick flick?"

"Yes!"

Rex and Milo weren't girls, but they were invited. Only Anna's cats had to stay home tonight.

Anna let go of Milo's leash. "Go see Rex on the pillow."

The dog ran toward his favorite doggy friend.

She pulled out a pink folded paper from her purse. "I

stopped by for a menu. We can phone in our order and then pick it up on the way to your house."

"You've thought of everything," Callie said.

"I've had time." Anna sounded resigned.

"Davis working crazy hours again?"

Anna nodded, an odd expression on her face.

Callie had never seen her friend this quiet about a guy she liked. Sometimes Anna wouldn't say much, but rarely did she say nothing. "Are you okay?"

"Fine." Anna's smile didn't quite reach her eyes. Maybe she was tired. "I'd hoped the holidays would be different this year."

"Kisses under the mistletoe?" That was something Anna had mentioned.

She nodded and then shrugged. "Nothing I can do about it."

"You still have time." Callie wanted her best friend to be as happy with Davis as she was with Brandt. "Maybe as Christmas gets closer, Davis's workload will lighten."

"Maybe." Anna handed her the menu. "What do you want to eat?"

As Anna ordered, Callie locked the tablet in the office and removed the laundry from the dryer. Another load remained, but that could wait until the morning.

"How are things going with Brandt?" Anna straightened the bags of organic and gluten-free dog biscuits.

Callie couldn't stop her smile from widening. "We made cookies with his aunt yesterday."

"You guys are too cute."

"He is." Callie thought about their call when she'd gotten home last night. Once again, she hadn't wanted to hang up, but yawns had gotten the best of them both. "I keep trying not to think about him leaving in a couple of weeks."

"Maybe he'll stay."

She shrugged. "I'm not even going there. We have to make the most of December."

"What about when your family is here?"

Callie had invited Brandt to bake cookies with her family. "He's going to meet them, but I have no idea how to introduce him."

"Just say he's Brandt. If someone asks, let him answer."

"Putting him on the spot like that wouldn't be fair. Saying he's a friend might be best."

Anna rolled her eyes. "Whatever's going on between you is more than friendship. You see him all the time."

"When we decided to spend more time together, neither of us was interested in dating. We agreed to take things day by day and not label whatever was happening between us."

"I hope it works out for you."

Her, too. It had sounded so simple only a couple weeks ago, but now…

Didn't matter.

She couldn't ask Brandt to change what they'd decided, could she?

A dog barked from the front window.

Not Rex.

Anna froze. So did Callie.

"Milo," they said at the same time.

Anna ran to the window. As she grabbed the dog out of the display, his leash dragged behind him, pulling over more decorations before Callie could get there.

"I'm so sorry." Tears pooled in Anna's eyes. "I have no idea how Milo managed to get up there with his short legs. I thought he was on the pillow with Rex."

"So did I." Callie surveyed the damage. The metallic tree had toppled onto the waterfall. Lights had been twisted. Decorations were out of place.

How had Milo done all that so quickly?

"Not that many things were knocked over." She didn't want Anna to feel bad. Repairing the damage shouldn't take long. "Judging is a week away. Plenty of time to fix or replace items."

That didn't stop Anna from shaking her finger at him. "Bad dog, Milo."

The little guy panted happily. Silver tinsel was caught in his white fur.

"At least he had fun." Callie righted the Christmas tree, attempting to put back the items she could without too much work. A few silver balls were missing from the tree branches. She searched the display area and found a couple, but not all.

"We can finish cleaning up the mess before we go."

Callie's stomach grumbled. "That's good enough for tonight."

"Seriously?" Anna touched Callie's forehead as if checking her temperature. "You never leave things undone."

"This is the new likes-to-have-fun attitude. No more saying I'm all work and no play," Callie joked. "I'll fix the rest tomorrow."

Anna hugged her. "I'm so proud of you."

Callie brushed her hands together. "Our food should be ready."

She attached Rex's leash to his collar, pulled on her gloves and jacket, and then took one final glance around the doggy daycare before turning off the lights. Slipping her purse strap over her shoulder, she locked the front door.

"Hold the dogs while I get our order." Anna handed over Milo's leash. "Treating you to dinner is the least I can do after my dog messed up your spectacular window."

"It's our window, but go for it." As Anna went into the restaurant, Callie gave Milo a pat. "Because of you, I'm getting a free dinner. That's nice of your mom to do, but I'd rather you mind her."

Milo barked.

Rex stared at her as if she'd lost her mind.

An image of Brandt appeared. She didn't care what Nick Baxter had said. Maybe Brandt didn't like making commitments, but he'd never promised her more than the time he was in town.

Forget about losing her mind, but she could easily lose her heart, even knowing Brandt was leaving, if she weren't careful.

THE NEXT MORNING, Callie's cell phone buzzed. Another text notification followed a few seconds later. And another.

She glanced at the digital clock. A little after six. Her alarm wasn't set to go off for another fifteen minutes.

More buzzing.

What could be so important?

She picked up her phone, squinting to glimpse the messages on the screen.

Her eyes shot open. Her heart slammed against her chest. Air rushed out of her lungs. She bolted upright. Unlocked her phone. Called Sam.

Please, oh please, let this be nothing.

Callie crossed her fingers.

He answered on the first ring. "You need to get here now."

His texts had mentioned water damage. "How bad?"

"I left a message for your insurance agent."

That was bad. Callie swallowed around the lump in her throat before realizing she was still in bed. After putting the call on speakerphone, she scrambled from beneath the covers.

"What's damaged?" she asked, tugging on a pair of jeans.

"The lobby and window display."

Okay, Callie could work with that. She shoved a turtleneck over her head. "That means the dog areas are okay. We won't have to close today."

"They can't get through the front door. The lobby is a mess."

"We painted over the travel agency's door. It should be fully functional, but we'll need signs directing clients on which door to use and a new check-in table."

"I'll get on that," Sam said.

"Thanks." Closing wasn't an option. Callie couldn't afford to lose the bookings. Her employees needed money for rent, bills, and the holidays. So did she. "Do whatever you have to do so we can open on time today. I'm on my way."

❦

LESS THAN FIFTEEN minutes later, Callie stood in the lobby. A weight pressed down on her shoulders. Bad didn't describe what had happened.

As she surveyed the damage, her stomach knotted.

Somehow, the waterfall's reservoir had overflowed. The plastic layers she'd laid on and beneath the platform as a backup plan hadn't made a difference against the twenty-five gallons of water. That hadn't sounded like a lot when she'd filled the waterfall, but the amount had been more than enough to cause havoc. The entire window display platform had collapsed. Soggy and broken pieces lay on the lobby's floor.

One breath followed another. A conscious effort on Callie's part. She needed to remain in control and not let emotions get to her. Not with so much to do.

Sam and Mary Jo, who he'd called to help, were setting up a folding table to be the temporary check-in counter next door. Callie removed the wet-dry vacuum from the storage room. As she picked up water from the floor, she couldn't stop herself from staring at the waterfall. Rocks had broken off, but the pool section was in one piece.

Why had it overflowed?

The water feature had worked fine yesterday. No splashes. Nothing out of the ordinary even after Milo…

Oh, no.

Callie turned off the vacuum, ran to the waterfall, and peered into the bottom portion.

Silver ornaments.

The ones that had been missing from the tree last night.

The balls must have fallen into the pool, blocking the drain.

Callie hadn't thought her heart could sink any farther. She was wrong.

My fault.

Last night, she'd known ornaments were missing, but she'd left the doggy daycare anyway. If she had stayed to find them…

Callie's shoulders sagged. Her knees threatened to buckle. Knowing she couldn't support her weight much longer, she leaned against the wall.

What had she done? Rather—what had she *not* done?

She should have made sure every ornament was back on the tree. Instead, she'd wanted to leave and have a fun evening. Something she'd done before, but never at the expense of her business. That had always been her number-one priority.

Not last night.

Something had shifted since Brandt entered her life. There was nothing wrong with having fun, but she needed to balance her personal and professional life. Instead, she'd gone from one extreme to another, allowing herself to be distracted by him, her friend, and so many other things.

Now, look at the results.

Nothing remained of her Christmas window display. The lobby was a disaster area.

Forget winning this year. She had nothing to be judged.

A vise tightened around her heart.

Her hard work—the dreams of winning the award and having her best year yet revenue wise—had been destroyed. When her family saw the shop in ruins…

Callie's heart lodged in her throat.

They would want to drag her back to LA.

No! She wouldn't allow that to happen.

Pull yourself together.

She blinked away the tears. Making sure Wags and Tails survived and thrived had to be her focus. This was her business. Her livelihood. Employees counted on her for their jobs.

She rubbed her face. Sniffled.

She'd made a mistake last night, but she wouldn't allow that to define her today.

Callie continued vacuuming and draining the water when the container became full until she'd gone over the entire lobby. Then she started over. Mold would spell disaster to the business, so she had to remove as much water as she could.

Anna entered the lobby from the back. That meant Sam and Mary Jo had set up the alternative entrance, and they could open for their clients. Relief rushed through Callie.

"Hey." Anna's arms wrapped around her stomach. Her

eyes gleamed. "Milo did this, didn't he?"

Anna's voice was raw and full of regret.

Callie abandoned the vacuum to hug her best friend. "What happened was an accident."

"I should have checked..." Anna sobbed.

Callie hugged her tighter. "Me, too, but we'll get through this."

"The window display?"

"We'll start planning for next year's competition once everything is back to normal."

Anna backed away. "But you wanted to win for your family!"

"They've harped on me for the past twenty-eight years. What's one more?" Callie tried for a lighthearted tone. Her dream of winning the window display award was over. The important thing was taking care of her friend and the other employees. "Maybe I should tell them to postpone their trip until next year."

"Don't do that."

Callie half-shrugged. "I'll figure it out."

Though once she mentioned this, her parents and her brothers would view her as a total failure. Proving what they'd always believed—she couldn't do anything on her own.

Maybe they were correct.

Despite her research and backup plan, the waterfall had failed and ruined everything.

The Christmas window display and the lobby.

She sighed.

Brandt. He'd been right about the water fountain. That reminded her. She needed to let him know what happened. Would he give her the support she desperately needed? Or would he say he'd told her so?

She guessed she would soon find out.

Chapter Twenty-Two

A TEXT NOTIFICATION woke Brandt. He stretched his arms over his head, waking up his tired body that longed for more sleep. He'd only gone to bed a couple of hours ago after working on his game. Yawning, he reached for his cell phone.

> **Callie:** *Water damage at shop. Window display destroyed. Waiting for insurance agent to arrive.*

Wait. What? He blinked before rereading the text. The words remained the same. Brandt bolted upright, the bedding falling to his lap. He dragged a hand over his aching eyes as if that would make him alert.

No problem. He'd functioned on less sleep. The only thing that mattered was Callie. She needed him. No way would he let her down. He typed a reply.

> **Brandt:** *Just woke up. Be there ASAP.*

Brandt wanted to tell her everything would be okay, but she didn't need platitudes. She needed his support and his help. He was ready to provide both. Whatever it took.

He showered and dressed quickly, told his aunt he'd let

her know what was going on, and then drove to First Avenue. He wanted to have his car nearby if Callie needed anything.

Brandt: *Just parked. Do you need a latte? Breakfast?*

Callie: *Raine delivered both. But thanks. xoxox*

Hugs and kisses were a good sign, but as Brandt approached Wags and Tails, his heart dropped. Not only was the window display lying in a heap of broken boards and wet decorations, but water had seeped between the panes of glass and frozen. Most likely due to age and wear.

He hurried inside the store. More than half the floor tiles curled on the edges. Orange safety cones marked a path leading across the lobby to the doorway in the back. Callie stood with Mr. Lee, one of the local insurance agents in town, deep in conversation.

Callie nodded. Her eyes weren't red and puffy, but a sadness clouded her gaze.

Brandt tapped his foot, not caring if he wore down the tile. It needed to be replaced anyway. He couldn't interfere, even if he wanted to. Callie needed to handle this. Wags and Tails belonged to her.

As soon as Mr. Lee left, Brandt embraced her. He loved how she fit perfectly against him like she was his matching piece. He tightened his arms around her, wanting to let her know he was here and not going anywhere. "I'm so sorry this happened."

"I still can't believe it." She went limp in his arms. "The damage is covered by insurance even though it was my fault."

He pulled back to see her chin quivering. "What do you mean?"

"Last night, the metallic tree tipped over. A few ornaments were still missing, but I put off searching for them so I could go home. Turns out, the ornaments fell into the waterfall pool and blocked the water return. If I hadn't left..."

He used his fingertip to tilt her chin up. "You didn't know that would happen."

"But it did."

Her anguished tone clawed at his heart. "Things look bad, but you're not facing this disaster on your own."

Rising on her tiptoes, she kissed his cheek. "Thank you."

"What do you need me to do?"

"We need to find a contractor ASAP. Mr. Lee gave us a list of who they recommend, but Mary Jo said we should get bids on our own, too." Callie's gaze kept drifting to the window. Each time, the lines around her mouth deepened. "Anna has a list of names and numbers. Would you mind helping her call—"

"I'm on it." He missed the shiny silver and bright white lights that had been in the window. "Are you going to try to salvage the decorations?"

"I'll dig through to see what I can find. Otherwise, everything's going in the trash."

He kissed the top of her head. "When I finish the calls, I'll help you."

She smiled up at him. "By the time you make the calls, I

hope to be done."

His Callie was back. He doubted she'd been gone for long. "Good luck."

She held up her hand, showing him her crossed her fingers.

Definitely back.

SO MUCH FOR luck. Brandt wasn't having any. He sat on a folding chair in the storage room—the quietest place they could find with the dogs having too much fun in the large play area. Anna sat on the floor with her legs out in front of her, lowering the phone from her ear.

Groaning, she dropped her phone onto her lap. "Why is every contractor and handyman in town booked solid when Christmas Eve is a week away?"

"I thought this was the slow period for construction." Brandt pulled up a new search of licensed contractors within a fifty-mile radius. "Let's expand the search to include other towns."

"That'll be more expensive."

If Callie's insurance wouldn't cover the travel costs, Brandt would if she'd let him. First, they needed to find someone who was available to do the work.

"Not getting the repairs done until the new year might end up costing her more." He texted the new list to Anna. "I'll start on the top."

She picked up her phone. "I'll go from the bottom."

An hour later, Anna groaned again. "This is ridiculous.

No one has any openings until after Christmas."

"Same here," Brandt said. "I even offered a bonus, but no takers."

She scrubbed her hands over her face. "What do we do now?"

"I'm going to talk to Callie." Brandt stood. "I have an idea if she's open to asking for help."

Anna shook her head. "It's nice of you to want to try, but… Not. Going. To. Happen."

Yeah, he had a feeling this would be a long shot, still… "Desperate times."

"I'd wish you luck, but you're going to need a miracle."

All he could do was hope. Maybe he should cross his fingers like Callie had. "It's Christmastime, so that's a possibility."

Anna bent her knees and wrapped her arms around them. "We're talking Callie Andrews—Miss Independent-I'll-help-you-but-I've-got-this."

He threw up his hands. "It's all I've got."

Brandt headed into the lobby to find Callie on the phone.

"Of course I understand, Mrs. Sellwood." Callie wiped her forehead with her arm. "I only want what's best for Madden, too. If the construction noise will upset him, I'm happy to cancel his reservations for the rest of the month with no penalty fees."

Not only did she have to worry about repairs but also her bottom line. Brandt's heart hurt for her.

"I'm sorry, but I don't have any recommendations…

There is another doggy daycare thirty miles away, but I know nothing about their services. Okay, Mrs. Sellwood… Merry Christmas to you, too."

Lowering the phone, Callie turned the knob on the Christmas tree figurine until the song played. She stared at the window with a desolate expression.

"Hey." He came up behind her, wrapped his arms around her, and pulled her against his chest. The vanilla scent of her hair made him want to buy a bottle to have handy when he missed her. "Rough morning?"

"That was the seventh client cancelling their reservations for the remainder of December." She leaned her head back. "I don't get it. None of the doggy playrooms are affected. The experience is the same as it's always been except having the dogs enter through a different door with no lobby."

"Dog snobs," Brandt joked. This wasn't a laughing matter, but he wanted her to smile if only for a few seconds. "The owners, not the pups."

She laughed, so it worked. "Did you and Anna have any luck finding a contractor?"

He held Callie tighter. "The earliest anyone can schedule an estimate is on the twenty-sixth."

Her muscles tensed. He rubbed her arms.

"Mr. Lee said the holidays were a tough time to have repairs done, but the twenty-sixth…" Callie sighed. "Nothing I can do if no one is available. Waiting is far from ideal, but I have savings I can tap into if need be."

Brandt had no doubt Callie had not only savings, but also a contingency plan. "If you want another option to consider, I have an idea."

She faced him, hope reflecting in her green eyes. "What?"

"You said how much you like being part of the community. That's what Silver Falls is all about, right?"

Callie nodded. "But how does that relate to another option?"

"Going through normal channels for repairs is going to affect your bottom line, so why don't you put out a call for help instead?"

She tilted her head as if considering the idea. "Ask for help?"

"Yes." At least she hadn't shot him down right away. That was a good sign. "There are retired people in the area who still have their contractor licenses, as well as handymen who only take jobs through word of mouth. If you ask for help, you'll get it."

She crinkled her nose. "You don't know that for sure. I mean, maybe that could happen. But I'm not comfortable doing the asking."

"I'll do it for you."

"No." The word shot out fast and decisive.

He touched her shoulder. "What other choice do you have?"

"To wait until after Christmas." She sounded crushed by having to do that.

No way was he letting her wait or give up. Wags and Tails meant too much to her. "And have your business affected so you have to cut your staff's hours and lose money? Asking for help will solve all your problems."

She stiffened. "Don't tell me what to do."

Brandt didn't understand her firm tone. He wasn't a dog who needed commands to follow. "I'm trying to help you."

"I appreciate that."

Except she wasn't acting like she did. The tone of her voice and tense muscles suggested she was annoyed with him. "Do you?"

"It's just…" She shrugged his hand from her shoulder. "You of all people know how hard I've worked to stand on my own two feet."

"And you've done a wonderful job, but there's nothing wrong with getting help when you're in trouble." He wasn't going to let her stubbornness keep her from doing what needed to be done. "I'm here. I can help. I have money—"

Anger flared in her eyes, the gold flecks shooting like flames. "I don't need you to take care of me."

He reached for her, but she angled herself away from him. "You're important to me. I want to take care of you. Help."

She took a step back. "I've always been able to do things myself. I'll figure this out, too. On my own."

"I know you're capable, but there's no reason you have to handle this all on your own."

"I do because that's who I am."

"Then stop being so stubborn and change who you are."

She flinched. "Change?"

"Trying to be so self-reliant is going to hurt you."

"Or make me stronger." Her voice hardened, matching the expression on her face.

"Or keep you repeating the same old pattern because you don't learn your lesson."

"At least I stick around. I don't keep running away," she fired back. "That's what Nick said you've always done. Even you admitted doing it."

Brandt's blood ran cold. "You've been talking to Nick?"

She lifted her chin. "He stopped by yesterday to tell me his side of what happened with NiBrTech."

Hurt ripped through Brandt. He cared for Callie, wanted only the best for her, but Nick was a smooth talker. He could convince anyone of anything. "Why didn't you tell me?"

"We were both busy last night. I was going to tell you today, and then this..." She stared at the mess in the lobby. "He and Robin wanted to warn me about your tendency to run away. They don't want me to have my heart broken."

Brandt inhaled deeply to slow his rapid pulse. "And you listened to him?"

Her nod was a knife to his heart.

"That doesn't mean I believed him," she said.

"Why would you give Nick the time of day?"

"I told you I knew him and his wife. He came to me as a friend."

"Nick Baxter shouldn't be your friend."

Her eyes widened. "Wow. First you try to tell me what to do...and now you put limits on who can be my friend?"

"That's not what I meant."

Her gaze pinned him. "Then tell me what you meant."

Disappointment mixed with anger. His frustration kept

growing, too. Brandt could tell her numerous reasons why Nick Baxter wasn't who she thought he was, but Brandt wanted to put the past behind him so he could move on. He didn't want to list his grievances. Not again.

"You heard my side. You know what Nick did." Brandt thought she understood how hard talking about what happened was for him. "I shouldn't have to explain more."

Not to Callie. If she cared about him, believed in him, loved…

But she didn't.

The realization tore his heart in two.

No, she didn't love him. Not with the way doubt creeped into her eyes and she kept angling her shoulders farther away from him.

If she'd felt more for him, she wouldn't have given Nick a moment of her time. Maybe someday Brandt would forgive the guy, but what was happening now went beyond his issues with his former best friend.

This was between Brandt and Callie.

He couldn't trust her.

Not after this.

And that colored the last three weeks in a different light.

A dark one.

He'd thought their connection and friendship had been special, but he'd been wrong. Everything they had shared, from time spent together to kisses, had been a mistake.

He blew out a breath. "It doesn't matter. You've known him longer than you've known me."

"I only listened until I realized he didn't think I was capable of taking care of myself." She wasn't making Brandt feel better. "The same way you do."

His jaw tensed. He stared at her in disbelief. "I'm nothing like Nick Baxter."

"No, he stuck it out in Silver Falls while you ran away." Her eyes darkened. "That's what you're doing in a couple of weeks, right? Leaving—again. I didn't want a label on us, but if I had, it wouldn't have done any good. You want to be able to make a clean break for whatever job comes next. Forget commitment or wanting to take anything one step further."

Her words struck at his core, devastating him. He had to protect himself. Fire back. "You're one to talk."

Her brows drew together as if confused.

"Moving to Silver Falls to escape your family counts as running away, too," he continued without giving her a chance to say anything. "But kudos to you for only running away once. Maybe you can win an award for that instead of the window display one."

That was a low blow, but he couldn't help himself. Not after she'd compared him to Nick Baxter. Brandt should say something, but what?

She remained silent. Her lips pressed together in a thin line. No emotion showed on her face or in her eyes. No hint of regret or of sadness. She'd shut down.

And he had no idea what to do that wouldn't make things worse.

The situation was hopeless. There was no future for them. Maybe there never had been.

Six years ago, Nick's betrayal had shattered Brandt. He'd done what he could to numb the pain to protect himself. Today, the loss wasn't as physical as losing his company or his best friend, but the pain cut to his bones. He hadn't known Callie long, but she'd meant something to him.

The possibility. The hope.

And like the last time, Brandt knew what he needed to do.

He left Wags and Tails the same way he had NiBr-Tech—without a word or a glance back. But this time, he wasn't sure how his heart would survive.

Chapter Twenty-Three

ON HER KNEES, Callie threw decorations into the garbage can. Dogs barked. Sam shouted from the room next door. She focused on what she was doing. Not that working was helping her feel better.

The mess only added to the pain inside her.

Somehow her heart kept beating and her lungs expanded with air, but an emptiness threatened to consume her.

Brandt was gone.

He wasn't coming back.

What they'd said to each other…

Her vision blurred.

She'd worked so hard to be her own person, yet on the worst day as a business owner, Brandt had tried to tell her what she should do.

Her anger had spiraled. She'd lost control. Comparing him to Nick hadn't been fair, but neither had what he said about her.

A heaviness weighed her down. She swung from wanting comfort to needing to be alone. Both were impossible right now.

Which left her cleaning and too much time to think

about what had been said.

Brandt had acted the same as her parents and brothers did toward her. The only difference was her family loved her. Brandt may have liked her, but that didn't give him the right to ask her to change.

Not when she'd been searching for acceptance. Something she thought she'd found with him.

But she hadn't.

Not even close.

Tears rolled down her cheeks. She brushed them aside, not wanting to cry over him. Over anything that had happened today. But her eyes wouldn't stop watering.

Anna kneeled next to her. "Where's Brandt?"

"Gone." Callie sniffled. "It's over."

Anna placed her arm around Callie. "What happened?"

"He said stuff. So did I. It was bad."

"Emotions are high," Anna said in a calm voice. "After things calm down—"

"Some things can't be taken back. There was more..." Callie hiccupped and then tried to calm herself. "I thought he accepted me for who I was, but he doesn't. He told me I was hurting myself if I didn't change."

Anna sucked in a breath. "I'm sorry."

"Thanks." Callie hadn't found something special with Brandt. She'd escaped into a fantasy, a daydream for a couple of weeks, nothing lasting or meaningful. Her heart splintered more, but she ignored the pain. "Whatever was happening between us was going to end when the new year rolled around. We shut it down early."

"Still hurts."

Emotion tightened her throat. "I had no idea how badly."

"What are you going to do?"

"Work." Overwhelmed, she eyed what needed to be done. "I have so much to keep me busy I won't have time to think about him."

At least, Callie hoped she wouldn't.

THE NEXT DAY, Brandt forced himself out of bed. Stubble covered his face. His eyes hurt. So did his heart. Something smelled. Probably him considering he wore the same clothes he'd worn when he'd walked away from Wags and Tails.

From Callie.

The last time he'd cried had been when he'd lost NiBr-Tech, but the tears had poured out last night against his pillow. He hadn't remembered them stopping, so he must have cried himself to sleep. That would explain how much his eyes and his head hurt.

A crying hangover.

Nerd.

Getting drunk would have been better.

He made his way downstairs.

Aunt Margot sat on the couch with her e-reader in hand and her two dogs at her feet. Neither Angus nor Sadie raised their heads. "You're alive."

Was he? A role in a zombie movie seemed all he was capable of at the moment. "Barely."

"I'll get you a cup of coffee." She placed her device on the end table before standing. "Caffeine might not be the answer, but it'll help."

"Thanks." Forehead throbbing, he plopped onto the nearest chair. That was better than standing. Not moving for the rest of the day sounded like a decent plan.

A few minutes later, his aunt returned with a steaming cup and a plate containing two cranberry scones—his favorite from the bakery. Guess she must have gone out while he was asleep. That brought a rush of guilt, but not enough to keep him from picking up a scone.

"Drink and eat," Aunt Margot encouraged.

Brandt ate like a man who hadn't eaten in over twenty-four hours. Which he hadn't.

His aunt stood next to his chair. "Yesterday, you wouldn't talk to me. Given how restless you were last night and how awful you look this morning, I'd say something happened with Callie."

His throat tight, he nodded.

"What are you thinking?" Aunt Margot asked, her tone full of loving concern.

Surprisingly, his mind was clear, though his heart was shattered. The pain was real, but through that and the never-ending regret flowing through him, the past six years crystalized into a single point. "I'm tired of running."

Aunt Margot rubbed circles on his back the way she'd done when he was a kid. When he was younger, the word of a friend had been something to put stock in…to trust. Nick had known that about Brandt even then.

"Then stop."

He nearly laughed even though his eyes stung. "You make it sound so easy when that's all I've been doing."

That was also clear to him. He hadn't been trying to put NiBrTech behind him. He'd been trying to pretend nothing had happened.

"Stopping will be as hard as you make it." She squeezed his shoulder. "Even after you left, Silver Falls was still your home. You might not have thought it was, but this is where you belong. Where you've always belonged."

"But Callie…" A knot burned in his chest. "I messed up."

"Nothing is unfixable," Aunt Margot said in a no-nonsense tone.

If only… "What I said hurt her."

What had he been thinking? He scrubbed his hand over his face. She'd told him about her family issues, about being told what to do and how to do it when all she wanted was to be accepted for how she was.

But he hadn't done that.

He'd told her what she should do—even flat-out said she should change.

No way would she forgive him.

Brandt wouldn't if he were her.

"Everyone has said the wrong things at one time or another," his aunt said. "All humans do, because we're flawed. Imperfect. Give Callie and yourself time. Nothing is going to change overnight."

"Even if I wish it could?"

Aunt Margot smiled softly. "Even then."

Questions swirled in his mind, making his head hurt more. He'd need to pack up his apartment, find a place to live here, and get a job. The thought made him dizzy. "What will I do if I stay?"

"Whatever you want." Margot laughed. "You earned that money from the sale of NiBrTech. It's not blood money or tainted in anyway."

"I've spent some."

"On yourself?"

He hadn't so didn't answer.

"Start your own company," Aunt Margot continued, not missing a beat. "You enjoy working on apps and mobile games."

"For fun."

"That's what quilting has always been for me—fun—but let me tell you what a fulfilling career it has been."

Starting his own company wasn't something he'd considered doing again, but this time he could use the lessons he'd learned and do it right. A challenge yes, and he'd be putting down massive roots if he hired employees. The thought should scare Brandt. Instead, the idea appealed to him on multiple levels. "I could do that."

"You can and will. Now eat the other scone." She motioned to the remaining one on his plate. "You need to feed a broken heart."

His heart and soul had been engulfed by a black hole. He had no idea when he'd stop feeling this way, but it wouldn't last forever.

At some point, he'd want to move on from this emptiness. Until then, he could make plans for staying in Silver Falls.

Because whether he stayed or left, he wouldn't be with Callie. This town was small, but he would have to learn to live with that.

Somehow.

TUESDAY NIGHT, FANS blew on the wet areas in the window and lobby. December twenty-sixth might as well be next year, but Callie had been doing what she could with no contractor available. And she'd keep doing whatever work needed to be done.

Muscles she didn't know existed ached. Callie ignored the bruises she'd gotten from working. Thankfully gloves and a long-sleeved shirt kept her hands and skin from being cut.

"What's next, boss?" Sam asked. They had removed the debris from what had once been the window platform while Becca, Mary Jo, and Anna were with the dogs that had been dropped off. Less than half their normal weekday attendance.

If this kept up, the business was going to be in trouble.

Callie stared at the window.

The empty space matched the emptiness in her heart, but that had nothing to do with Wags and Tails.

Don't think about him.

"We've done all we can for now." Unfortunately.

Callie, however, wished she and Brandt could go back to

how things had been before the day when everything went wrong. Ugly words had been spoken, but she missed him.

Sam sighed, seeming more like the teenager she'd hired. "There has to be something."

He was right.

She had no time to wonder if she'd made a mistake with Brandt or not. Her business and staff were her only priorities now.

Which meant she needed to do something other than waiting for a contractor. If what she tried didn't work, she'd do something else.

Wags and Tails was too important to her.

So were the people who worked for her. Brandt's words came back to her.

Asking for help will solve all your problems.

Callie took a breath and another. "There is."

Sam perked up. "What?"

She would do what Brandt had suggested. At this point, she had nothing to lose. "Give me a few minutes."

Callie went into the grooming area where Anna was cleaning up after bathing a dog. Thankfully, those clients hadn't canceled their appointments.

Anna wore a rubber apron over her normal cotton one. "What's up?"

This wasn't a time to let ego or pride get in the way. Callie might want to do this on her own, but Brandt had been correct. She couldn't. "I have a favor to ask."

"Name it."

"Could you please call Davis and ask if he has connections to someone who could help us out? Time of day or shift doesn't matter if someone wants to moonlight. I need the work done ASAP."

Anna's face paled. "I…"

"What?" Callie asked.

"Davis broke up with me." As Anna's eyes gleamed, her face scrunched. "Well, broke up suggests we were in a relationship, which I assumed we were, but he said we weren't and that I was too clingy."

Callie closed her gaping mouth. "When did this happen?"

"After I asked him to go to the church play."

"Why didn't you say anything?"

Anna crossed her arms over her chest. "You've been so happy with Brandt. It's no big deal."

"But you really liked Davis."

She dropped her head. "I did."

Callie hugged her friend. "I'm sorry I was so distracted and wasn't here for you when you needed me, but I am now."

"It's okay."

She let go of Anna, noticing her red eyes. This was not okay. "Forget I asked you to call him. I'll figure out something else."

"No." Anna spoke forcefully. Much stronger than she appeared at the moment. "Wags and Tails means too much to both of us. You're my best friend. Milo is the reason we're in this mess. I'll call Davis now."

With that, Anna grabbed her cell phone and headed into

the back.

With a heavy heart, Callie went out into the lobby. She hated imposing on her friend, but she'd done what Brandt had wanted—asked for help. Doing so might not change when the repairs occurred, but she needed to try for the people who counted on her.

Clutching her cell phone, Anna returned to the lobby. She wasn't smiling, but she had a hopeful expression. "Davis will be by later to see if he and his crew can squeeze this project in at night."

Relief surged through Callie. "He said yes just like that?"

Anna shifted her weight between her feet. "Not exactly."

"What did he say?"

"He said he'd take a look at the job if I'd get together with him so we could…talk."

"You agreed?"

She nodded. "He's the one who ended things. Whatever issues he has with me being 'clingy' or wanting to rush things still exist, but I'll do anything to help you out."

Even spend time with the guy who broke her heart. Callie hugged Anna. "You're the best friend ever."

Anna held tight. "So are you."

ON DECEMBER TWENTY-SECOND, Davis and his crew finished the repairs. With a thankful heart, Callie surveyed the store. "The lobby and window look better than before."

Anna nodded. "Davis did an excellent job."

"Did you have your talk?" Callie asked.

Another nod.

"And?"

Anna sighed. "He apologized for calling me clingy. He would like to go out again, but he also wants to date other people. Something he hadn't told me before."

"What did you say?"

"No, thanks." Anna laughed. "We're in different places. I like him, but I'm not settling for anything less than what I want."

"I'm sorry because I know how much you liked him, but you're making the right choice."

"I hope I agree when the clock strikes midnight on New Year's Eve and there's no one to kiss." Anna held up her chin. "About the window."

Callie stared at the space. "It's so empty."

"Yes, and if you don't put decorations up today, you'll be fined by the First Avenue Business Association." Anna strode determinedly toward the space. "We have the old decorations in the storage room."

Callie didn't want to pay a fine, but she still hesitated.

Anna's gaze narrowed. "What's wrong?"

"The judging is tomorrow. We can't win."

"You won by not giving up when the first display was destroyed." Anna spoke in an encouraging tone. "I'll bring out the boxes as soon as the dogs are picked up."

Once the closed sign was hanging on the door, Milo and Rex settled down to share the big pillow, while Sam, Anna, and Callie sorted the decorations.

Callie held up gold stars attached to fishing line. "Anything will be better than nothing."

Sam nodded. "That's the attitude, boss."

"What kind of theme do you want to do?" Anna asked.

Staring at the decorations, Callie sighed. "Let's skip a theme. Using years of leftovers doesn't give us many options. Let's make the window as Christmassy as possible with what we have."

Anna winked. "No one will judge you."

Callie laughed. "I doubt the judges will bother with us, but that's okay."

She would find another way to convince her family she was doing well on her own, even if the past week had been touch-and-go.

The bell on the door jingled.

Callie turned to see Mary Jo and Becca enter. Several of the First Avenue business owners followed, including Beth, Mr. Jones, and Taryn. Raine was there, too. A few carried bags. Others carried boxes.

Callie stood and then wiped her hands on the front of her apron. "What's going on?"

Mr. Jones stepped forward. "We heard you were redecorating, and we thought you could use a little help."

Her chest tightened. Tears stung the corners of her eyes. "Thank you."

That was all she could manage to say.

Taryn hugged Callie. "That's what being part of the First Avenue Business Association and living in Silver Falls is all about."

The bell on the door continued to ring as more people

entered with thermoses and liters of soda. Oscar, the deli owner, brought sandwiches, chips, and cookies.

As people laid decorations on the floor, someone turned on Christmas carols. The laughing and singing reminded Callie of a holiday party. That festive atmosphere continued to grow with each passing minute.

Her hand on her chest, Callie surveyed the scene. Her heart overflowed with gratitude. The generosity of these people reaffirmed everything she loved about Silver Falls, but something was missing. Someone.

Brandt.

No matter what had happened between them, her heart still wanted him. She loved him, whether it made sense or not.

None of tonight would be happening if not for Brandt. He wasn't here physically, but he might as well have been. He was the reason she'd asked Anna to call Davis. Brandt's words had hurt, but they'd also made Callie take a second and third look at herself. Made her push aside her fears. Made her remember what was important.

Without him…

She no longer wanted to be without him because if they hadn't argued…fought…broke up, she had no doubt he'd been in the middle of all this helping to pull the window display together. He should be here.

Swallowing her pride, she typed a text.

Callie: *Window repaired. Will you help me put heart into the new display?*

She hit send, not expecting a reply, but she'd…tried.

"WE'RE A PAIR." Aunt Margot stood in her living room with her arms on her hips. "My cell phone died, and it won't recharge. You're frowning as if you're stuck on Santa's naughty list and going to find coal in your stocking."

If only that was Brandt's problem. Nothing he did—perusing real estate listings online, writing a business plan, or seeing if he could start an afterschool or weekend coding club at the library—took his mind off Callie.

"At least there will be something in my stocking." Not that Brandt cared. He was miserable without her.

His aunt moved closer. "Brandt, you need help."

"I'm not running this time. I'm okay." Or he would be when he stopped thinking about Callie. She haunted his thoughts and his dreams. The memories of their times together wouldn't go away no matter how hard he tried to make them.

Aunt Margot touched his arm. "No, you're not."

"I will be." He sounded more confident than he felt.

"You should talk to her."

"I can't." Not after what he'd said. "Maybe in time…"

A text notification buzzed.

He stared at the screen. Callie. His heart slammed against his chest. Unlocking his phone, he read her message.

Callie: *Window repaired. Will you help me put heart into the new display?*

His hands trembled so much he nearly dropped his cell phone. "Callie texted me. She's redecorating the window tonight, and she needs our help."

Margot plucked a large grocery tote off the coatrack, grabbed the teddy bear from the rocking chair, and proceeded to shove it inside. "Let's bring some decorations in case Callie needs them."

Brandt grabbed a box. His aunt loaded it with the quilt off the back of the couch, the table runner from the dining room, and a couple of snowmen. Angus and Sadie waited patiently by the front door as if knowing someone was going out. It was obvious they didn't want to be left behind.

A few minutes later, all four of them arrived at Wags and Tails. The place was full of people. Lots of business owners, many he had seen but didn't know. Christmas decorations were spread out across the lobby, and themes were being debated.

Callie raised her hands to quiet people. "We have so many beautiful decorations. We don't need a specific theme. A cheery Christmassy window will be perfect."

A low murmur sounded. Most of the others wanted a theme.

He glanced at his aunt. "We got here just in time."

Brandt wove his way through the clutter to the counter and then lifted the Christmas tree figurine. "What do you think of using this to guide the theme?"

"That's the perfect inspiration." Aunt Margot clapped her hands together.

Everyone agreed.

Callie nodded. "That is the perfect theme for Wags and Tails, but our original theme was Silver Falls. I realize now that didn't have to be taken quite so literally."

People laughed.

"But Brandt has the right idea." Callie glanced at him.

The unsettled feeling hanging over him since Monday lessened.

"What if we keep the Silver Falls theme, but use items that represent the First Avenue shops and all of us?" she asked.

Excitement buzzed through the crowd. Voices got louder. Some ran out the door saying they had the perfect items that fit their stores. One by one, business owners set up a spot to represent their shops. With each one, the window display came together. Even after finishing their sections, people stayed. No one cared it was getting late on a Sunday night. More platters of cookies arrived. Large containers of hot cocoa and eggnog, too.

Mr. Jones twirled Raine around, laughing. "This is going to be the best Christmas window Silver Falls has ever seen."

Eyes full of happiness and what appeared to be hope, Callie stared at Brandt. "It already is."

BY TEN O'CLOCK, amid yawns and stretches and texts to loved ones at home, the window display was finally finished. So many people had come together to help Callie, and she'd accepted their generous support. If anyone had lost the meaning of Christmas, they could find it in Silver Falls.

Brandt couldn't have been prouder of his hometown. Callie, too. This was the place for him to put down roots, to grow a business, and to find a personal life.

As she stood by the door saying *thank you* and *goodnight* and giving each person a hug, her gratitude touched Brandt's heart. He wanted a hug. A kiss, too. But he'd wait until after he escorted Aunt Margot, Angus, and Sadie to the car and helped get the dogs inside.

"Are you sure you don't want me to drive you home?" he asked.

Aunt Margot shook her head. "You have something more important to do. Go win that girl's heart back."

He wanted—no, *needed*—to speak with Callie. "I'll give it my best shot."

His aunt kissed his cheek. "Good luck, dear."

"Thanks." He tamped down his worry. So far, tonight had gone well. Granted, he hadn't had the chance to talk to Callie. "I'm going to need it."

"Maybe not." His aunt stared at the doggy daycare. "But a little luck never hurts."

As he watched Aunt Margot drive off, Brandt took a deep breath. If Christmas magic existed, he hoped a few sprinkles had landed on him.

❦

STANDING OUTSIDE WAGS and Tails, ignoring the cold, Callie wiped happy tears from her cheeks. The inside of her doggy daycare was dark and empty except for Rex, who slept on his pillow behind the counter, but the spirit of Christmas remained, glowing as bright as the lights in her window display.

Not hers.

This Christmas window belonged to all who helped…to Silver Falls and to Brandt.

The display was nothing like she had planned, but she'd never seen anything more beautiful.

Heart.

She understood what he'd meant. This window defined heart. Christmas. Community.

Her chest squeezed tight as if caught in a vise. If only she knew what the future held for her and Brandt.

"The window is amazing."

The sound of his voice startled her. "I thought you left."

He stood next to her. "I wouldn't leave without saying goodbye. Not again."

There was so much she wanted to say, but she'd start with something simple. "Thanks for coming."

"You're welcome." He studied her. "You're shivering. You must be cold."

"A little." But seeing the window from the outside made the goose bumps and chill worthwhile.

"Let's go inside." He placed his hand on her back to lead her to the door. "We should talk."

We should talk.

A wave of apprehension rushed through her. Would this be goodbye? Or the start of something new?

The shiver inching down her spine had nothing to do with the cold now. She hurried into the shop, torn between wanting to get the talk over with and lingering in his company for a little bit longer.

The miniature white bulbs in the display provided enough glow that she didn't turn on overhead lights. A few chairs had been left out from the decorating party. She sat in one.

"What did you want to talk about?" Callie tried to sound casual, as if this wasn't the most important conversation her aching heart would ever have. She wiped her clammy palms on her jeans.

A beat passed. And another.

"I'm so sorry." The words were heartfelt. He reached toward her before lowering his hand to his side. "I should've never said what I did. I've regretted walking away, and I've been wishing for a do-over since Monday."

She hadn't known what to expect, but an apology hadn't been it.

"I forgive you." That was easy to say. This next part wouldn't be. "I hope you'll forgive me for listening to Nick and for not standing up for you. For not trusting my heart and ignoring everything else. I have a lot of baggage from my family, and I don't always hear what I'm supposed to. Other times, I put too much meaning into what I shouldn't. Regardless, that shouldn't have influenced my trust, my belief, in you."

"I forgive you."

He reached out again, this time not pulling back but lacing his fingers with hers. His skin was so warm and welcome. Tingles shot out from his touch.

The Christmas lights cast shadows on his face, but his affection shone through the darkness. "If you can forgive me for what I said, then I can forgive you for pretty much anything."

Tears of relief welled in her eyes. She blinked. Once. Twice. As she stared at the window display, her shoulders slumped. The tension that knotted her muscles all week disappeared as if she'd woken and realized the nightmare was over.

"I thought the way to prove I was capable and all grown-up was to do everything myself. I love helping others, but I wouldn't let anyone do the same for me." Saying these words were difficult, but he deserved to hear them. "When the shop was damaged, accepting help showed me how wrong I was. If I hadn't asked like you suggested, this place would still be a disaster. You're the reason everything got fixed this week, and for everyone showing up here tonight."

"Maybe the catalyst, but not the reason."

"Then you're the biggest catalyst ever," she admitted. "I didn't think anything was missing from my life except for my family accepting who I am, recognizing my success, and approving of what I'm doing. And then I met you."

He squeezed her hand.

"I was afraid of dating because I thought it would be one more person who'd want me to do things their way or not accept me," she continued. "I used my business to keep myself safe, but that's not what I want any longer."

"What do you want?" he asked.

"More. A relationship. I can have both a professional and

a personal life. It's not one or the other. I can have both. I want both."

Callie took a breath. She'd kept talking, afraid she might stop, but she'd said what she needed to.

"So do I." Raising her hand to his mouth, he pressed a kiss to it. "What about your family?"

"I was defining success by my family's definition, not mine. But no longer. I don't need to win the window display award to make my family or anyone proud. I'm proud of myself, of my business, and this town."

"You should be." He rubbed his thumb against hers. "You're an amazing woman. And I can't imagine my life without having met you."

"Same." Entire body tingling with warmth now, she smiled so big her cheeks hurts. "Meeting you was the best Christmas present ever."

"The first of many, I hope."

Her breath caught in her throat.

Brandt held her hand. "We haven't known each other long, but I fell hard for you. Somewhere over the past three weeks, I fell in love with you."

Her heart soared. "I love you, too."

He lowered his mouth to hers and then kissed her.

The touch of his lips was like coming home. His taste was her favorite now, and something she'd never be able to get enough of today or any day. As he wrapped his arms around her, she sank against him, relishing his strength and soaking in his scent.

He slowly backed away from her. The love in his eyes

told her this was only the beginning. The realization resonated in her heart and her soul.

Her dreams were coming true.

No mistletoe required.

Only love.

All of this did feel magical and perfect and right.

Something caught her eye. Glitter floated in her window display, suggesting something else might also be at play…

Christmas magic.

That would explain so much.

Chapter Twenty-Four

ON THE AFTERNOON of December twenty-third, Callie made notes on the profiles of two dogs who were new to the facility. The bell on the door rang. She glanced up to see three men. Not any guys—her brothers, all dressed in jeans, parkas, and hats.

"What are you doing here?" She hurried around the counter to greet each with a hug. All three were cold. "I didn't think you were coming in until tomorrow morning."

"You'd mentioned the window contest," Flynn said.

Keaton nodded. "We thought we'd surprise you."

"Surprise!" Garrett yelled.

"That's so sweet, but I won't be winning." Callie was okay with that. She explained about the damage, the last-minute redecorating efforts, and how she felt like that was enough of a win for her.

"Sounds like people take care of each other in Silver Falls," Keaton said.

"They do." Thinking about so many people coming to help her last night and being with Brandt after everyone had left filled her with happiness. "That's one reason I consider it home."

Keaton tilted his head, looking every inch the professor with a touch of philosopher thrown in. "The town is quaint. I understand the appeal after growing up surrounded by concrete, strip malls, and traffic."

Callie did a double take to make sure that was her brother talking. "Wait until you experience your first white Christmas."

"I don't know." Garrett made a face. "My lungs might explode with all this fresh air. Where's the smog?"

The bell on the door jingled. Mrs. Sellwood entered the lobby carrying a gift bag. "It's as crowded in here as it is outside with everyone waiting for the big announcement."

Callie stepped forward. "Can I help you, Mrs. Sellwood? Is Madden okay?"

The older woman released a long sigh. "He's not doing as well as he could be, but that's my fault. It's why I'm here."

Mrs. Sellwood was a complainer. Nothing was ever good enough for her and Madden, her spoiled dog. But Callie didn't understand. "Do you need help?"

"No, dear. This is for you." Mrs. Sellwood handed her the gift bag. "I've come to apologize for taking Madden to another facility while you did repairs. The place he went to was okay, but it's not as nice as Wags and Tails, and he was unhappy there."

Poor pup. "How does he act at home?"

"The same as usual." Red colored Mrs. Sellwood's cheeks. "I'd like to bring him back here after the holidays, if that's okay with you?"

This was an unexpected but pleasant surprise. "Madden

is always welcome. You know how to reserve a spot with the app."

The woman nodded. "Wags and Tails is far superior with the exception of one thing."

Callie drew back. "What's that?"

"You don't offer boarding."

"We will," she said without missing a beat. "I have the plans, and it's on my list of services for next year."

Mrs. Sellwood rubbed her hands together. "Then you're all set. I mentioned Wags and Tails to some of the people I met at the other place, so expect a few calls next week, dear. Merry Christmas."

Mrs. Sellwood turned and left before Callie could say anything.

"Wow." Garrett gave her a high five. "You have a customer for life."

Guess there *was* such a thing as Christmas magic. Callie glanced at the gift bag. Or maybe this one would count as a miracle. "I do."

"Impressive, sis," Keaton said.

Flynn's eyes widened. "I wasn't sure what to expect from your doggy daycare, but it wasn't this. Keaton's right. Very impressive."

Huh? She frowned. "I sent you pictures."

"What Flynn means is all we saw were the dogs, not the business itself," Garrett admitted with a sheepish grin. "You've done good, baby sis."

The baby part made her cringe, but she doubted they'd stop that. Still, she wanted to try. "Just sis would be fine."

"You'll always be the baby of the family." Flynn tousled her hair like she was five. "Even when we're old and gray."

Garrett nodded. "The entire time Mom was pregnant with you, she and Dad kept telling us our job as big brothers was to always take care of our baby sister."

"Not only our job," Flynn added. "Our responsibility."

Keaton nodded. "I was too young to understand until my two big bros helped me figure it out."

"Noogies work wonders on little brothers." Garrett laughed while Keaton rolled his eyes.

Maybe they acted like they did for a reason, but they could be more careful in how they spoke. "Well, your baby sister is all grown up with a business, employees, a house, and a dog."

"The famous Rex," Garrett said.

"Where is my four-footed nephew?" Flynn asked.

"In the back." She glanced at the time. "I'll get him in a minute, so he can go with us when they announce the winner."

"Don't count yourself out." Flynn glanced back at the window. "First Avenue is blocked off, so we had to park and walk. Your display has the most heart out of all of them."

Heart. That was what Brandt had told her she needed. "Then maybe we'll win even after everything that happened."

Flynn gave her a one-armed hug. "That's the right attitude."

She studied each of her brothers. Flynn, who saved lives with his skilled hands and was model attractive but appeared tired with circles under his eyes and lines on his face. Garrett, who had the face of a pretty boy but dressed as if he expected to get called before a judge at any minute even in jeans. Keaton, who had the handsome stuffy look down but looked more approachable and younger wearing such casual clothes.

Callie wanted to pinch herself. "I can't believe you're here."

Garrett tapped the tip of her nose, the way he'd done since she was little. "We thought you might need help before Mom and Dad arrived. Hosting Christmas is a big deal."

"I might surprise you." Callie was only half-joking. By the time her family left, they'd be asking her to do all their event planning. "But extra hands are always helpful."

Keaton wrapped his arm around her. "You saying that might be the biggest surprise yet."

She was happy to see them. "Let me grab Rex, so we can go hear who won."

"What about the other dogs?" Flynn asked.

"My staff will stay here with them," she answered.

Keaton elbowed their oldest brother. "She's the owner and boss, remember?"

A few minutes later, she stood with Rex and her brothers on First Avenue. Both ends of the block had been barricaded. A stage had been set up in the middle of the street. The high school choir, wearing Santa hats, sang Christmas carols.

"This is like a scene out of a movie." Garrett sounded dazed. "I didn't know towns like this existed in real life."

"Another world compared to LA," Flynn agreed.

Pride flowing through her, Callie raised her chin. "My

world."

Two familiar-sounding barks caught her attention. She turned to see Brandt and Margot approaching with Angus and Sadie. Brandt's eyes matched the clear blue sky overhead.

Her heart skipped a beat. Maybe two.

Brandt greeted her with a hug and a brush of his lips over her hat.

Flynn cleared his throat.

She glanced over her shoulder to see all three brothers, chests pushed out, shoulders squared, scowling at Brandt.

"My brothers are here," she whispered.

Brandt laced his gloved fingers with hers in what she considered to be a brave move given the dagger-filled glares being shot his way. "Introduce me."

Very brave.

But that was one of the things she loved about him.

"Brandt Winslow." She squeezed his hand. "I'd like you to meet my brothers in order from oldest to youngest. Flynn, the surgeon. Garrett, the lawyer. And Keaton, the professor."

"Assistant professor but soon to be on tenure track," Keaton corrected.

Her other two brother shook their heads.

Brandt let go of her hand to shake theirs. "Nice to meet you."

"You know Callie how?" Garrett asked.

Brandt pushed his own shoulders back. "We're dating."

Extremely brave.

Flynn grimaced. "I didn't know you were seeing anyone."

"Why didn't you tell us?" Keaton asked.

Garrett frowned. "Do Mom and Dad know?"

"I am." She grinned. "I'm telling you now. Mom and Dad don't know. Yet."

There, that wasn't so bad.

Margot sashayed closer with Angus leading the way. "Who are these handsome fellows?"

Angus sniffed everyone's shoes.

"These are my brothers." Each introduced themselves. "This is Brandt's aunt, Margot Winslow. She owns the quilt shop in town."

"The pleasure is mine, gentlemen." Margot studied each one. "So, are any of you single?"

All three men nodded to Margot's obvious delight.

"She wouldn't," Brandt whispered.

"She would." Callie kept her voice low. "I think she's planning her next match. Or matches."

They both laughed.

If Margot set her sights on meddling in her brothers' love lives, they wouldn't know what hit them.

The head judge, who was also the superintendent of the school district, stepped to the microphone. His Santa hat had LED lights built into the ball on the end, and it glowed with a rainbow of colors.

"Judging this year's competition was tough." He chuckled. "Though we say that every year."

The crowd laughed.

Flutters took over Callie's stomach. She shifted her

weight between her feet.

"Nervous?" Brandt asked.

"More than I realized," she admitted. "And I shouldn't be."

When she'd decorated the window the first time in late November, she'd wanted to win but for all the wrong reasons. After decorating the window with everyone last night, she wanted to hear what name would be called so she could cheer their victory.

The superintendent held up a large red envelope. "Are you ready to see who this year's winner is?"

Some of the crowd shouted *yes*.

Others cheered.

Some clapped.

"I'll take that as a yes." With exaggerated motions, he opened the envelope. "This year's holiday window display award goes to Wags and Tails."

Callie's jaw dropped.

As people applauded, she stood in shock, not believing what she'd heard. They won? That didn't make any sense.

She glanced at Brandt for confirmation. "Really?"

Nodding, he hugged her. "Get up on stage."

Margot gave her a slight push. "Go claim your prize. Then you can make goo-goo eyes at my nephew for the rest of the day."

Her brothers, eyes full of pride, laughed.

With heat flooding her face, Callie climbed the three steps with Rex.

The superintendent shook her hand. "Congratulations,

Callie."

"Thank you."

He handed her the shiny plaque, the one she'd imagined hanging on the wall behind the counter. She'd done it. Not in the way she'd expected or planned, but she'd won.

In the crowd, her brothers cheered. So did Brandt.

Joy overflowed from her heart. Love, too.

She stepped forward to the microphone. "To say this is unexpected is an understatement. Most of you saw the mess our window was only a couple of days ago. This wasn't a solo effort. Nor was it only my staff and me."

A lump lodged in her throat. She swallowed around it.

"So many people share in this award. First, I'd like to thank Davis Tucker and his construction crew from Summit Ridge for repairing the damage. My fellow First Avenue Business Association members, friends, and a few strangers, who showed up to help me decorate. They brought decorations, food, and drinks so no one would have to stop working for dinner. That made an enormous difference in being able to finish in time. Anna, Sam, Becca, and Mary Jo for the extra hours they worked this past week. Angus, Sadie, Milo, and Rex kept us company as we put the window display together and made us laugh with their antics. Without all that help, big and small, winning this award would have been impossible. Thank you, Silver Falls, for this honor and for your friendship."

Heart pounding, she stared at Brandt. "Merry Christmas, and may all your Christmas wishes come true."

Someone handed her a stocking. A glance inside told her

these were the other prizes that came along with the plaque. Holding onto everything, she left the stage in a daze.

Brandt hugged her. "Congratulations."

"Right back at you," she said. "You were a huge part of this."

Her brothers and Margot congratulated her.

"You know." Margot had a mischievous expression on her face. "Silver Falls is a lovely place for a wedding, especially in the springtime."

Everyone laughed. Brandt shook his head.

He eyed his aunt. "Please let me get Callie under the mistletoe before we start talking about what comes next."

Callie wanted to know what came next. Summer would be a nice time for a wedding. She grinned.

Margot handed him a sprig tied with a red ribbon. "It's a good thing you have me to help you out."

"Best aunt ever." Brandt held the mistletoe over Callie's head. "This okay?"

She nodded, anticipation thrumming through her. The dogs barked as if they agreed, too.

"This is our first Christmas together in Silver Falls," Brandt whispered. "There will be many after this. I promise. Nothing will make me leave you or this town again."

Brandt kissed her with his lips, but she could feel his heart, too. Callie soaked in the taste of him, a mix of warmth, peppermint, and his unique flavor. She wasn't sure if people were clapping or if her heart was pounding that hard.

She didn't care.

This was already the best Christmas ever, and the twenty-fifth was still two days away. How amazing would New Year's Eve be when Brandt kissed her at midnight?

Callie couldn't wait to find out.

The End

More by Melissa McClone

The Bar V5 Ranch series

Home for Christmas
Mistletoe Magic
Kiss Me, Cowboy
Mistletoe Wedding
A Christmas Homecoming

The Ever After series

The Honeymoon Prize
The Cinderella Princess
Christmas at the Castle

Available now at your favorite online retailer!

About the Author

USA Today Bestselling author **Melissa McClone** has published over twenty-five novels with Harlequin and been nominated for Romance Writers of America's RITA award. She lives in the Pacific Northwest with her husband, three school-aged children, two spoiled Norwegian Elkhounds and cats who think they rule the house. For more on Melissa's books, visit her website: www.melissamcclone.com.

Thank you for reading

The Christmas Window

If you enjoyed this book, you can find more from all our great authors at TulePublishing.com, or from your favorite online retailer.

TULE
PUBLISHING

Printed in Great Britain
by Amazon

34674979R00172